A BIGAMIST'S DAUGHTER

A Bigamist's Daughter

A NOVEL BY

ALICE McDERMOTT

PERENNIAL LIBRARY

Harper & Row, Publishers, New York
Cambridge, Philadelphia, San Francisco, Washington
London, Mexico City, São Paulo, Singapore, Sydney

Grateful acknowledgment is made to the following for permission to reprint previously published material:
New Directions Publishing Corp.: Excerpt from Scene VI from *The Glass Menagerie* by Tennessee Williams. Copyright 1945 by Tennessee Williams and Edwina D. Williams. Reprinted by permission of New Directions.

A hardcover edition of this book was originally published in 1982 by Random House, Inc. It is here reprinted by arrangement with Random House, Inc.

A BIGAMIST'S DAUGHTER. Copyright © 1982 by Alice McDermott. All rights reserved. Printed in the United States of America. No part of this book may be used or reproduced in any manner whatsoever without written permission except in the case of brief quotations embodied in critical articles and reviews. For information address Harper & Row, Publishers, Inc., 10 East 53rd Street, New York, N.Y. 10022. Published simultaneously in Canada by Fitzhenry & Whiteside Limited, Toronto.

First PERENNIAL LIBRARY edition published 1988.

Library of Congress Cataloging-in-Publication Data

McDermott, Alice.
   A bigamist's daughter.

   Reprint. Originally published: 1st ed. New York : Random House, c1982.
   I. Title.
PS3563.C355B5   1988   813'.54   87-45640
ISBN 0-06-097142-8 (pbk.)

88 89 90 91 92 FG 10 9 8 7 6 5 4 3 2 1

FOR MY PARENTS

A BIGAMIST'S DAUGHTER

I

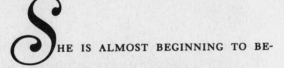

SHE IS ALMOST BEGINNING TO BE-
lieve him.

He's been here for nearly twenty minutes now, sitting across
from her on the edge of his seat, his forearms resting on her
desk, his hands folded before him, the right hand covering the
left, the left a fist that he occasionally taps, ever so lightly, upon
the gray steel to give his voice emphasis. His voice is Southern,
slow, but with a rising quality that makes her feel it's being
rushed from behind, that something is pushing him to get the
story told faster, to get it finished. Perhaps it is only her slow,
habitual glances at the clock on the edge of her desk, or the
quick sounds of the typewriters outside her office.

But his voice will not be rushed, and his face, that light,
open, seemingly featureless face that only very blond people
can have, very blond people with pale skin and colorless lashes,
remains unchanged.

"He seemed to look different each time we saw him," he tells
her, reciting. *"Not a difference in weight or dress or disposition,
not even the difference that can come over someone at different
seasons, but a true, somehow internal difference. At times, he
would look kind—God, so kind it made you want to kneel, filled
you with an optimism, a joy, that was almost religious. At other
times, he would look fierce, savage, so that you knew if he were*

3

to touch you, as we'd seen him touch his wife (who was only one of his wives) and a shopgirl, and even a dog at these times, there would be no humanity in it, no connection of blood and living skin, no recognition. Just weight and direction; the blade of the tractor meeting dry earth."

He speaks slowly, carefully, and his voice, like his small blue eyes, seems to search the air, the pale sunlight coming from the window behind her, as if some response should be found there. As if each word were a cue.

"One summer we saw him in town. He was driving a gray Mercedes with Montana plates and it was the first any of us had seen of him for nearly a year and a half. He pulled up in that car that was like a flash of black water thrown onto the dry, dusty street, stepped out, and then stood there, seeing no one, but waiting, as if for our vision to clear. He seemed thinner, even taller than we'd remembered him and he wore white duck trousers and a loose white shirt. He was tan and his hair had begun to turn gray.

"He walked slowly into the liquor store, all of us watching him and him knowing we were watching, came out with a bottle, got back into his car and drove out to his home that, as far as any of us knew, he hadn't seen in the past year and a half. And all of us, despite what we'd been saying when we saw his wife —who was really only one of his wives—moving through us like a whipped dog, despite the pity we'd been giving her, the puzzled shame we thought we'd seen her wearing, despite that, any one of us, man, woman and child, would have sold his soul to have been there in that darkened house on the Fainsburg Road that night, to have been there waiting to receive him."

Like a medium, he searches the air as he speaks, and although she's sat at this desk, in this white office, and has listened to the drone of countless other voices, countless other stories ("Do you have a story to tell? Have you ever told yourself: 'I should write a book?' Vista Books seeks new authors

4

with manuscripts of all types."), she has been, in these past twenty minutes, intrigued, interested, verging on belief.

"And the other women, his other wives, whom we could only guess about, only imagine as we waited for him to return to our town again, those women became as real to us as the women who we knew to be his wives, and we always imagined them crying. Crying in different rooms, in different cities, on different days of the week. One, we would say, is fat, with curly hair, and she cries in her kitchen and wipes her eyes with a gingham apron, a small whimper always at her throat. Another is thin, sharp-nosed. She places long, bony fingers over her face and cries sitting on the edge of a cream-colored couch in a darkening living room. Another, we would tell one another, winking, smiling a little, is blond, shapely; she lies flung across her bed, crying with awful, shuddering sobs, one red slipper on the floor, the other still dangling from her polished toes."

The phone rings, and she almost expects him to make the sound part of his story, the way a dream will sometimes gather the real world into itself and build a meaning around it.

He merely smiles, pulling his lips together, and nods when she says, "Excuse me."

It's Ann, her secretary. "Elizabeth, you've been in there nearly a half an hour," she says in a low voice. "Do you need to be rescued?"

"Fine." Elizabeth reaches for her pen. "Give it to me again, slowly." She notices her movements are sluggish, drowsy.

"Should I give you about fifteen more minutes?" Ann asks.

She nods, writing nonsense, illegibly. She's not sure she wants to get rid of him so soon, but Ann's call and her response to it are automatic, cues and stage directions in a scene she knows so well that even to improvise would mean to pick up a pad and a pen and pretend to be writing. "Fine," she says. "Got it."

"It's twenty-five after ten," Ann tells her. "If he's not out by ten forty-five, I'll come in and say there's a meeting."

Elizabeth writes, "This is the day that the Lord hath made," and nods again, wondering where in her mind the phrase came from. "Well, that's fine," she says, "but tell them not to start without me."

Ann laughs a little. "Okay, I'll tell them."

She hangs up the phone and stares at the pad. Remnants of Catholic brainwashing or God trying to get a message to her? She scribbles a bit more, as if she has something urgent on her mind, and then looks up. "I'm sorry, Mr. Daniels," she says. "Please go on."

He smiles a little, eyes on his hands, and she's suddenly ashamed, afraid that he's seen through the phone call. "Well, it's all in the book," he says and then, looking up, "Why don't I just let you read it instead of reciting it to you?" He smiles, a weak smile that somehow reaches to the very corners of his mouth, squaring them. His teeth are small and white and straight, his skin smooth, beardless, his narrow eyes a very light blue. There is, she thinks, something uncomplicated and pleasant about his face.

"Yes," she says, smiling back at him, placing her hand over the thick yellow envelope before her. "Why don't I read it first and then we can talk?" She pushes her chair back slightly, places her hands on its arms. He stands. She stands too, and holds out her hand. "I'll call you as soon as I've read it all. Maybe we can have lunch."

They shake hands across her desk, above his manuscript in its yellow envelope, and for just one moment she catches a certain facetiousness in his eyes, as if he's seen through more than the phone call. She suddenly feels like a little girl caught dressed up in her mother's clothes, gravely playing grown-up. It's a feeling she often gets when acting the businesswoman around people her own age.

"I'd appreciate that," he says and smiles again. He is a broad

6

young man, nearly stocky, and as she walks him to the door she notices that he is only an inch or two taller than she. He wears neat khaki pants and a navy-blue blazer. Loafers and no socks. She briefly imagines him naked, but can think only of a pale, rather knotty backside.

"How much longer will you be in New York?" she asks, as they walk down the corridor, the typewriters clicking on either side of them. Ann peers over the green, smoked-glass partition, watching him carefully, as if she suspects he may bolt at any minute, make a run for it back to the office, where he will demand more time. She seems ready to block the door if he dares.

"I have some shopping to do," he says. "And some old friends to visit. Actually, when I come to New York I usually just stay until I get tired of it. Once I was here about four hours, once for over six months."

The idle rich. She imagines the price of his contract edging up over the $5,000 mark.

They stand in the small reception room and shake hands. It's a sleazy room. Dark paneling, brown-and-orange Danish modern furniture, beige linoleum. It's so much like a front, like the fake offices they used to set up for *Candid Camera,* she often wonders how their "authors" fail to see it. The first time she sat here, when she came up for her interview two years ago, she could think only of illegal abortions and unlicensed electrolysis, of Allen Funt suddenly revealing that nothing is what it seems to be.

As it's not, in here. Vista Books is a vanity publisher masquerading as a real one. Making the dreams of every would-be writer come true, for a while. And then sending them the bill.

"I'll call you," she says to him. "Soon." They stand looking at each other, smiling somewhat awkwardly. She knows what he's waiting for. "Tomorrow," she says, giving it to him.

Now he really smiles. "Great. I hope you like it."

She reaches for the door and holds it open for him. "I'm sure I will."

He says, "Have a good day," and walks out. He has an odd little bounce in his step, and he walks with his hands straight at his sides, like a well-behaved child.

Bonnie, the receptionist, sits behind a small window opposite the door watching her, sucking on a red-and-white straw stuck into a can of grape soda.

"Yuk," she says as Elizabeth turns back into the room. The straw doesn't leave her mouth. "He's a creepy one." There are bright red pimples spread across her forehead like strawberry jam. She is fat, painfully homely; nasty with homeliness.

"You think so?"

"Yuk," she says again, and then adds, biting the straw, "Ned wants you in Production."

She goes the back way, through the stockroom, a large gray area that smells damp and oily like an old garage. There are rows and rows of books, some in opened boxes, some wrapped in brown paper, others piled loosely on metal shelves, their jackets sooty and torn. Hector, the stock boy, is on one of the wooden skids, disco-tap dancing to the music from his transistor. He waves to her. She waves back. She fights her recurrent fantasy of the entire room in flames.

As she enters Ned's office, a small, windowless room between the storeroom and the large area where the six members of Vista's production staff actually work, she can tell this is not going to be a pleasant session. He has a large, sloppy manuscript on the desk before him; judging from his face, it is giving off a terrible odor.

"You signed this book?" he asks. *"The Coy Caitiff?"*

She moves to his desk and looks at the title page. "By Blanche Willis. Yes, I signed it. It's a good contract."

"I don't suppose you've read it." His eyes and forehead are small, pushed together, but the rest of his face is wide, long, exaggerated like a cartoon character's. He's spent the last ten years with a trade publisher, and after six months at Vista he's still a little surprised at what goes on at a vanity press.

"I didn't read the *whole* thing," she tells him. "But I read some of it. Why?"

He sits up in his chair, sighing, playing with the buttons of his shirt. "The copy editor I gave it to just brought it back. He can't make any sense of it. He says the main character keeps changing his name. And his sex. He says on one page the author's calling him Fess and on the other page she's calling him Bess, and sometimes she describes the clothes as male, sometimes as female. I've just looked at it and I can't make any sense of it either." He pushes the manuscript away from him, toward her. "How am I supposed to send it to the compositor if I don't know where it's supposed to be B-E-S-S and where it's supposed to be F-E-S-S, where it's supposed to be he and where it's supposed to be she?"

She begins to laugh a little. Ned doesn't, and she wishes he would. She realizes that Ned takes his job seriously because he has a wife and five children and a mortgage, but she also believes a certain amount of laughter is important, for perspective.

"It's really very simple," she tells him, pretending to be serious. "It's all explained in the outline." She sits on the edge of his desk. Blanche Willis, she knows, has already become a celebrity in her small New Jersey town, and her husband, who is an executive for the telephone company, has just given her an office in his own building, where she can begin working on the sequel. She had called just yesterday to ask Elizabeth what she thought of Dustin Hoffman starring in the movie version of her book. Blanche wondered if he was "serious" enough.

"In the beginning of the book," she tells Ned, "Bess and Fess are twins, male and female. Bess marries a doctor and they drive cross-country for their honeymoon. Fess goes along with them because he's gay and wants to live in San Francisco. On the way, there's a car crash and Bess is killed. Fess is castrated."

"Shit," Ned whispers.

"So," she goes on, "to calm the broken-hearted doctor, Fess proposes that he become Bess and the two of them live as man and wife. This pleases Fess because he's always wanted to marry a doctor, and it pleases the doctor because he's always liked Fess better anyway. The story goes on from there."

"It's not supposed to be a funny book?" Ned asks.

"No," she says. "The author believes it's a reflection of the way we live now. That's what she wants on the jacket."

He breathes another "shit" and then asks, "So what do I tell the copy editor?"

"Tell him it's easy to figure out. When Fess and the doctor are in public, Fess is called Bess. When they're alone, he's Fess again because the doctor knows he's not really Bess. In public, Fess is she, in private, he's he, unless the doctor is kidding him and calling him she in private. I think the same goes for Fess's mother because she knows Fess is Bess, too."

Ned looks down at the manuscript and then looks up at her. Laughing a little, she slides off the desk and straightens her skirt. "Does it ever occur to you to reject a manuscript on the grounds it's ridiculous?" he asks.

She laughs out loud, again wishing he would smile. "It occurs to me every day," she tells him. "But if the author's willing to pay us to publish it, what can I do?"

He shrugs, dismissing her. As she turns to leave, she sees Kevin, their art director, standing behind her. He grins through his freckles and whispers, "Bess and Fess, what a mess," as she passes by. They both raise their shoulders and giggle into their hands. Ned ignores them.

Ann is in her office when she gets back, gathering papers from Elizabeth's OUT basket and twisting her head around to read the name on the yellow envelope.

"What's his name?" she asks as Elizabeth walks in. "Tupper?"

"That's what it says."

"As in Tupperware?"

"Yup."

She sits down at her desk and picks up the envelope. The label says Tupper Daniels, Monteagle, Tennessee. She slides the manuscript out. It's on nice paper, neatly typed, and she suddenly feels strangely embarrassed, as if he'd accidentally left something very private in her office, like a pair of rosary beads or a worn sock. Ann leans over her, her large breasts pressing softly against Elizabeth's shoulder and arm. She almost wants to block the manuscript from her view.

"What's it about?" Ann whispers.

She shrugs. "Bigamy, I think. He just recited most of the first chapter to me."

"Oh God," Ann says. She straightens up. She is a big woman, huge actually, but her face is thin and she dresses well, so Elizabeth only notices her size when they are standing side by side in front of the bathroom mirror, or when, like now, she stands close enough to block out one entire side of the office.

"Bigamy?" Ann says. "My, my, he didn't look the type." And then she laughs that staccato, sophisticated laugh Elizabeth loves her for. "That's an answer to the divorce problem. I wish Brian had thought of it." She's been divorced from Brian nearly seven years now, but his name still haunts her conversations; she seems to hold it in her mouth like a dog with a bit of coattail: the only part of the thief that didn't get away.

"You would have preferred Brian to be a bigamist?"

She shrugs, hands on her wide hips. "Why not? Half a man's better than none at all. And think of the freedom; he'd have to work double-time being two husbands, but I'd only have to work part-time being half a wife. It's the working girl's answer to a demanding marriage. Don't get a part-time job, get a part-time husband! I love it."

Elizabeth tells her she's got a point. Had Brian been a

bigamist, she knows, Ann would have made herself believe this. She has a marvelous way of turning every rotten thing her once-husband did into some kind of sly joke in which she is ultimately the winner. Her poetry, which she used to let Elizabeth read, was full of such twists.

"Well," says Ann. "Are you going to sign old Tupperware?"

"Probably." She flips through the manuscript and then drops it onto her desk. "And I told him I'd call him tomorrow, so be a dear and get me his file so I can make out his contract. Type a folder for him too, and find me a time tomorrow afternoon when I can see him—he'll probably sign then."

"Right-oh, chief," Ann says, saluting and turning to walk out the door. The "chief" is to remind Elizabeth, nearly six years her junior, that she's getting carried away.

"And then take the rest of the morning off," Elizabeth calls after her. An apology.

"You're a sport," Ann calls back.

Tupper Daniels' background file consists of his first letter to Vista, the questionnaire he was asked to fill out, the summary he was asked to submit and the two letters arranging this morning's meeting.

His questionnaire says he's submitted to all the major houses, the real publishers, and was turned down by each one. It doesn't say why. It says he finally decided to come to Vista because he feels a writer should believe in his work enough to pay to have it published. He also adds that Stephen Crane published his own first works himself, and he's always admired Stephen Crane.

She sits back, lights a cigarette. She recalls having read it all before, just yesterday probably, but it had no meaning then. She reads hundreds of these backgrounds a week, hundreds of letters from people with books that Vista simply must publish, no matter what the cost. Housewives with desks full of poetry, businessmen with exposés they're sure will change the world, old people, so many old people, with memoirs and philosophies they want urgently to be preserved, recorded. So many pathetic people with dreams of immortality and a spot on the *Tonight Show*.

In the beginning they had depressed her with their sad stories and hopeless ambitions, but gradually she came to see that, like anyone who dealt with *the public*, she would have to keep her sympathies, and her imagination, in check. How, she reasoned, could even the most humble shoe salesman accomplish his work if each socked or stockinged foot he held brought visions of this little piggy and pedicures and calluses earned in vain pursuits? Of mortician's tags hung from cold toes?

She picks up his summary. It's sketchy, but enough to allow her to discuss his book with him for hours; her own special talent.

"This is an intriguing story in the tradition of some of our greatest Southern writers. It deals with a young man who suddenly appears in a small Southern town. He camps on the outskirts of town, then buys the land under him and begins to build a home. When the home is completed, he disappears for nearly a year. On his return, he marries a young girl who is engaged to someone else, puts her in his home and then leaves again. He comes and goes with monthly and yearly intervals for nearly fifty years, fascinating the townspeople and marrying two other women from the town as each wife dies.

"The townspeople are convinced that he has other wives and families across the country, and along with the story of this man's comings and goings the novel consists of various townspeople's theories of who and what he has elsewhere, told from the point of view of the women themselves. So the novel is actually many stories with the same mysterious man as the center of each."

He'd told her it was based on fact, on a man who had lived in the town where he grew up, a man later proven to be a bigamist. He'd said he was having some trouble with the ending.

She gets up and walks to her small window. A dozen cars are parked on the roof across the street. She's been in this office nearly two years and has yet to see one car actually moving on that roof. They're either there or not there; she never sees them coming or going.

Bigamy. She tries to remember some old joke, something about two women in love with the same man asking him, "What would you say to screwing us both?" and the man answers, "I'd say that's big of me."

No, she thinks, that can't be it. She's sure it was funnier than that.

A huge tractor trailer is backing out of the garage below. There are three little men in the street behind it, holding up their hands, waving, yelling, shouting directions. There's something unnecessarily frantic about their movements, as if they're trying to wear themselves out. Perhaps, she thinks, so they'll feel their day was well spent; like her, right now, laboring over a simple contract she need only type a name and number on: Tupper Daniels, $6,000. The simplest procedure in her delightfully simple job.

The first day she worked here, the miracle of being hired as an editor of Vista Books without any experience and only a college minor in English making her overly grateful and terribly anxious to please, she sat down with a pile of manuscripts before her and began to read, slowly, carefully, giving her full attention to each word. She was still on that first manuscript —a love story about a pioneer werewolf—when Mr. Alvin Owens, president of Vista, and son (with a name change) of Barney Goldfield, Vista's founder, came into her office. He quickly snatched up the manuscript before her and put one piece of paper in its place.

"Sweetheart," he said, breathing his spearmint-flavored

breath on her, "you read the summary so you can talk to the author, you look at the manuscript so you can count the pages. While you're counting the pages, you check the manuscript for pornography or slander or anything that looks like mail fraud. If it's clean, you send the author a Congratulations letter—you know, we loved your book, we loved this sentence, this chapter, whatever. Follow the form letter until you get the hang of it. Then you fill out the contract." He pulled one of the long, four-page documents from her desk and drummed his hairy fingers over it. "If you can find reason for the book to cost more than five thousand—it's long, it needs illustrations, the author is a doctor—you get ten percent of the difference." He put the contract on her desk and patted it with his hand, as if to establish a rhythm. "One contract, fifteen minutes, plus the time you spend stroking the author's ego. You make money, I make money and we can all go home at five o'clock."

Since then, she hasn't read one manuscript from beginning to end. She hasn't had to. She merely smiles at the authors and sends them contracts and acceptance letters. They, in turn, cry in her office, kiss her hand, send her gifts. They tell her: Now I know why these things happened, why I was lonely, hurt, why my child died, my husband left me, why I lost, missed out, messed up: *So I could write about it.*

She looks down into the street, at the three little men who are now sitting, exhausted, on milk crates at the entrance to the garage. She imagines titles for the books they might write: *Semi-Retirement on the Lower West Side*; *How I Backed a Tractor Trailer Out of a Garage, Once*; *My Life: In and Out of Mental Institutions.* The last is a title Vista really has published. Kevin dug it out of the storeroom and left it on her desk one morning a couple of weeks ago with a note that read, "Perhaps this will provide some insight as to why we are here." The jacket, in two colors on cheap paper, showed a long path leading to a wide door. The print, the path and the door were all dark green, but the rest of the jacket was light blue, as if the path led not to a mental institution but to the sky or a large lake.

Kevin had taped a sketch of her on the back of the book, over the author's picture. It was a very good sketch, even though he had made her cross-eyed. Kevin is a good artist. Under the sketch was a photo of a man with large watery eyes and big ears and a dent that looked like a huge thumbprint right in the middle of his forehead. His face was also light blue, and if it hadn't been for that, and for the dent, he would have looked like Bing Crosby. It said in his biographical note that he'd once been hit on the head by a subway train and lived to tell about it. She pointed this out to Kevin and they laughed about it all that day.

One of the little men gets up off his milk crate, stretches, and walks slowly down the street, west toward the river. She thinks of the Steinberg poster of the New Yorker's view of the world: the Hudson, New Jersey, Chicago, California, Russia. She thinks again about Tupper Daniels' novel, wondering how such a story can end. What happens to a man who comes and goes for nearly fifty years? Does he come home one day and simply never leave again, making his poor wife frantic, month after month, because she'd been sure he'd be gone by now, sure by now she'd have the house to herself again? Or does he, like her own father, go away one day and come back dead? Or does he simply turn a corner as the reader turns the last page (which, she supposes, is the same as going away and dying, coming home and never leaving)?

She turns from the window and goes back to her desk. His manuscript is thick, on expensive paper, professionally typed. The author has already invested in his work, he believes in it. If Mr. Owens were here, he'd tell her to hit him for seven.

One contract, fifteen minutes, and $200 is in her savings account. She passes Tupper Daniels and his mysterious man on to production (Won't Ned love how neat it is, how much it looks like the real thing!) and goes home at five o'clock.

Home to her studio apartment and her casual glances at the calendar, to her calculations that in about three more weeks it will be a year since Jill's party, a year since she's had anyone in her bed. Back to her studio apartment and her memories of that morning nearly a year ago, when she threw him out—Greg was his name, she thinks. Yes. Greg. Threw him out because he smelled of smoke and slept with his mouth open, because waking up with the feeling, Oh shit, who's this? makes for wonderful jokes but lousy mornings and lousy days. Because right there and then on that Sunday morning, with her apartment a mess and her sheets looking gray and feeling greasy and a strange, bearded man sleeping next to her with his mouth open, she had vowed—shaking him, telling him to leave—that there'd be no more casual sex, that next time she had someone in her bed it would be for love.

Now, nearly a year later, she's willing to settle for a fine friendship or even a true concern. Although Ann has suggested a one-night stand might help get things moving again, a one-night stand who arrives late and agrees to be gone by morning.

She glances at her clock. It's almost lunchtime. She should pick up the contract, roll it into her typewriter, get it over with.

But there is something about this book, the image of that man, the bigamist, as Tupper Daniels talked him into existence, that remains with her, intrigues her still.

Maybe, she thinks, there is Ward's voice, three summers ago now, talking into the gloom of that damp, tree-shaded porch on that darkening summer evening. There is the sound of his voice as they sat on the creaking wicker chairs and watched through the screens the speckled light that fell sparsely across the front of her mother's house. His voice, deep and puzzled, a voice, she tried to imagine then, that her mother heard in moments of passion, loneliness, in the small, mundane exchanges of early mornings and late afternoons. (Ward, my mother's lover: Even now the expression is only ludicrous to her, a hilarious joining of words that suddenly made possible a host of other inappropriate couplings: my mother's sexuality, my mother's orgasms, my mother's immorality. My mother and Ward.) There is Ward's voice telling her about her mother's fears, her theories. Ward's voice never saying the word bigamist (for, she is certain, he would have to know how silly it would sound, how obsolete the word had become) but still, somehow, filling the air with the word, so she could feel it forming on her own tongue.

"Your mother has worried," he said, sitting in the wicker chair with its dark-green paint seeming to crack and snap each time he moved, leaned forward to see her more clearly, leaned back to watch the deepening shadows. "She has confided in me about your father's long absences, his constant distractions. She has no proof, but her intuition is strong."

And she had felt the dampness rising from the concrete floor, from the growing shadows of the trees. The cool, bitter air of the Maine woods at night, in late summer.

"She has confided in me that she felt each time your father left he was leaving for something more solid and formed and more compelling than he ever admitted to. Something more than a job. Which made it more difficult for her to see him go. More difficult than you've probably ever realized."

And the word, she is sure, was there between them, on the damp air.

Or, no. It wasn't there then because then there was a roll of thunder and Ward unfolded himself from the old chair and got up to stand closer to the screen. Then the rain began, gathering first in the leaves of the trees and then falling on the roof and in the dirt around her mother's house, its sound somehow diminished by the filter of trees and yet somehow made more terrible by it. And then her mother's car came into the driveway and she ran to the porch, pulling the light screen door open with more force than was necessary, and Ward took her arms and they both laughed about how wet she'd gotten as they went inside for her to change, turning on the lights as they passed through the rooms.

So there was no time then for the word to form between them, no time for her to feel it fully on her lips.

But now, with the idea, the image, of a bigamist here in her office in New York, two years later, she can recall that day, recall Ward sitting in that chair, speaking of her father, his long face pale in the dark air on the porch of her mother's home, and she can remember it as if the word had been there.

She picks up Tupper Daniels' bright, neat manuscript and slips it back into the yellow envelope.

Different women crying in different rooms in different cities, on different days of the week. One fat, one thin, one buxom, one small and wiry like her mother. A trail of broken-hearted women crying because he is gone, again, but all the while knowing he will return, again, to leave, to return; and all the townspeople wishing to be in her place, to receive him, again. A trail of broken-hearted women with before them a lifetime of sad partings and joyous reunions; of heartbreaks that do no damage and happy endings that end nothing.

Perhaps, she thinks, it is only frantic arm-waving when a simple direction would do; perhaps her job has become too easy and she's feeling the need to wear herself out. Perhaps this stubborn celibacy has left her with a need to wear herself out in other kinds of frantic, inconsequential acts. Perhaps she is merely curious.

He told her his book was about a bigamist, a polygamist, a chameleon of a man who balances women like so many spinning plates on so many tall sticks; a man, he said, whom every woman will be intrigued by. As she slips his neat manuscript into her brief case, she's almost beginning to believe him.

II

W HEN I GOT TO MAINE THAT AUG-
ust, my mother was thinner than I'd ever seen her. Muscular,
somehow, although undoubtedly aged, as if she had shed so
much of herself, her old plumpness, until this tight core, which
had always been there, was all that was left. The house where
she was living was nothing like the house we had lived in on
Long Island, with its painted red bricks and white shingles, its
wrought-iron porch and fake black shutters, the house I had
last seen her in. This was a small, squat cottage set in a shallow
valley among heavy oaks, off a road that was really only a
half-mile extension of Ward's driveway, a road that ended in
my mother's driveway and a narrow footpath that led to the
beach. The house was covered with rough maroon and green
shingles, and there was a low, sloping screen porch across the
back and a small, dilapidated greenhouse to the right. The land
around it was soft with layer upon layer of dead leaves, and even
on the hottest days there was a damp coolness about the house;
it had a smell that alternately struck me as fertile and tomblike.

I was twenty-three-years old and I had just left the man I'd
been living with. I say "just"; I mean I had called my mother
at six o'clock that morning from the Buffalo train station, my
three pieces of American Tourister (a high school graduation
gift from her), my two coats and a shopping bag full of shoes

making a fortress around me, and said I was coming to see her. I didn't know how long I would stay.

I hadn't seen her in nearly two years, the two years since I'd moved in with Bill, the two years since she had sold our house on Long Island and moved to Maine. Of course, we'd spoken on the phone since then. Short, long-distance conversations full of pauses that always ended with one of us saying, "So, what else is new?" We were close in that we had shared my father and much time alone together in our small house, but we had never been given to whispered, late-night conversations about ourselves or to crying on each other's shoulders, and knowing this helped me feel as I waited for the train that morning that I was truly just stopping by to visit, not crawling back to her with my life in pieces.

Ward, my mother's landlord and neighbor, picked me up at the train station in Boston. He was a tall, thin man with buck teeth and sharp blue eyes. Had his mouth been smaller, his face fuller and his ears not quite so thick, he might have been handsome; as it was, he was merely homely. The type who you knew immediately had always been optimistically homely, who had always held the promise of an ugly duckling but never quite made the transformation, never had that moment when he blossomed or filled out or even looked a little better than you remembered him. Still, there was something very gentle, nearly gallant, about the way he approached me in the station and bent over me to take the suitcases from my hands. I disliked him immediately.

"This is quite a surprise," he said as we pulled away from the station. His car, an old, boxy Plymouth, was terribly neat and reeked of the sweet, genderless perfume of its deodorizer, a cardboard skunk that hung from the radio's tuning knob. I opened the window a little and smiled at him.

"I guess so," I said, shouting the "so."

"When Dolores came up to my house this morning and told

me you were coming, I actually asked if she hadn't dreamt that you called." He laughed a little or perhaps just cleared his throat. "She said what amazed her the most was not that you were coming but that you were up at six A.M." He glanced at me briefly. "Guess you're not an early riser."

"No," I said, wondering why my mother had sent him, why she had not come herself or at least come along with him. "I'm not."

We were driving over a dark bridge, Boston behind us, the narrowing harbor on either side. When we stopped at the toll booth, Ward said "Hiya," in what seemed an exaggerated Maine accent.

"Dolores tells me you two haven't seen each other for a while." He seemed to repeat my mother's name unnecessarily, as if he were trying to prove to me that he knew her well.

"That's right," I said. "I guess we've both been pretty busy."

He sucked his teeth, nodding a little. "Dolores has had a hard life," he said softly, and then, louder, "She's done well up here, your mother has. She's quite a woman." I watched his profile, the sallow skin, the gray stubble on his cheek. The thick white hair, nearly yellow in places. He shook his head again. "After all she'd been through, to have come up here and started a new life for herself. You have to admire her. After all the hard times she'd had."

I folded my arms in front of me and stared out the window. Fast-food restaurants, trailer parks, topless discos, motels with four-wheeled rent-a-signs in their parking lots advertising vibrating waterbeds and adult movies. And then, just beyond this strip, white colonial houses, green lawns. Suburbia.

"You really do have to hand it to her," Ward said. "With the hard times she's had."

I laughed a little, implying I knew far more than he. "Oh, things were never very hard," I said.

He glanced at me again. I'd swallowed his bait. "Children often mistake their own happiness for that of their parents. When your mother came up here, she started her life over again. I believe she needed to."

I shrugged and laughed a little, but he was beginning to annoy me.

My mother's life at home had been made up of morning TV shows and shirtwaist dresses, meetings of the Mothers' Club and afternoon naps. Waiting patiently for my father.

My clearest image of her then is of a plump woman in a yellow dress, humming, peeling potatoes at the sink at five o'clock on a winter evening, the water running, the radio giving the traffic report, the table, set by me, ready for the two of us. And it was this image that made Ward's talk of suffering ludicrous.

Yet, when we got to Maine and I saw where my mother was living and how thin she had gotten and how she wore her graying hair tied back in a low ponytail, like some old male hippie, it was this image that my mind turned to, held onto, as she embraced me and kissed my cheeks.

"You'll find your mother's changed," Ward had said to me in the car as we passed from New Hampshire into Maine. "She's happy." He hadn't said if she was changed *and* happy or happy merely because she was changed.

My father had seldom been home. Sometimes he was gone for days, sometimes for months, and he and my mother were always so casual about his trips, his "jobs away," that it was years before I realized our lives were unusual. When I did realize it, I saw my friends' predictable gone-at-seven, back-at-six fathers as dull and burdensome.

Even now, I'm not sure what he did on his jobs away. Once, when I asked him what his occupation was, he told me he was a gigolo, and I dutifully reported the news to my friends and to Sister Immaculate Rose, my second-grade teacher. When the nun smiled kindly and told me to ask him again, he said to tell her he was with the government. We were in the kitchen, I on my father's lap sipping his beer, my mother at the sink washing something. I remember she turned and smiled and told my father not to teach me to lie, but she offered no alternative answer.

A year or so later, my mother and I ran into Sister Immaculate Rose as we were coming out of church. She noticed my father wasn't with us and mentioned that I'd said he worked for the government.

"That's right," my mother answered coolly.

"How interesting," the nun said. "In what capacity?"

My mother stared at her a long time and then slipped her sunglasses from the top of her head, over her eyes. "I'm not at liberty to say," she whispered. Her lips barely seemed to move. The nun glanced at me and I tried to make my face as grave as my mother's. Then, without another word, we both walked stiffly, mysteriously, away. At home we said nothing about the encounter and I presumed the answer, though still not true, was no longer a lie.

The nuns, it seemed, were always fascinated by my father. Perhaps they sniffed some tragedy, some rich life of sin behind his disappearances, or found my mother's devotion to a man who was seldom there similar to their own calling; whatever the reason, they often asked me about him and gave me deep, searching looks whenever I, or anybody else, spoke about fathers in class.

On the day he died—that is, the day we heard he was dead —my mother gave me a picture of him to take to school with me after the funeral. She said the nuns at Blessed Virgin, the "all-girl" high school where I was a freshman, would probably take me aside when I got back and ask a lot of questions, so I should show them the picture to curb their curiosity.

A week later, on my first day back at school, I was called from my homeroom the minute I got to my seat. Sister Illuminata, the principal, Sister Lucille and Sister Reine Regina, our religion teachers, were waiting for me in the "Rap Room," a former storage closet that had been set aside for "rap sessions" between the nuns and the girls in the school. It was decorated with the felt posters an art class had made and was closed the following year when one of the nuns found an unopened condom among the cushions and bean-bag chairs.

The three sisters hovered around me, their hands between their breasts or up their sleeves, and asked me how my mother was, how I was, and was it business my father was on when he died? I mumbled yes and then whipped out the snapshot my mother had given me. They passed it around, saying how handsome he was and nodding at one another as if that's what they'd expected.

A year later, I was taken aside again by Sister Loretta Belle Lynn (the nuns had started using their real names by then), a gaunt, ancient nun who occasionally taught Latin and often called girls into her office for "spiritual guidance counseling." She sat me in her small, dusty cubicle, asked me about school and what sports I liked, and if I had a boyfriend, and then, leaning so low across her desk that the blotter made her chin and bony throat reflect green, she whispered, eyes wide, "I saw your father last night."

Although I was beginning to read Freud and Nietzsche by then, beginning to drink heavily on weekends and to argue cynically about anything, I had nearly ten years of Catholic training and just enough Irish blood in me to drop my mouth open and begin to tremble. Immediately, I pictured the dark, cell-like room where the nun must have slept and my father's pale, wispy form slowly gathering in it.

"You did?" I whispered back.

She smiled and I thought I glimpsed something serene and

mystical about her yellow teeth and smooth, thin lips. "He said he misses your mother very much."

I felt my heart beating. My mother, not me. I wondered if he had seen me Saturday night at Jack's party.

"It's very hard for him being without her."

I nodded, my mouth was dry.

"That's why he needs your help. You must do everything you can for him." She ran the words together like a chant. "You want to help him, don't you?"

"Yes, Sister," I whispered.

"Well," she went on. "It was about seven last night when I saw him." I thought it oddly early, but decided she must have been in chapel, after dinner. She paused, played with her worn, married-to-God wedding band. "I was just coming out of the drugstore and your father was just coming in. He had a bag of groceries with him and he said he had to pick up some cold medicine. The poor man hadn't even gotten home from work yet." She leaned forward a little. "Now, Elizabeth," she said, "you could very well do the shopping when you get out of school at three and not leave it to your father. I know you probably want to be with your friends after school, but with your mother gone, you'll have to make some sacrifices, for your dear father's sake."

I looked down at my hands. "Yes, Sister," I said. Frances Connelly's mother had died a few weeks before. Sister Loretta had gotten the last name right but "E" comes before "F" in the school files, so she'd sent for me. "I'll do my best, Sister," I said. I left the office with her blessing, feeling I had done both Sister Loretta and Frances Connelly a great favor.

When I told my mother about the incident, she merely shook her head and said she would light a candle for poor Sister Loretta that night when she went down to St. Elizabeth's for the Altar Rosary Society meeting.

My mother, by then, had become very active in our church,

probably because it provided her with enough holy days and conferences and missions and bazaars and meetings to absorb her need for expectations, something to look forward to, just as hopeless crushes and later, hopeless love affairs, absorbed mine. It was a need my father had established in both of us.

While my father was alive, we lived in a constant, subtle state of expectation. We'd wake up every morning thinking this might be a day he'd come home, and go to bed at night thinking we might awake at any time to find him leaning over us, smiling. We were happy to have each day begin and happy to have it behind us, to have been brought one day closer to the day he would return.

When he did return, whether it was for a day or long enough for us to grow confident in his presence, casual in our references to him (but casual in the same self-conscious way I have since heard the newly rich refer to their help and their summer homes), our house was blessed by that strange aura that guests or Christmas or even just having all the lights on at three A.M. can give a place. My mother would put the special white chenille bedspread on her bed, and I would lie awake at night listening to him snoring in her room, trying to interpret the deep, throaty sounds he made, imagining it was his own secret way of speaking to me.

On the morning we got the call from Wisconsin, telling us he was there and he was dead, I stayed home from school and my mother and I had breakfast on tin snack tables in the living room. We watched all her favorite morning shows, shows that school usually deprived me of, and she said how good it was to have someone there who appreciated Hugh Downs' good looks and soft manner as much as she did. We cried together when we changed the channel and caught the last half hour of *Now, Voyager.* That afternoon my mother got dressed and went down to church to talk to the priest, who convinced her to join the Altar Rosary Society. Two weeks later, I fell madly in love with Rosemary Hart's brother Tim, who drove us home from school one day. He was a senior at Pius X Seminary and well on his way to the priesthood, but I never knew when he would show up at school to drive us home again.

By the time I left for college, my mother was known to nearly every priest and nun in the Rockville Centre diocese as good Mrs. Connelly, and she'd had lunch with the bishop three times. When she took a weekend off to drive me up to school, I felt rather like some mongrel who'd interrupted the meditations of Saint Francis to be let out to pee. She did it graciously, willingly, because she loved me, but it was clear she had more important things to get back to.

She kept our house and her faith until I graduated from college, and then, on the day I returned with my steamer trunk and my arctic parka, my diaphragm and my résumés, she said I'd have to find an apartment of my own because she was selling the house and moving to Maine.

She said nothing about giving up her religion, but when I arrived in Maine that August and went into her bedroom to unpack my bags, I saw no crucifix above the bed, no rosary beads on the night table, no prayer book, no holy cards, not even the statue of St. Jude, patron of hopeless cases and her favorite apostle, perched on the wide windowsill.

There was only the white chenille bedspread on the big, fourposter bed and, on the heavy dresser, in a new silver frame, a blurry snapshot of my father.

"I've cleaned out the two top drawers for you," my mother said, pointing to the dresser. "And half the closet."

She pulled open the closet, which was actually an old wooden armoire, and showed me the empty side, the tangled hangers rattling within it. "That should be enough room."

"Sure," I said. "I guess so." I glanced at my three suitcases, my coats, my shopping bag, all my worldly possessions.

"Of course," my mother said, "you'll have to leave some

things packed. Just push the suitcases under the bed when you're through with them." She had her hands on the hips of her gray, baggy trousers and her rolled-up shirtsleeves made little wings on her elbows. I was used to seeing her plump, her hair teased into curls, her face round and somewhat surprised-looking. I had a terrible impulse to wail, I want to go home!

She crossed the room and embraced me again. Even her smell was wrong, not perfume but soap and woodsmoke. "It will be all right," she whispered, in her old way, and then she backed away, smiling, as if she had given me some secret message and now must carry on with her part. "You must be hungry," she said, "I'll make us something to eat."

I smiled, too brightly perhaps: an intruding houseguest pretending her welcome was sincere. "That sounds great," I said and she nodded and patted my arm, leaving me alone to unpack what I could.

My mother had been raised to believe that to ask any personal questions was to pry, to presume there was something that would not be told voluntarily, and, as I was growing up, she had passed the belief on to me. It seems ironic in light of our Catholicism, which makes a ritual of prying, of exposing your private life to another, albeit in a quiet, guarded atmosphere, a yellow-lighted darkroom of sorts, where the exposure will not be too great and the listener is sworn to secrecy, but even now I am surprised and somewhat offended by strangers who can sit beside me at a party or on a train and ask me about my love life and my sex life and my deepest fears. I am somewhat envious, too, of those who can answer such questions easily, although I often wonder what so much discussion, so much exposure, does to the quality of those feelings.

That evening, over grilled cheese sandwiches and tea, we discussed Ward ("He's a dear man," my mother said, "but so ugly.") and Lillian, an old woman my mother had met on the beach, and some of my friends from high school and even the service on Amtrak. But she did not ask me why I had left Buffalo so suddenly, nor did I ask her why she was living here, so far from all her old friends and neighbors, from Brooklyn and Long Island where she had spent her life.

Whatever you need to know about a person, my mother used to tell me, you'll find out eventually if you pay attention.

Life as a play, not a press conference.

Later we sat in the small living room, she on the overstuffed reading chair by the window, I on the corduroy day bed where I was to sleep, and watched a TV movie about two girls trying to make it in Las Vegas. We were both in our robes, and I was very tired, but I could still feel the motion of my long train ride and I could see, as if from the corner of my eye, that the events of last night and early that morning were still with me, and so I was not ready to go to sleep.

I liked, too, seeing my mother in the thick quilted robe she had worn at home, that now, too big for her, gave her some of the bulk and familiarity she had been missing. She was still not the same as she had been before, not to me, but in the hours I'd been there this new image of her had begun to merge slowly with the old, and I wondered if her hair hadn't always been this gray, if she'd ever really been that heavy, if those deep lines that looked like dark parentheses around her lips had not more or less always been there. I had trouble recalling how she'd looked when her hair was short and curly.

The TV helped, too, the sound, the light. After my father and our old house, it was the thing my mother and I had shared the most, back home.

When the movie ended—one of the girls became a serious actress, the other mistress to an eccentric millionaire—my mother looked at me and grimaced and said, "Junk." I agreed, although I had enjoyed it.

"We should get to bed," she said. "No one stays up this late in Maine." She stood and gathered the blanket and pillow that she had set out on the rocking chair. "If you need another blanket during the night, just come into my room and take one from the closet. It gets rather cold at night."

"Okay." I took the bolsters and the corduroy covers from the bed. The sheets underneath were plain white and smelled cold. "It must be brutal in here during the winter."

"Oh, it's terribly cold," she said. She put the pillow under her chin, slipped it into the case and threw it on the bed with a deftness I knew I could never match. My mother again.

"Last winter," she said, "there were drifts that nearly covered the roof." She turned down the bed, smoothed the top sheet over the edge of the gray blanket.

"Is it warm enough for you?" I asked, hearing her own tone as she'd approved each of my winter coats and the apartments I'd had up at college. "I mean, is it winterized and everything?"

She looked over the bed and then looked up at me and smiled. "No," she said. "Not at all. I stay at Ward's house during the winter."

She pushed a piece of my hair back behind my ear. Although we were the same height, the gesture made me feel very small. Even her robe smelled of woodsmoke, although the cottage had no fireplace.

"Isn't that scandalous?" I asked, trying to laugh.

"No," she said. She held herself before me rather delicately, as if her center were made of fragile glass. It made me feel childish, or fat, clumsy—a woman without a lover facing a woman with one. I glimpsed, for a moment, what Ward must have found so fascinating and tragic about her: that odd and delicate core, full of secrets. "We old people," she said, "are easily forgiven our indiscretions. Especially during the long, cold winters. In the summer, Ward likes to stay here, so it works out nicely." She hugged me again, quickly this time. "It is good to have you here," she whispered. "I hope you'll stay a little while."

She went into her bedroom, closed the wide white door between us. When I turned off the light, and then the television, the room was completely black and the sounds outside, the crickets, the ocean, what might have been a buoy, seemed to rise. In bed, I tried to think of this as my mother's house, and thus, in some way, my house too, but I was unable to bring any of it together.

I felt for my ring and realized I could have been anyone, anywhere, starting from scratch, from the womb, from the gates of Ellis Island, surrounded by strangers.

I'd taken the ring off on the train that morning. I'd made a ceremony of it. As soon as my suitcases were stored above my head and my two coats arranged neatly on the seat beside me and the train had started moving with the rhythm that was to keep me feeling strangely renewed and unfamiliar to myself the entire way to Boston, I walked back to the club car and bought a small bottle of wine. Back at my seat, I'd cracked it open, or at least twisted the cap until the plastic seal broke with a pleasant cracking sound, and poured half of it into my clear plastic cup. I took a quick sip of the wine and put the cup on the white tray before me.

I twisted the ring on my finger, brought it up to my knuckle, thinking things like: to love, honor, cherish. To love forever, despite everything. To say this is the one I love, will always love. Everything will change but this, in me. Trying to bring tears to my eyes. But I could remember only that it was a ring I had bought for myself, one of many on a tall, black-velvet finger in a Buffalo jewelry store, on sale. I'd worn it home and waited for Bill to notice it the way Lucy would have waited for Ricky to notice her false eyelashes or blackened front teeth: fearful of his reaction, aware of my own foolishness. And when I'd explained, so coolly, that I thought it would save me a lot of explanations, he'd merely shrugged, although months later he said that he'd noticed a lot of women wearing them, women who, like me, were merely living with someone, not interested in marriage. He said there was something dishonest about it.

I pulled the ring off my finger and saw the white band of skin, the ghost of a ring, it had left there. I put the ring on the tray, took a large swallow of wine, let the tears fill my eyes. It was a lovely moment of pale light and changing colors, of the train's sad attempts at homeyness: the carpeted floors, the soft blue-and-gold chairs, the headrests like expensive paper towels. I looked at the gold ring on the white table, the clear glass with the pale-yellow wine, the green bottle beside it, all of it trembling, swaying with the motion of the train. Perfectly, the train whistle blew.

I looked at the white scarlike mark on my finger and I took another sip of wine, quickly, like a sad woman, a woman with a broken marriage. I lifted the ring, held it in my fist, a final embrace, and then slipped it into the small ashtray at my side.

I drank some more wine and imagined the reaction of the conductor, the engineer, the black man who cleaned the trains, whoever would find it. I imagined him taking it home, standing in his small kitchen with the ring in his palm like a beautiful dead bird, his wife drying her hands on her apron, looking at it shaking her head, and then turning back to the stove and wondering what would be the fate of her own worn band; his children peering over his thumb, wanting to ask if they can have it, the boys to store it with their foreign coins and two-dollar bills, the girls to slip it on their own fingers, to pretend it is a gift from their own imaginary lovers.

Bill had once accused me of inventing my life, re-creating it, making it into a movie or a play. He'd said he knew me too well to provide a gullible audience.

"Your mother made a new life for herself," Ward had said in the car. "When she came here, she started over." Among strangers, he should have added, gullible strangers willing to believe in tragedy and romance, a hard life in a comfortable home with fake black shutters and a wrought-iron porch. A marriage ending sadly on a train to Boston.

Two weeks later, I left my mother's house for my own apartment in New York.

III

TUPPER DANIELS' NOVEL HAD NO
ending. The last page ended with half a sentence in the middle
of a paragraph in what seemed to be the beginning of a chapter. The night before, she had read the first twenty pages and
then, abandoning her resolve to read the whole thing, scanned
the rest and skipped to the end, where she discovered there
wasn't one. She'd drunk half a bottle of wine by then, so she
gave up and went to bed. If she'd been looking for her father
(as she'd been told by books and articles and countless young
men that she should be), she hadn't found him in Tupper
Daniels' long, complex sentences.

Now he smiles at her across her desk when she asks if
perhaps there are some pages missing.

"No," he says, shaking his head a little. "It has no ending."

"I see." She looks down at the manuscript, straightens its
pages. "You don't want it to." She tries to make it sound like
both a statement and a question. If he tells her this is his own
unique literary device, she wants to be able to say that's what
she thought it was—how marvelous, what a fascinating idea.

He makes his pale eyes wide, raises his eyebrows. "No," he
says, "I want it to have an ending. I just haven't written it yet."

She leans back. She can't do a page count and put a price
on the contract until she knows how long it's going to be.

"Well," she says hesitantly, "are you writing the ending now?"

He is sitting back in his chair, his elbows on the armrests, his legs crossed. Today he is wearing lime-green corduroy pants and a yellow sweater; his blue blazer is draped over his lap. He seems to be making a great effort to seem casual. "No," he says, matter-of-factly. "I didn't tell you I hadn't written the ending because a couple of other publishers refused to look at it until it was finished." He leans forward, crossing his arms over his crossed knees. "You see, I'm stuck. I don't know where to go with it. It's the same thing I told the other publishers: If I could just get some help on it, just a good editor to work with me, I know I could finish it." He smiles at her again, coyly, drawls: "Have *you* got any suggestions?"

She smiles back at him. This is a new one. Many authors ask for help but none of them really want to be told anything, except that everything they've written is perfect. "I guess I have a few ideas," she says. Mr. Owens: "Sweetheart, you never tell an author no. You say maybe, perhaps, we'll see, let me look into it for you, but never no."

Tupper Daniels sits up on the edge of his chair and slaps her desk. "Good," he says. "I knew I was doing the right thing coming to Vista. I knew if I had a publisher behind me I could get the thing finished." His forehead seems to sink a little. "That is, if you're willing to publish me."

"Oh, yes," she says, on safe ground again. "I loved the book. You have a wonderful style, it echoes some of our greatest Southern writers." She pauses, looks thoughtful. "But you know, it goes beyond them too. I honestly think your voice takes the Southern tradition a step further, into a new decade, so to speak. Faulkner, Flannery O'Connor, Mark Twain, were all Southern writers of their time. You, it seems to me, are a Southern writer for our time."

He is holding his lips together as if his mouth contained some small animal struggling to escape. "And the story," he says, looking at his hands, "do you think it moves well?"

"Beautifully," she tells him, nearly whispering the word. "I was up all night with it, couldn't put it down. Your character, Beale, the polygamist, is so fascinating, not only for what he does, but for what he represents—as a symbol of life's transience, unpredictability."

Tupper Daniels is so elated his cheeks seem to bulge. Were she to put a match to him, she's sure he would explode.

"And the women," she goes on, having fun now. "I'm amazed that a man can write about women with such sensitivity. Honestly, not since Henry Miller have I seen such understanding."

He deflates a little. "Henry Miller?"

She laughs. She's overdone it. "Miller? Did I say Henry Miller?" She searches her mind. "James. I meant Henry *James.*"

He grins. "You were probably thinking of *Daisy Miller.*"

"Yes," she says. "Not since James have I seen women dealt with so well."

His neck is flushed beneath the turned-up collar of his white alligator. She fully expects him to yell, "EEE-Ha!" but instead he cries, "How about lunch? I'll even buy. My treat to you!"

She checks the clock. It's only eleven-thirty, but her expense account is limited and a free lunch is a free lunch.

She puts on her jacket and picks up her purse. As they walk out the door, he puts his hand on her elbow. Ann peers up over the partition and Elizabeth waves and tells her she's going to lunch. Ann winks. Bonnie, a folded red-and-white straw stuck like a thermometer into the corner of her mouth, scowls at Tupper Daniels as they leave.

In the elevator, they stand apart. She notices he is wearing socks today, gray ones. He has his hands crossed over his fly. She wonders what he thinks the relationship between an editor and an author should be. At the third floor, a young Puerto

Rican woman gets in. Elizabeth has seen her before, she works in the styrofoam factory in the building. She chews gum impatiently and dances a little as the elevator descends. Tupper Daniels glances at her from beneath his eyelids. Elizabeth wonders if she wears her bright green high heels while she makes styrofoam.

"Well," Tupper Daniels says when they get outside. "You're the New Yorker, where is there a nice quiet place?"

She looks up and down the street, as if deciding. The September air is cool, full of sun and grit. There's a strong wind blowing in from the river and the street is filled with gray trucks. This far west, there are more parking garages than quiet restaurants.

"There's a place down the block," she tells him, shouting over the trucks. He puts his hand out for her to lead the way.

Inside at their table, he looks around and compliments the place as if she had decorated it herself. He likes the white tablecloths, the short oak bar, the bare floors, the ferns in the one small window. He likes the candlelight at lunchtime and the waiters who wear black bow ties and white bibs. He likes the wine and the bowl of black olives and celery sticks. She wonders if this is his way of repaying her for complimenting his book. She wonders how long he's waited for such compliments.

"So," he says, after having raised his glass and whispered, To a wonderful relationship. "How do you usually work with your authors? Should I come in every day, every other day? Do we have lunch together a couple of times a week?"

She takes a sip of her wine. It hadn't occurred to her that he'd actually want to spend time with her. "Well, it mostly depends on what's convenient for you," she tells him, improvising. "Maybe you should just write an ending, or a couple of endings and then show them to me."

He nods and spits an olive pit into his cupped hand. "Well,

I thought maybe we could just talk about it first. You know, kick some ideas around."

"Fine," she says, "if that will help." She can't have him in her office three or four times a week. "Why don't we start right now?"

He laughs a little, showing his square smile. "Good," he says. "You're dedicated. That's what I need. I'm a terrible procrastinator—like most writers, I'm told. If it had been up to me, we'd just sit here and get drunk and get to know each other." He sits up, smoothing the white tablecloth before him, serious. "Okay. You said you had some ideas. Shoot."

She wonders if he thinks she's a bore. She sips her wine again. "Well, first I'd like to know how you're thinking," she tells him. "How do you see the ending?" A good move, she thinks, throw the unanswerable question back to the questioner, just like the teachers used to do in college. She wonders if she might have made a good real-life editor after all.

He raises his hands and makes a tight-lipped grimace. "I don't see it at all," he says. "Bailey, the man who lived in Gallatin, where I grew up, the one the book is based on, is still alive. As far as I know. I left town when I went to Andover and the next year my family moved back to my grandmother's house in Monteagle, so I never heard very much about him after that. Except that his second wife, Luanne, died—which is already in the book—and then that he was found to be a bigamist, which I don't want to include in the book because I don't know how to write good courtroom drama. I've tried."

She puts one of the black olives into her mouth and then wishes she hadn't. It seems to make an awkward bulge in her cheek and the harshness makes her tongue wrap around itself. It tastes salty, foreign. She sucks the pit as he goes on.

"I've even done some research. I called a few people I still know in Gallatin and asked about Bailey, but they couldn't tell me anything new." He pours her some more wine. "So I'm stuck. I guess the novel has no end because Bailey doesn't seem to have one either."

The waiter brings them their soup and Tupper says, "That looks good." She slips her pit onto the white plate under the bowl. It's cold cucumber soup, laced with a flavor like walnuts.

"Have you ever had this problem before?" he asks. "An author without an ending?"

She shrugs a little. "I've had them with bad endings," she says, rather world-weary. "But never without an ending at all."

He laughs. "I guess you do see a lot of bad stuff. There are so many people who think they can write."

"True."

He sips his soup and looks at her over his spoon. "Do you come here with all your authors?" he asks.

She feels her stomach drop, as if the entire restaurant has just gone over a sharp hill.

"It depends," she says.

He laughs a little, spooning his soup. She wonders if she's blushing, squirming. "This is a loaded question," he says, studying the soup, "but I'm curious. I'm curious about women in power, I guess. How they handle it. Maybe you should think of me as Henry James doing research when I ask you this."

"What is it?" she says, perhaps a little impatiently.

He looks up at her. "Well, what if an author you're working with comes on to you? Do you think"—he makes a stupid, almost cross-eyed face and she wonders if it's supposed to be hers—" 'God, he just wants me to publish his book,' or do you give him the benefit of the doubt? I mean, you *are* a very attractive woman and you do have a certain amount of power. Do the two things sometimes give you problems?"

The waiter clears their plates. "Not really," she says over his arms. "It's easy enough to separate the two."

"That's good," he says. "After all, men do it all the time, don't they? Separate the two, I mean. Home and office, work and play."

"Yes," she says, "that's true."

They were in his office that was all oak and leather and rich browns. Even the light from the one lamp seemed beige, golden brown.

The waiter brings them their lunches. Cold smoked chicken, asparagus salad, tomato aspic.

"Sometimes," Tupper Daniels says, "I think I may be missing something, never having had a nine-to-five job, an office, power, regular lunch hours."

Before the office, they'd had dinner here, at a table farther back, where he could still watch the door. A married man's oldest habit, he'd said, watch out for it whenever you meet someone new. He was publishing a book of poetry, under the pen name Conrad Sikes. She'd only been working a few months and had not yet been trusted with an expense account, so when he asked to buy her dinner, she saw it as the job's first fringe benefit. And she'd pitied him. Mid-sixties, somewhat wealthy, probably once handsome but now simply a nice dresser with a permanent tan, a round, old belly. Most of his poems were about his sixteen-year-old son, his only child, who was severely retarded, living in an expensive school near Philadelphia. The one poem she'd read all the way through told how hard he found it to praise the boy for writing his name on a piece of lined paper, in large, gross letters, at a time when his friends' sons were being praised for making the football team and the National Honor Society. How he sometimes prayed that the boy would die.

They drank cocktails, two kinds of wine, brandy. The waiters nearly bowed to him. Whenever he mentioned his son, he would duck his head and say, "But you don't want to hear about my troubles," and then, minutes later, bring him up again. He wanted to discuss poetry, but he knew far more than she.

"I decided to be a writer while I was at Vanderbilt," Tupper Daniels is saying. "And when I graduated, my parents gave me an office in one of our guest bedrooms and a weekly salary. They said the Daniels family had not yet produced a writer."

She smiles at him, nods.

It was December. The wind from the river was bitter and she had four long blocks to walk to the subway. His car, a silver-gray Cadillac, was right there. And did she mind, he asked as they drove smoothly up Eighth Avenue, if he stopped at his office for a minute? It was on the way.

She tries to remember: Was she playing innocent? Was she truly naïve, drunk?

"My first novel was awful, I began it at Vanderbilt. It was, I'm ashamed to say, terribly *macho*. Hunting and fishing and violent intercourse."

She laughs. "Really?"

He had his own keys to the building. The walls of the lobby were gold, the floor a beige marble. He took her arm as they walked toward the elevator; her heels clicked and echoed.

"Actually, it was like *Deliverance,*" Tupper Daniels says. "Lots of action. But totally heterosexual."

Upstairs, the silence was frightening, exciting. To their right there was a glass wall and a set of glass doors with gold lettering. Everything behind it was black, and as he opened the glass door with another set of keys she stood by the elevator, wondering what she would do if he told her to step into that blackness. She decided she would run, but wasn't sure if it would be forward or backward, into whatever he was planning or away from it.

When he got the door open he said, over his shoulder, "Just wait here a minute." She was strangely disappointed. Her reflection in the glass embarrassed her. Her long hair was tangled, her raincoat was wrinkled along its hem. She was standing in a bare hallway, alone, left out, denied entrance.

"The two main characters were trappers, you see. Handsome, virile. But they had been Rhodes scholars too, so when they started trapping, they noticed that there was a kind of organized crime controlling the fur business from start to finish."

Finally, a soft light went on behind the glass. He was standing by a big round desk, and he waved for her to come in.

"Sorry," he said as she entered. "I couldn't find the switch."

The light was under a large blue-and-green oil painting that nearly covered the far wall. It left the rest of the room in light shadow. The carpeting was a sea green, the four round chairs and two round couches were blue and green, set in two semicircles opposite the green reception desk. She felt she was underwater, submerged in a goldfish bowl. She was finding it difficult to breathe.

"They only trapped for sport, and enough money to support themselves. One was a painter, the other an aspiring writer."

He took her arm again and led her down a dim corridor. It smelled of paper, aftershave, ink. She heard herself chattering, sounding more drunk than she was. Her legs ached.

He opened a final door. Turned on a light. The brown office. Leather, shining oak, the softest browns. Large ferns by the heavy brown drapes.

He went to the huge desk at the far end of the room. "I'll just be a minute," he said.

"The climax was a wolf hunt where they became the ones being hunted."

She stood by the door. The only light was from a tall lamp beside the leather couch. The light was beige, golden brown.

He turned from the desk, some kind of portfolio under his arm. He smiled. "That's all," he said. "We can go."

He walked toward her and she turned to let him open the door. She noticed the gold tie tack in his red-and-blue silk tie, saw his long, tanned fingers reach for the doorknob. Then he turned a little more, slipped the portfolio onto the table behind him. He put his hands on the lapels of her coat and the touch made her stomach flinch, as if it had been kicked from the inside.

"I would like so much to see you," he said, his voice soft, suddenly hoarse. She smiled a little, politely.

"My son, my wife. There's not much beauty in my life. I promise I won't touch you. I'd just like to look at you."

She knew it was not the type of thing she would do. He worked intently on the buttons of her blouse, biting his lip childishly. She pushed his hands aside and undid them herself. He knelt before her as he took off her shoes and stockings and she could see his skull just under the thin hairs; it seemed soft, painfully bare. She told herself she pitied him.

When he looked up at her, his eyes were filled with tears. "I won't touch you," he assured her again. He stood up and went to his desk, sat stiffly behind it. "Just let me look," he said. "I just want to look at you."

She stepped over her clothes and into the middle of the floor. The carpet was beautifully soft against her feet. She moved around the room, looked at some books on a shelf, brushed her hand along a wall. She felt beautiful. Beautifully white, pure white, bright. She stretched out on the leather couch. It was soft glove leather, wonderfully cool. The golden light was all over her skin.

Later she felt that the incident had been some strangely erotic dream. Perhaps even the beginning of a strange affair. But from then on he had his secretary sign all his letters and make all his phone calls to her. She didn't speak to him again and she saw him only once, when he'd come to the office after his book was published. He pretended not to notice her.

Tupper Daniels orders coffee as the waiter clears their plates. "Too *macho* for today's market," he is saying. "You really have to appeal to women these days." She drains her last bit of wine and he glances at his watch. "Which brings us back to my book," he says. "I guess I've avoided working on it with you after all."

She smiles at him. "Are you busy tonight?"

He smiles, slyly, it seems to her. "Nothing that can't be canceled if I say I have to see my editor."

"Well, why don't you come over to my apartment tonight, say eight or nine or so? We can talk about the book then." Some part of her is wondering what she's doing. Other parts seem to know perfectly well.

He nods. "Sounds fine," he says, his voice low. "I can see why you have no problem with power."

She shrugs and picks up the check, hands it to him. "Then don't ask to arm wrestle for the bill." She can see he likes that: Kate Hepburn to John Wayne.

She wonders how many poses this "relationship" can inspire.

It was the *Playboy* fantasy, although not from the playboy's point of view. It was the fantasy she had foreseen as a child, sharing a stolen copy of the magazine with her girlfriends, seeing the women—pretty women they thought, beautiful princesses and Miss Americas and Cinderellas—draped over leather couches and dark beds, glowing white and beautiful in the leather and oak and deep brown nests of men.

Young as they were (eight? twelve? sixteen?) they studied those pictures, compared their own bodies to them, lifting their blouses, examining one another and later, standing alone before their mirrors, naked, posing, puckering their lips, mussing their hair, smiling. Alone.

They were always photographed alone, those women: beautiful and naked and unafraid in a world where everything was masculine, where the men were kept behind the camera, in the next room, in some shadow.

It was not pity alone that had made her do it. It was because he didn't touch her that night as she stretched out on the couch and felt her own golden skin. It was because he stayed behind his desk, in shadow, admiring her, while she alone was in the light. Because it was a perfect moment of selfishness, self-love, a moment she'd been taught all her life to long for.

That's why she undressed for him that night, why she enjoyed it so.

Maybe.

Maybe not.

Maybe, she thinks, she's only making excuses. Maybe she is merely perverse, maybe the night was merely sick, her own problem, her own weakness.

It all sounds so much like an excuse: I did it because I'm a woman, because I'm a repressed Catholic, because my father was never home.

Maybe she is simply sleazy and would, given the opportunity, take her clothes off for every old man, in every office. Maybe she was simply afraid to say no, too lazy to say no.

Maybe, she thinks, it was just me, my fault, and any other interpretation is merely an excuse.

Ann is standing in her doorway, smiling. "How was your Tupperware party?" she asks.

"Fine," Elizabeth says.

Ann moves into the office. Her matching skirt and blouse, navy blue and white, billows.

"Why is it," Elizabeth asks her, "that as soon as I figure out why something I've done shouldn't make me feel guilty, I feel guilty for making up excuses?"

She frowns down at her, her green eyes puzzled. "You mean like working here?" she asks.

Elizabeth returns her look.

"You know," Ann explains, "we tell each other, 'Look, we're not robbing these people, we're giving them what they want and getting paid for it. If we didn't publish their lousy books and take their lousy money, somebody else would.' Which is true, of course, but sounds an awful lot like an excuse for robbing people."

Elizabeth shakes her head, not pleased with the analogy. "I was thinking more of women," she says. "We're really not responsible for so many of our attitudes about ourselves, but"—she slaps her desk—"Jesus, even a statement like that sounds like an excuse. Of course we're responsible."

"Okay," Ann says, nodding. "I'm beginning to get your point. Like last weekend, when I met that guy Ray, remember? The one who was so nice and so good-looking and he bought me a drink and we talked for a while and then he said, 'So, you want to go someplace and fuck?' Remember I told you?"

She laughs. "I remember."

"So, when I asked him if that was all he was interested in and he said, 'You're fat, what else is a guy going to be interested in? Showing you off to his friends?' That was his problem, right? He was a rude moron, right?"

"Of course."

She puts her hands on her hips. "So why did I starve myself for the next two days?" She pinches her rear. "I'm all hips and breasts, I know that. It's the way I'm built. But I watch what I eat and I exercise and I like the way I look. At least, I thought I did. But then some jerk in a bar tells me I'm fat, and I starve myself for two days. I kept telling myself he was an asshole, but something else kept telling me that I was using that as an excuse for my lousy shape. That it was really *my* fault—like if I were skinny he wouldn't be a jerk."

Her voice is high now, shrill. Her eyes are sparkling. They both begin to laugh.

"I mean it," Ann says. "I ate nothing all weekend but a grapefruit and a bowl of soup. I kept thinking, 'If you weren't fat, you wouldn't think he was such an asshole—you'd be out with him tonight, he'd be showing you off.' Isn't that crazy?"

Elizabeth nods. "So," she says. "To repeat the question: Why do we feel guilty about knowing why we shouldn't?"

Ann looks at the ceiling. "Because," she says, ticking off the logic on her fingers, "if you feel guilty, you feel responsible; if you feel responsible, you feel there is something you can do about it. You've got some control. But no guilt means no responsibility, no control, no power. So we make ourselves feel guilty even when we have nothing to feel guilty about. You should have taken that course at NYU with me. We were always talking about women and guilt." She frowns again. "So what did you do to Tupperware that makes you feel guilty?"

"I invited him to my apartment tonight," she says and then quickly adds, "But that's not what I'm talking about."

Ann slaps her hands together. "Oh, good," she says. "Are you going to sleep with him or just let him look at you?"

She's a little startled. "Look at me?"

Ann laughs, taking a thin manuscript from the OUT box. "God, when you two walked out of here, he was watching you as if you were pure gold."

"That's because I'd just told him what a masterpiece he'd written."

She looks at the manuscript in her hand, reads the title page. *"Heart Murmurs.* Poetry, hey?" She shakes her head. "No, it was more than that. Pure adoration."

Elizabeth shuffles some papers, trying not to look too pleased. "Oh, great, that's all I need."

Ann shrugs, looking up from the poems. "So go to bed with him. Do what I did to Brian. Fuck the adoration right off his face." She turns and walks to the door. Blue and white. Hips and breasts. She turns suddenly. "Oh, dear," she says. "Speaking of adoration, that's what I came in for. Mr. Palmer is here to see you."

She moans. "Does he have an appointment?"

"You made it with him. That day he called to tell you his brother had just dropped dead on Beaver Street."

She remembers the day. Elizabeth had been one of the first people he called. His brother had been his last surviving relative.

"You felt sorry for him," Ann says.

"I know. Well, call me in fifteen minutes."

"Will do, boss." She swings out of the office, all hips.

Elizabeth tries to remember the logic: guilt, responsibility, power. This from Ann who turns every rotten thing Brian ever did into her own sly maneuver.

Mr. Palmer's bio card has little information. Jonathan Whitney Peale Palmer. Author of *Apocalyptic Calculations Based in the Third Dimension.* Lives in the Hotel Belvedere. Signed a $6,500 contract but is still making slight changes in his manuscript. Graduated from Harvard sixty years ago.

Another wealthy young man whose family paid to let him be a writer, or, actually, an apocalyptic mathematician, so that now, sixty years later, the sole survivor, he can publish a book that will give the family name immortality. If a name on a hundred books sitting in a dusty storeroom can be considered immortality.

But she'd felt sorry for him. It happens. In her two years here, she's learned to control her pity, but still, at times, it escapes, grows from her heart like those thin, flesh-colored bubbles that occasionally, unexpectedly, blossom between Bonnie's chapped lips: transparent, pulsing, achingly thin. Not that her authors deserve or even want it. Not that it does any of them any good.

She had pitied Conrad Sikes and he, the next time he saw her, ducked his head and raised his tanned fingers to his brow, like a reluctant star. As if, that night, he had been the star.

She returns Mr. Palmer's card to her file and goes out to the reception room to collect him. He is sitting on one of the Danish modern chairs, partly sunk into it, his battered brief case and black homburg on his lap, a faded blue ascot wrapped around his thin throat. He looks badly in need of a dusting.

"Mish Connelly!" he sputters when he sees her.

"Hello, Mr. Palmer," she shouts, holding out her hand, helping him out of the chair. "Nice to see you again."

He reeks of Old Spice and she can feel drops of spittle falling on her outstretched arm as he speaks. "Ash beautiful ash ever," he says, beaming, his yellow upper plate slipping from his gums with each word. His thin hair glistens with tonic.

"Thank you," she says. "You're looking well yourself. Come inside."

He goes through the door ahead of her and as he does, she notices Bonnie. Her hand is over her mouth, her eyes and blood-red forehead wrinkled with laughter.

Mr. Palmer walks slowly down the corridor, his free hand brushing the wall. Taking his elbow, she guides him into her office, into one of the brown chairs.

"Now, Mr. Palmer," she asks, smiling, closing the door. "What can I do for you?"

He lifts both hands and taps them on his brief case. "Thish is my manuscript," he says. "I want to show you the changes I made."

He fiddles with the latch and then hands the brief case to her, smiling apologetically. She opens it for him and passes it back across the desk. It's an old leather bag with the initials JWPP printed on it in worn gold letters.

He takes out the moth-eaten manuscript and she moves to the chair beside him so he won't have to lean across her desk.

"That'sh a lovely dress," he says softly before he begins.

"Thank you," she says.

He hands her the manuscript, then searches in his brief case again. She imagines Ned's reaction when *Apocalyptic Calculations* hits production.

Mr. Palmer extracts a small, wrinkled sketch from his bag. It is on dirty tissue paper and seems to be a grid of some kind.

"Thish," he says, pointing to the paper with a trembling finger, "goesh here." He taps the front page of the manuscript and she marks the spot with a red pen.

"Fine," she says.

"That'sh very important, you know."

She nods, looking grave, and he turns a few pages of the manuscript. "Theesh numbers here are all wrong," he says, pointing to a row of them.

She crosses them out with the red pen and he says, "Very good."

"What should they be?" she asks him.

He taps his fingers against his brow, rolling his eyes, wafting Old Spice through the room. "Eshleben," he says finally.

She repeats it and he nods and she writes 11 on the page.

"No," he cries, smiling. "Eshleben." Spittle hits the page like tiny raindrops.

"Seven?" she asks. He nods and she writes 7.

"No, no," he says again, laughing. He is being very patient with her. "Eshleben."

She points at the 11 she's just crossed out. "Eleven?" she asks again.

Very gently, he takes the pen from her hand and writes, in large, shaky letters: 29. He hands the pen back to her and points to the number. "Eshleben," he says, smiling.

She nods and he pats her gently on the shoulder. "Oh," she says loudly. "Eshleben."

This goes on. Five is 9, twenty-two is 50. He shouts numbers at her and she writes them down. Only twice is she right. Every other time, Mr. Palmer gently takes the pen and patiently writes the number for her. It's like learning to count all over again.

"See?" he asks, and she says, "Yes, twelb," nodding and pointing to a 93.

When the last number is changed (selenty-sel is 33), he sits back, sighs. "Now it'sh finished," he says. "It'sh a very good book."

"Yes," she tells him. And he smiles at her with all his perfectly yellow false teeth.

"Yesh," he says. "I know."

IV

WHEN SHE LEAVES WORK AT FIVE, she walks down to Penn Station. It's starting to get dark earlier now, and the crowds around Thirty-fourth Street are moving quickly, crossing the street in clumps, like conventions of blind people. A woman in a red coat stands in front of her as a group of them wait for the light on Eighth Avenue. The woman has a black attaché case tucked under her arm. "I'm sick of this," she tells another woman beside her. "Sick, sick, sick." The other woman laughs.

Downstairs in Penn Station it is dirty and bright. People are running stiffly, as if it had begun to rain and they have a specific shelter in mind. The whole place smells of doughnuts.

The bar is unbelievably dark, a yellow, muddy kind of darkness, and it takes her a while to see Joanne. She is in their usual booth, right next to the hot hors d'oeuvre. She flutters her fingers at Elizabeth, and Bert, the tall black man who carves the ham and dishes up the meatballs, says, "Here she is, here she is," as she approaches.

Joanne slides out of the booth and they hug. Although Elizabeth is nearly four inches taller, Joanne seems to lean into her a little, as if she were the one who had to bend for the embrace. They haven't seen each other since her wedding a month ago, although before that they met here for drinks nearly every Friday night. Joanne has a party to go to when she gets home tonight and Elizabeth has Tupper Daniels coming over, but they made this date two weeks ago and neither of them wanted to break it. They'd promised each other that Joanne's marriage wouldn't change their very old friendship, and this meeting is their token attempt to keep that promise.

"How *are* you?" Elizabeth says, sliding into the booth, slipping off her jacket. "You look great."

Joanne laughs, puts her thin fingers to her face. Her thick, shining wedding band. "Do I still have my tan?"

"You do," she says, looking closely. "How was Aruba?"

"Hot." She rolls her eyes. She has a narrow face and big, bulging brown eyes. Nervous hands. When they were in grammar school at St. Elizabeth's, people used to say that Elizabeth was the Irish version of Joanne and Joanne the Italian version of her. But since then Elizabeth has grown taller and wider and her nose has gotten sharp. Joanne has simply grown breasts, large ones; everything else about her has seemingly stayed just about the same.

The waitress comes to take Elizabeth's order and Joanne asks for another vodka and tonic, although the one before her is nearly filled. Elizabeth notices that the black bowl between them contains only popcorn kernels and is nearly empty.

"How long have you been here?" she asks.

Joanne shrugs. "Not long. So what's new with you? Did Toby ever call you?" She picks up one of the kernels and bites it between her front teeth.

"No," she says. "I didn't really expect him to." Toby was her partner at the wedding. They'd kept up a polite banter throughout the whole thing and eventually got ridiculously drunk together, but she was sure he'd only asked for her number because all the other unmarried ushers were asking all the other unmarried bridesmaids for theirs. "I think he just took my number because he was kind of caught up in the spirit of things."

"What do you mean?" Joanne asks, looking at her carefully, almost cautiously.

"Oh, you know, the wedding and the drinking and the dancing. And you and Tommy looked so cute together, I think everyone wanted to get married, or at least be in love." She laughs. "And when your father got up and sang "Stay as Sweet as You Are," to your mother—"

"He was drunk," Joanne says.

She laughs again. "God, who wasn't?" It had been a wonderful, extravagant wedding. Eight bridesmaids, six limousines, three hundred guests, a nuptial mass, and seven rolling bars. Joanne's father, a short, burly man, almost suave in his brown tuxedo and ruffled yellow shirt, had cried openly during the ceremony and then danced with every woman at the reception, frequently grabbing the microphone away from the band leader to shout insults at his friends. Insults that always ended with, "Ahh, I love ya!"

There had been a cocktail hour with a twelve-foot table of hors d'oeuvre and a fountain of champagne. A six-course Italian dinner, a Viennese dessert table. Tommy's family sang German and Irish songs, Joanne's sang Italian, all of them did the hora and sang *Hava Nagila*.

"You should see the hem of my dress," she tells Joanne now. "Ripped to shreds."

Joanne looks concerned. They'd spent a year finding those blue Qiana dresses and another six months deciding what to wear in their hair and what flowers to carry. "Is it ruined?"

"No," Elizabeth says. "I can fix it. Don't you remember? I showed you at the wedding."

She shakes her head. "They say the bride never remembers anything." "Are you on drugs?" Elizabeth had asked her at one point during the reception, she was smiling so, her eyes were so bright. Joanne had just smiled back at her, lights snapping around them.

"How did the pictures come out?"

Joanne pushes her glass to the end of the table and pulls the new one to her. The small red napkin beneath it is soggy and she lifts the glass a few times, blotting it. "I don't know," she says, watching the glass. "I haven't looked at them."

"What?" Elizabeth laughs a little. "After all the posing we did? How could you not look at them?" She suspects Joanne is joking.

She takes a sip of her drink. "I don't like thinking about the wedding," she says solemnly. "I don't even like to talk about it."

Elizabeth puts her hand on Joanne's wrist. A reflex. Like when they used to play lightning tag when they were young: If I'm touching home and you touch me, you're safe, I'm safe. If I'm touching you and you're out, I'm out too. They always tried to be near each other when they played.

"What's wrong?" she asks, touching Joanne's wrist, trying to absorb what she feels. "Is something wrong between you and Tommy?" She wonders briefly if she's prying.

Joanne laughs a little, shaking her head. "No," she says. "It has nothing to do with Tommy. It's just me. My mother says it happens to everyone. Tommy's great. I love him."

"Then what is it?"

She sucks her bottom lip. Twelve years old again. The two of them sitting on the curb outside Elizabeth's house, knees and thighs touching. Joanne sucking her lip, eyes filled with tears, Elizabeth watching her, thinking death, divorce, she's moving, whatever we fear most for our friends at twelve. "My father threw a cup at me," Joanne had finally said.

She says now, in the same tone, "I just can't stand that it's over."

"What's over?" And already she's searching for some antidote, some sad part of her own life to hold up beside Joanne's. If you're out, I'm out. "At least your father's home to throw a cup at you," she had said that day on the curb. "My father's never even here." Just what her mother would say to their neighbors when she sat with them in the kitchen, drinking beer or coffee. "At least your husband's always home." Not that either Elizabeth or her mother would have changed places with any of them—replaced their sometime father/husband with any of their friends' permanent tyrants. But neither would they have said the others were right, that they had a right to complain, that their husbands/fathers were bastards, oafs. No, only the subtle lie: At least he's home, at least you have that.

"The wedding," Joanne says. She breathes once, a laugh, a sob, and puts the back of her hand to her mouth. "I know it's stupid, but, God, I just can't stand it." She swallows, shakes her head. "It was the biggest day of my life and it went so fast. And now it's over. Forever." She looks directly at Elizabeth. "I waited all my life for that day."

"And it was beautiful." At least you have that. "Perfect."

"Yeah," she says, stirring her drink. "So now I'm back and my parents are yelling at each other again and Mr. Havers is bitchy again and work is the same and I don't even have flowers on my desk any more."

"But you're married now," Elizabeth says. "You're living with Tommy."

"I know," she says wearily. She's heard it before. "I know. And I ride the train home to Westbury instead of Valley Stream. And I live in an apartment with Tommy instead of at home with my parents. But what do I have to look forward to? Everything's over."

"Oh, Joanne." She tries to think for her: She has her job, but she's an executive secretary already, has been for the past four years. Good salary, nonpromotable. She has children to look forward to, but not for a while, not with Tommy just out of law school, still struggling to pay off his loans. She may buy a house someday, but when, how far away?

"What does anybody have to look forward to?" she says, feebly. "And you're married. You're lucky."

She stares at her drink. After a while, the waitress comes and they order two more. Joanne glances at her watch but says nothing.

"You want something to eat?" Elizabeth asks. She nods.

At the hors d'oeuvre table, Bert hums as he puts the tiny meatballs into a small white dish. "How you been, darling?" he asks.

"As good as I can be," she tells him, glad to smile, to joke a little. Feeling guilty that she's glad. He laughs, his teeth whiter than his tall chef's cap. "Well, you can't beat that," he says. "You just got to do your best."

A man in a dark suit steps in front of her, holding out a small plate. "Yes, sir," Bert says. "Have some of this nice ham here."

"You know what it's like?" Joanne says when she returns to the booth.

Elizabeth offers her a toothpick and she takes it, holds it. "It's like when I got busted in high school, remember?"

She laughs, spearing a meatball. "I remember you telling me about it." Joanne had gone from St. Elizabeth's to the public school just down the street, "the incubator of atheism," as one of the nuns called it, while Elizabeth went on to Blessed Virgin High. They parted ways for a few years then, while Elizabeth learned why she was sick of the Catholic Church and Joanne discovered why she couldn't live without it, and were reacquainted in their senior year when they both started going to the same bars; as if, despite the efforts of the nuns and the atheists, they had both ended up looking for the same thing.

Not, Elizabeth recalls, that Joanne ever had any trouble finding it. Boyfriends. Dates. Sex. Romance. Her appeal to men has always been legendary and puzzling. "She's such a homely, wiry little thing," Elizabeth's mother used to say, and her girlfriends at college, who were dazed by the number of men Joanne met each time she came to visit, decided she was, "Not pretty, but attractive, sexy." Elizabeth has always attributed it to every man's fantasy of a twelve-year-old with breasts.

She was with one of her many boyfriends, parked by a reservoir somewhere, when a policeman, just checking, found three joints in her pocketbook, in the plastic case where she stored her tampons. The charges were eventually dropped, but her father told her then and there that she would never be allowed to go away to college, or to leave home until the day she was married.

"Well, after that," Joanne says now, "I made myself sick wishing I could go back to that night. Do it over. I just kept thinking if I could only relive it, go backward and do it over right."

"Yeah," Elizabeth says, chewing the tasteless meatball, glad to have an answer for her, a point to make. "But that's because you wanted to do it differently, so you wouldn't have gotten caught. You wouldn't want to do your wedding any differently."

"Yes I would," she says quickly. "I'd pay more attention. I'd make it seem to last longer. Maybe I'd even put it off for another year. Maybe even two years."

Elizabeth smiles at her. "But it would still have to be over, eventually."

"No," she says, childish, stubborn. Then, softer. "I waited all my life. I mean, how many times did we play bride? And have weddings for our Barbie dolls? Remember I had the five-dollar gown with the veil and the bouquet and the little blue garter? And I'd always pretend her husband got hit by a car or drowned or something so she could get married again?" She laughs a little; not a real laugh, but one that tells Elizabeth that she knows all this is beginning to sound a little silly. "Jesus, Liz, I've been planning my wedding since I was three years old!"

Elizabeth laughs, touches her arm again. "Oh, Joanne," she says. "Everybody probably goes through some kind of depression after they get married. They probably even have a name for it, like post-partum blues."

"That's what my mother told me. She said she had it too. But I still just can't accept that my wedding is over. I feel like somebody died. Maybe even me."

Elizabeth laughs again, patting her hand. "Oh, really," she says kindly. "Come on, it's not that bad. At least you've had your wedding. Look at me, I'll probably never have one. Having your wedding over is better than never having one at all."

At least. It could be worse. Don't complain.

Joanne smiles a little, somewhat sheepishly. "I know," she says. "I'll get over it."

Elizabeth knows Joanne is only trying to appease her, Joanne doesn't believe it herself, and suddenly she regrets being so rational. But, she wonders, what else can she do for her? Moan with her for the impossible? Cry with her over the irretrievable? Joanne is lucky to be married to someone like Tommy. They'd all said so at the wedding, they'd all envied her. She has no reason to be so unhappy now.

She looks into the dark bar behind Joanne, the tables filled with young women and businessmen of all ages. The blue glow of the jukebox. She looks again at Joanne, and sees the beginning of those changes they'd promised each other would never occur.

Joanne finishes her drink and checks her watch. "I'd better go," she says.

Out in the bright station, they embrace again.

"You have to come over," Joanne says.

"I know, let's arrange something. I'll give you a call."

They kiss again and Joanne heads toward her train. The announcer is calling it already and she jogs a little, somewhat awkward in her high heels. From the back, she could be ten, nine. A little girl playing dress-up in her mother's shoes. There's a crowd at her gate, moving slowly through it. She joins them, pauses. A tall man beside her turns, looks at her, and then bends to say something into her ear. Two more men come up behind her so Elizabeth can't see if she replies.

She goes up the stairs, out of the station. It's darker now, and the crowds have thinned. The bums and shopping-bag ladies are stationed in their doorways. Women gather at the windows of various shoe stores. The streets are littered with pamphlets and newspapers.

The air is growing colder but it's refreshing after the bar in the station. She can feel the drinks at the back of her throat and she decides to walk most of the way home. It will be good exercise and she'll still have plenty of time to prepare for Tupper Daniels. She wonders if she'll sleep with him, decides not to. Wonders what Joanne would have done, before. Fallen in love and then slept with him? Slept with him and then fallen in love? For Joanne, the two had always gone together. She'd been in love so many times before Tommy.

She crosses Fifth Avenue, pauses in front of Altman's windows. Sleek manikins in sheer silk dresses. One wears a narrow yellow gown, slit to her thigh, mandarin collar. On her right side there are three rows of silver sequins from shoulder to hem. One hand is placed seductively just over her bare thigh.

"Must be cold in that window," the man beside her says to the woman on his arm. "Look at their nipples."

The woman laughs, pulls him away. He is fair, she is dark. They are both tall and sleek. They take long strides together.

Elizabeth smiles a little, turns back to the window. All the manikins are cold, or aroused, standing there under those blue and red lights, in silk dresses that shine with hundreds of tiny mirrors. She wonders how Tupper Daniels would react if she were to answer the door tonight in a dress like that, her nipples erect.

She turns, continues walking. Remembers Joanne in the bridal shop where she finally found her gown. Up on a platform before a semicircle of mirrors. Her mother and the saleswoman and the eight of them in the bridal party grouped around her, watching her, or one of the five images of her. The same scene repeated six times around the busy shop, six different brides, all shapes and sizes, all young, up on little platforms, before five images of themselves. Thirty images in white silk or satin or lace or Qiana or polyester, some turning to check their hems, some running their fingers across their chests, along their waists, some standing oh so still, arms out, smiling back at themselves. Mrs. Paletti had cried when Joanne had said, "Yes, this is the one." And all of them had smiled, sat up a little, made a wish.

No one being rational then, saying perhaps this is a little silly, perhaps all this fuss and fanfare will outshine the event, leave you disappointed, bitter that it's over. None of them, not even Joanne's mother, who had been through the disappointment herself, reminding her that this is a fantasy, that when it's over there will still be your parents fighting and the papers on your desk, and a lifetime of wondering what you should look forward to. Not saying it, not even thinking it, but thinking instead of their own moment up there on the platform, in the white gown, their own moment, in the past or in the future, that they'd been told all their lives to prepare for.

Told so often and so well that even now she can dismiss Joanne's unhappiness, admit that yes, even now, she wants her own moment up there in the white dress. Even now she believes it will somehow change her life forever.

End it, Joanne had said. But she'll get over it; everyone goes through it. She has no reason to be unhappy. She has Tommy, love.

She turns down Fiftieth Street, heads crosstown, believing that Joanne should be happy, will be happy. And yet, as she decides that maybe she will sleep with Tupper Daniels and feels, like the fresh air, like Friday night, like her freedom to turn at Park or York, Sixty-first or Seventy-ninth, that the decision need not be final, she knows she would not trade places with her.

V

*E*IGHT TEN AND THE DOWNSTAIRS buzzer rings.

He answers "Tupper" when she asks who it is, and when she opens the door he stands there with a bottle of wine and a cone of flowers. Rosebuds and baby's-breath, the kind they sell on the street, near subway entrances. The kind that always make her think of businessmen stopping on their way home to buy the wife some flowers after eight hours of lusting after their secretaries.

"Madame Editor," he says, presenting her with the bouquet, the facetiousness again in his eyes, again making her feel caught. His eyes look very blue.

"How sweet," she says. Bette Davis to Robert Montgomery. "Do come in."

A new blazer tonight: dark green. Navy sweater, jeans, loafers.

"Not exactly posh," he says, looking around her room. "But nicely done. Your elevator isn't working."

"I know," she says with a laugh. "It seldom is."

He takes off his blazer. His shoulders *are* rather broad. His aftershave is smooth, pleasant. He leans to look at some of the Folon prints over her couch. "How long have you lived here?"

"Two years," she says, watching him, wondering why she's

perspiring so. Why he seems so comfortable in her apartment and she suddenly feels like a stranger. She looks at the room. Although she is pleased with it, has copied it almost exactly from an apartment shown in *Mademoiselle,* it suddenly seems lacking. "I'm looking for a better place now," she says, wondering what she's talking about.

He points to the prints. "Are these from a book?"

"Yes," she says, holding the wine and the flowers in her arms. "I never buy prints separately. I just cut up art books." She laughs, foolishly. "Can I get you some wine?"

"Certainly," he says and sits on the couch. "It *is* nice in here." The room is his.

She walks into the kitchen, turns on the cold water, runs it over her hands, which are trembling slightly. She wishes she hadn't invited him. She fills a vase, puts the yellow rosebuds and baby's-breath into it, carries it, dripping, to the table just outside the kitchen door.

He is sitting on the couch, flipping through an issue of *Time.*

"They're pretty," she says, standing back to look at the flowers. "Thank you."

She goes back to the kitchen, opens the wine, pours two glasses, brings one glass and the cheese board out to him. He puts the magazine down, says, "Thank you," watching her. She returns to the kitchen for her own glass and then sits on the opposite end of the couch, sipping the wine before he can make another toast.

"This tastes good," she says, leaning back. "It's been a long day." This is her habit: Whenever she is uncomfortable, she finds an extreme and sticks with it. Extreme boredom, extreme interest, extreme weariness, pleasure, love. Her first month in high school she yawned so often the nuns mentioned it to her mother.

"I enjoyed our lunch," Tupper Daniels says, sitting back. "Although I'm sorry we didn't talk much about the book."

She laughs a little. "I often wonder if anyone gets any business done over a business lunch." This as if she has them everyday.

"Yes," he says. "But I wouldn't have minded it much if I'd learned a little bit more about you. I did all the talking."

She remembers Ann's "He was watching you as if you were pure gold."

"All right," she says. "What would you like to know?"

"Well," he says. "Where are you from, for instance?"

"Long Island," she says.

"And how long have you worked at Vista?"

"Nearly two years."

"What did you do before that?"

She hesitates, sips the wine (which is a little too sweet). "Spent some time with my mother in Maine, lived in Buffalo for a while, lived in Queens for a while, went to college—outside Rochester—went to high school—back on Long Island—grammar school, kindergarten. How far back do you want me to go?"

He laughs. "That's far enough. Have you ever been to the South?"

"Just Florida during spring break."

"Florida's not the South," he says. "It's a colony of New York City. I mean the real South, like Tennessee."

She shakes her head. "Never."

"Ever been married?"

She has a strange impulse to say yes, but instead she says, "I came close once but backed out."

"Why?" He seems truly amazed. His eyes, she thinks, are a lovely blue. Somehow darker in this dim light.

"It just wasn't right. Isn't that what they say?"

"And now you're single? Perfectly single?" He raises his eyebrows. There are women, she is sure, who would consider him handsome.

"Perfectly," she says, raising her chin, flirting.

He puts his glass on the coffee table in front of him. "That's really good," he says. He takes the glass from her hand, puts it beside his own. He is smiling a little and she is looking at him wide-eyed, helpless. She wonders why she must always pretend to have this moment of helplessness before she allows herself to be seduced.

He turns to her, one arm stretched over the top of the couch, the other on his own thigh.

"Listen," he says, and she makes her eyes wider, listening. Still helpless, nearly cute. She thinks vaguely of her diaphragm —do they deteriorate when not in use?

His hand brushes her hair, slips around her head, onto her neck.

"I want to make love with you," he whispers. "It has nothing to do with my book. I just find you ungodly attractive."

"All right," she says, surprising herself. She pats the couch. "This is my bed. Just pull the coffee table over by the window and throw the pillows on the chair. I'll only be a minute."

She gets up quickly and goes to the bathroom, wondering if he'd expected an argument, knowing she'd expected to give him one. When she tells this story to Ann or Joanne, they'll laugh about what she just said, how she took control, surprised even herself. Ann will say, "God, were you horny." Joanne will ask if she's in love. She holds the diaphragm up to the bright light over the sink. It seems fine, a little dry, but fine. She undresses, slips it in, stands before the mirror.

She'd said next time would be for love. No more one-nighters, no more strangers, no more of that disappointment, that feeling of loss each time she thinks how much better it would have been if she'd been in love.

She said never again until it was for love, but she is standing here naked with no intention of walking out there and telling Tupper Daniels that she's changed her mind, that she was only joking, that he really should put his clothes back on and fold up the bed because she's waiting to fall in love. She is standing here remembering how men have said that her breasts are lovely, that her hips, her ass, are perfect, that she looks better naked than clothed, that she is a joy to make love to. She is standing here thinking of selfishness and narcissism and all that she has missed this past year.

He is by the bed, his back to her. Narrow waist, broad back. Muscular, compact. No trace of a tan. He turns and smiles, both glasses in his hands. Hands one to her, shakes his head. Adoring. Pure gold. Runs one finger from her throat to her navel, shakes his head again, smiling. "Sit down."

She sits on the bed. He lifts her ankles, takes her glass, makes her lie down. He goes to the foot of the bed, looks at her. She smiles back at him, beautiful, untouched. Then he kneels.

He begins with the soles of her feet. Then moves up onto the bed, kissing ankles, calves, behind each knee. Up over her.

She closes her eyes and begins the slow, downward movement, the saddest, the loneliest. With Bill, she would sometimes grab at him, sink nails and teeth into him, trying to bring him with her. And sometimes, as she remembers, he would be there.

Hips, stomach, breasts. She turns and is slowly turning down, into herself. Absorbing every sensation, and bringing it down into her, to her burrow, her lair, her nest. Hoarding every sensation until the air seems to stop in her ears and all the sensations are internal, moving from her, down into her, until she is just a small center, receiver, sender; a heart, a depth, a small center without color or sound or light; until she is only reflexes that multiply themselves to a stillness, a numbness, to a point where movement surpasses itself, feeling surpasses itself. Where joining confirms its impossibility. All of it into herself until the closeness becomes only loneliness, selfishness, strikes at that impenetrable core: Me, alone, me.

And here, she knows, if there were love, not merely this stranger above her, here would be the crying out, the reaching up, the sinking of nails and teeth, the cry of outrage against such loneliness: There is more, at the center, the depth, the heart, there is more than I myself alone.

Bill. Again. And still.

Tupper Daniels turns on his side and wipes the tear from her face. He kisses her forehead. This pale stranger, this odd man.

"That was fabulous for me," he says. "How about you?"

She nods. She hates this checking of notes, this comparison of itineraries. *I was in Istanbul while you were in Greenland. How was it? Good. How was it for you? Good too.*

"You seemed to enjoy yourself," he says, pleased. He lies back, crosses his legs. "You remind me of the first girl I ever had intercourse with. I mean, the way you cry."

Strange voice even, she thinks, the accent suddenly too clear. She crosses her arms over her breasts and hugs herself, sad.

"I was a sophomore in college." He turns to her. "Which you probably think is ridiculously late to start."

She shrugs. It seems the older she gets, the more people she meets who were late to "start." She wonders if it's just her, or if they're all finally getting old enough to tell the truth.

"I was terribly shy," Tupper Daniels is saying, "but probably the horniest little bastard in the state. I had a constant erection, but could never get up—excuse the expression—enough courage to do anything about it." He laughs a little, his eyes on the ceiling, searching. "Finally, Beau Winston who lived next door to me in the dorm asked if I'd go out with his little sister when she came up to visit the school. Beau was going to Chapel Hill for the weekend so his sister could have his room and get to know Vanderbilt. She was a senior in high school and was supposed to start there in the fall.

"I saw this as my big chance, and as soon as she arrived,

Margaret was her name, I think, I started plying her with Boone's Farm Apple Wine. Of course, she was out cold by nine o'clock Friday night and sick most of the next day, so Saturday night I took her to a bar and told her she should drink vodka and Kahlúa and milk—white Russians. I think I told her something about it supplying her with lots of vitamin B along with the hair of the dog. Anyway, she was pretty sloshed again by the time we got back to my room. But not too sloshed. And was she hot! Jesus, all I kept thinking was what they say about little blond high school cheerleaders must be true. Damn, she had her clothes off and my clothes off before I could even lock the door, and she's kissing me and feeling me." He looks at her from the corner of his eye. "I was still a scrawny, ugly little kid then too." His eyes return to the ceiling.

"Anyway, I thought I was going to blow to pieces right there, so I kind of pushed her onto the bed and went at it. And pretty soon she started moaning and saying, 'Oh God, Oh God,' and I just thought I was a natural and kept doing what I was doing."

He laughs, shaking his head. "When I think of what I must have looked like, my little bare ass pumping up and down. Anyway, she started crying. Now I'd heard about that, how some women cry, so I just thought they were tears of joy and I was so proud of myself, I came like the dickens and collapsed, smiling I'm sure. But she kept on crying. So then I thought maybe I'd hurt her, which in a way also made me feel pretty proud too (I figured I was somehow much bigger than I looked) and I asked her what was wrong. 'My mother has cancer,' she said."

"Oh my God," Elizabeth says.

He shakes his head. "I guess I said I was sorry to hear that, but she just started crying again. Then she said, 'I promised God I wouldn't do this anymore if she would get better. Now she's going to die!'"

She laughs, wondering if she should, if it's funny that a girl would kill her mother just to screw some scrawny boy. But she fears he thinks her somewhat dull already and is herself annoyed at people who take jokes too seriously. And there is, she must admit, something charming about the way he tells a story. Boyish and self-deprecating. The bashful Southern gentleman. She suspects he knows it too.

"Jesus," he says, shaking his head. "It was terrible." He turns to her again, brushes a hair away from her face. "But I still kind of like it when a woman cries." He touches the corner of her eye. "In fact, tears are one of my leitmotifs, in the book." He makes his mouth round, as if he were crooning to her. *That spring, the land seemed to draw itself from her eyes and her tears, which were, by then, her most tangible memory of him, seemed to bestow on every peripheral object a certain fragile evanescence.* He smiles. "Tears as a creative force, as a point of view. Remember?"

She smiles, reaching down to change the subject, and they begin to make love again. It's slower this time and she keeps her eyes open, her mind on what she's doing, what she might do. No significance, no implications, no tears.

But it's good. Therapeutic, somehow, like a back rub.

Later, she notices his neck is flushed red. The way it had been that morning in her office, when she was praising his book. As if sex and praise stirred the same blood.

"Are you hungry?" she asks him, sitting up.

"A little," he says, eyes closed.

She swings her legs over the side of the bed. "There's this great little place down the block. Why don't we go?"

"You want to get up already?"

She stands, turns to him. Even this little exchange makes her uncomfortable; it sounds too full of intimacy. Almost more so than the love-making.

"Yes," she says, the decisive editor. "I'm hungry." She walks into the bathroom. Her hair is ratty at the back, her mascara is smeared under her eyes. She washes her face, reapplies her make-up, giving him plenty of time.

She knows she will regret this every time he shows up at the office, but right now she feels fine. And she looks so much better, like she's had a facial and a sauna and a whirlpool and basked briefly in the sun. She wonders why she went so long without it.

When she returns to the living room, he is sitting on the opened bed. He is holding one of his loafers, dangling it between his knees.

"We're going to have trouble with this," he says and for a minute she thinks he means the shoe. "You're the type who likes to get up and get going after making love. I'm the type who likes to linger."

She smiles. "I'm just hungry," she says, avoiding any reference to their love-making, trying to recoup some distance.

He puts the shoe on, gets up, goes into the bathroom, kissing her as he passes. She picks up her glass—his glass?—and finishes the warm wine.

When he comes out, his hair is neatly combed (her comb?), making him look surprisingly boyish, fresh out of prep school. He kisses her again (her toothbrush?) and she feels that slight turning at the base of her spine.

Outside, it is the same cool night that she had walked home in earlier, but it seems darker now, or the lights seem brighter. He takes her hand and his feels warm and wide. They smile at each other. They pass an old woman who lives in her building and she smiles, eyeing Tupper. She is a wide, male-faced woman with bow legs and yellow hair. She has never smiled at Elizabeth before.

Another couple passes them and then a group of young men, neatly dressed. One of them looks at her and smiles a little, then glances briefly at Tupper. He and his friends turn into a small bar crowded with young people.

Friday night on the Upper East Side, and the streets are filled with illustrations for every tense of the verb "to fuck." She tells Tupper this and he laughs, labeling others as they pass. A tall, attractive woman in a gray suit "has fucked," two women just a little younger than Elizabeth "will fuck," a plain-looking couple holding hands are simply "fucked."

She puts aside all thoughts of closeness and distance. This walking together, being silly, holding hands, feeling truly hungry and washed clean, is all part of what she's missed this near-year of celibacy. She will simply enjoy it and let Monday be as it may.

The restaurant is one of those small, glassed-in places on a corner. On the menu, they call it a sidewalk café. It's all yellow candlelight and green plants and the piano player softly plays show tunes.

"Well, here we are again," Tupper Daniels says. "Across a candlelit table. Twice in one day."

She smiles, nothing to say.

"So, maybe while we're here, I can get you to answer the question you didn't answer this afternoon."

"What's that?" she says softly, playing the lover.

"What are your suggestions for my book? For the ending?"

The piano, she thinks, should have struck a sour note. "Shop talk?" she says.

He shrugs. "Just briefly. So I won't spend all night trying to second-guess you. Like I did all day."

She shakes her head, hesitates.

"Do you think I should end it in a trial scene? You know, Bailey's trial. You looked a little unhappy today when I said I didn't want to do that."

She wonders what he's talking about.

"Or"—he shifts a little in his seat, puts both elbows on the table—"and this occurred to me today, after we had lunch:

How about if I end it with a chapter about Bailey himself? You know, maybe even pull a John Fowles, do the self-conscious ending, say there can be no ending because Bailey is still alive. Or do a total point-of-view switch and tell how one of the boys who used to watch him grew up and moved away. And then say I wrote a book about him. The little boy, I mean, not me."

Despite herself, she says, "Why don't you make something up?"

He looks at her, taken aback, she thinks. "What do you mean?"

She should say fine, any of those ideas is fine. Why don't you write them, any one of them, get it finished, sign the contract? "I mean, why do you have to find out what really happened to Bailey or talk about what happened to the little boy? The guy in the book is named Beale, isn't he? Why don't you just stick with him, have something happen to him. You know, make something up."

He rests his cheek on his knuckles, watching her. If she likes anything about him, she decides, she would have to say it's his eyes. Although his chest is smooth and hard and his arms somewhat appealing, crossed with thick veins. His legs.

"Make something up, huh?" he says. She wonders if he's patronizing her. "Okay, like what?"

She doesn't want to talk about this.

She shrugs. "I don't know. You're the writer. Have him decide to mend his ways. Maybe he could fall permanently in love with the fat wife."

He grimaces. "And they live happily ever after?"

"Why not? Or maybe he can meet someone else, say a lady bigamist. *Are* there lady bigamists?"

He smiles at her; the smile seems to say, Oh, I get it, you're being cute. "I've never heard of a lady bigamist," he says.

"Well, then. There you go. Make one up."

He sits back, straightens the napkin on his lap. "You

don't want to talk about this, do you?" he asks.

"Tupper, I leave work at five o'clock."

He looks up at her, reaches across the table, takes her hand. "I hope," he begins, then pauses, pursing his lips. "What just happened, it didn't have anything to do with my book. I mean, I'm not trying to get you to help me more than you should by going to bed with you. You know that, don't you?"

The waitress arrives with their crêpes so she answers a quick, "Yes, of course." She's beginning to see that she will soon remember this night as a lesson learned: Do not mix your play-pretend occupation with what appears to be your real life.

"It's just that I talk about this stuff all day," she tells him. "I like to leave it alone every once in a while."

"I understand," he says. He looks away, his face sad, struggling, it seems, with some frustration, some desperate tragedy.

It occurs to her that he thinks she's lying to him; that he thinks she's convinced he is interested only in her *power*. He believes she will never know that his motives for being with her are anything but selfish, she will never trust his good intentions.

It's rather a sad, romantic fantasy and she decides not to bother to refute it. Instead, she imagines a scene in which, some day, she turns bitterly to him (they are in her apartment, or in a restaurant having lunch, or, better yet, in a cab at night, returning from the opera or the ballet or even from a carriage ride around Central Park) and says, angry tears in her eyes, her voice a steady hiss: You never loved me. It was only your book that you cared about. You only wanted my ideas, you only wanted to steal my ideas, rob my mind.

She recalls Ann's "It sure sounds like an excuse for robbing people," and marvels at how she has imagined herself into the victim; how she has just turned her schemes to use Tupper Daniels into his to use her.

"Okay," he says, facing her again. "I'm sorry I brought it up." He smiles at her, an ingratiating smile. "So let's talk more about you. I know where you've lived and where you went to school. What about your parents. Where are they from?"

"Well, my mother was born in Brooklyn."

"Brooklyn?" he says. "God, I don't think I've ever met anyone who was really from Brooklyn."

"Your loss," she says coolly. "And my father was born and raised in England."

This he is impressed by. "Really?" he says. "How did he end up with a girl from Brooklyn?"

He says Brooklyn as if he meant Uganda. She marvels at the rude ignorance of inbred WASPs.

"My father came to New York when he was about fifteen or so. He lived out on Long Island with an aunt, but he had friends in the city and he met my mother at a party."

"So you're English and Brooklynish," he says.

"Irish," she tells him.

He laughs, waves his hand. "Same difference. And what did your father do while you lived on Long Island?"

She pauses, flips through her stories like a pack of cards. Government, traveling salesman, actor, on the lecture circuit.

She laughs. "He was a bigamist," she says. And there is the word, pointing at him. She doesn't like it.

Tupper Daniels' eyes grow wide. Light up, she would say. "You're kidding."

She doesn't like it. Her parents loved each other. Her father was a good man. "Yes, I'm kidding. He worked for the government."

He seems disappointed. "What did he do?"

"He traveled a lot. Some kind of intelligence." She decides to put an end to this line of questioning. "He died when I was fourteen."

"Oh, gee," he says. "I'm sorry. What did he die of?"

She turns her glass. "Car accident."

"Was anybody else hurt?"

She looks up at him. "No, he was alone."

"Gosh," he says, shaking his head, "that's too bad. It must have been hard on you."

She shrugs. "He wasn't around much anyway." She stares down at her glass. She feels him watching her, feels him questioning the hidden depths of her despair, her sense of abandonment. God, she thinks, he's a romantic. Or at least she's imagining him to be.

"Why did you say he was a bigamist?" he asks. A whisper.

She shakes her hair away, smiling. "Just kidding," she says. "I thought maybe it would get you thinking about the end of your book."

His voice is dry. "I'm always thinking about the end of my book. But I thought you stopped work at five o'clock."

She laughs. "I guess I never really leave. Do you want to go?"

He straightens up, calls for the check.

As they walk back to her apartment, she wonders where she should turn him away. At the corner where he can grab a cab, at the entrance to her building, at the door to her apartment?

He puts his arm around her as they walk. It is heavy, makes walking difficult. He comments on the cold and she realizes for the first time that he is not wearing his blazer. Clever trick.

"Did you leave your jacket in my apartment?" she asks.

"Yes," he says. "I forgot how cold it was getting."

"Oh," she says. "As long as you didn't leave it in the restaurant."

He laughs. "We Southern boys aren't used to these Yankee autumns," he says.

Rehearsed, she thinks. Oh, clever.

And so they are back in her apartment and yes, there is plenty of wine, but no, she says, she really is very tired. And although she doesn't want to end up in bed again, she doesn't want to be left alone in her apartment at eleven o'clock on a Friday night either, and so: All right, she says, a back rub sounds nice and yes, one more glass of wine. And his hands are strong enough and there is just enough pain in the way he grips her shoulders and her neck and kneads her back and sides. So it is another reversal—the literal back rub now feeling like making love, but now, with him fully clothed and her only clinically undressed, only her blouse off, her front hidden against the mattress, the back rub is somehow more desirable, exciting.

And so she turns, feels his soft sweater against her, his face, the almost imperceptible beard. Then the slow undressing. This will be the last time, she tells herself, the kiss good-by, the graduation drunk, the bachelor party, Fat Tuesday.

"Where in England was your father born?"
"London, I think."
"You think?"
"Well, I wasn't there. But, yes, I'm sure it was London."
"And he came over here when he was fifteen?"
"About that."
"And he lived with an aunt?"
"Yes."
"What was her name?"
"I don't know. Betty, I think."
"How can you not know?"
"She died before I was born."
"Didn't he ever talk about her?"
"A little. Not much. Anyway, he always called her his aunt."
He gets up, shaking his head. Goes into the kitchen. "There *is* more wine," he yells. Comes back with the open bottle. Her bottle. The one she'd bought on the way home. To seduce him with, maybe.

He pours two glasses, puts the bottle on the end table. Sits cross-legged, opposite her. His body is all primary colors: white, red, blue—no muted shades. Especially his feet, which could be sketches from a medical book, an encyclopedia. White from the ankles to toes, red around the side, blue veins crossing through it all. The hair on his pale legs seems blond enough to be transparent, his genitals are red, almost an angry red, veined in blue; his hairless chest is pure white without even a freckle or a beauty mark to contradict what seems to have been chosen as his color scheme. Surely, she thinks, even a medical illustrator would have added a brown freckle or two.

"Was she married?" he asks. "Aunt what's-her-name?"

"Yes. That's why she lived out there, on Long Island. It's where her husband was from."

"Was she born in England too?"

"No. Ireland, I think."

"How can you say, 'I think'? She's only one generation away. Gosh, I can name all my relatives back four or five generations."

"Probably because you've got huge oil paintings of every one of them hanging all over your mansion. I bet you've got headless ghosts in gray uniforms, too."

"I don't live in a mansion," he says. "And all our ghosts wear heads and frock coats."

"Even the lady ghosts?"

He nods. "The Daniels women," he says, in an exaggerated Southern accent, "were never above perversity. Some of our loveliest belles are transvestites in the hereafter. We all have our own idea of heaven."

She laughs and he looks at her severely, "What's yours?"

She shrugs. "I don't know. Typical Baltimore catechism stuff. God with a long white beard and a dove on His shoulders, angels with curly blond hair and blue wings instead of bodies. Lots of clouds."

"And where do you fit in?"

She looks down at herself, lounging so casually against her pillow, naked, her legs outstretched, spending an intimate evening with someone she hardly cares about and barely knows. With an author, of all things.

"I guess I'm in the crowd just under God's feet, right below the clouds, reaching up."

"Hell?"

She smiles. "No, purgatory. Not quite bad enough for hell, not quite good enough for heaven. Just kind of mediocre. I have a feeling everybody I know will be there too."

"Your father?"

She looks at him, slightly amazed that he would ask such a tactless question. But he is looking at her seriously, as if it were important to him.

"My father," she says, "could be anywhere. Heaven, hell, purgatory. Wisconsin."

He smiles a little. "What did he look like, your father?"

She brushes back her hair. "Dark hair, like mine. Blue eyes, like mine. My nose exactly, I'm told. But his face was thinner and he had a mustache. A small one, like Clark Gable's."

"Was he tall?"

"Yes," she says. "And thin. Why are you so interested?"

He shrugs, rests his glass on his stomach. "I don't know; you get kind of defensive when you talk about him. I don't think you liked him."

"I was crazy about him," she cries. "I lived for the days he came home. Honestly, I think he spoiled me for any other man."

"Is that why you're not married?"

She laughs. "Could be. He's as good an excuse as any. If I need an excuse."

"There could be a correlation," he says, seriously. "If your father represented impermanence, then anyone who wanted to marry you would mean permanence, just the opposite."

"Very good, Mr. Freud," she says dryly, although, suddenly, her stomach is dancing, as if she were a child again, playing hide-and-seek, hiding in someone's dark, cool basement, feeling the searcher come near, stop, turn, walk away, and then walk back. "But not very original."

"No," he says, refusing to joke. "You should think about that. I should think about it too, if I'm going to get involved with you. I always look at a woman's father; it's usually a good indication of how she feels about men."

"Jesus," she says, laughing. "Do you want a character reference too? Birth certificate? Fingerprints?" She doesn't tell him that his basic premise, that they are to get "involved," is his first mistake.

"You see," he says calmly, pointing at her. "You get touchy when you talk about your father, even though you say you liked him. And you called him a bigamist."

"I was joking." Her voice is higher than she wants it to be. Sounds touchy.

"Yes, but you see," he says, "if you don't like your father, then it says something to me about how you feel about men like him."

She gets out of bed, goes to her pocketbook for a cigarette. Although she tries not to smoke in her apartment, this gives her something to do, something that might remind him of her professional status. "Perhaps my 'touchiness,'" she tells him, blowing smoke through her nose, "has more to do with my dislike for you, not my father. You are, you know, being totally obnoxious, analyzing me when you know nothing about me, looking into my ancestry to discover my temperament. Jesus."

He throws his head back, looks up at the ceiling. "I made you angry," he says, his voice full of self-disgust.

She laughs at the ploy. No, you didn't, she's supposed to say. It's okay, really, I don't mind. At least you're interested. "Maybe you should go," she says instead.

He gets off the bed, stands by her, hands at his sides. Eyes mournful. "I'd like to stay."

She shakes her head. "I think you should go."

She walks to the closet, puts on her robe, goes to the love seat. "Really, it's getting late." She sits down, waiting.

Slowly, he puts on his jeans, his shirt, his sweater. Then he sits on the edge of the bed, before her, and puts his hand on her knee.

"Listen," he says, "I'm sorry. Maybe I was prying, maybe I was being, I don't know, calculating. But I thought maybe . . ." He rubs his thumb along her knee. "When you said your father was a bigamist." He holds up his hand. "I know you were kidding, but you did say he was never home, so I thought maybe he could be a clue for how to end my book. I mean, Bailey has no ending, but your father, well, he might give me a different perspective. Maybe I could use something that happened to him, or even you."

She doesn't know if she should scream or laugh, slap him across the face or merely brush him aside. "It's an unusual way to be used," she says quietly.

He seems to take this as some sort of acquiescence because he smiles, shaking his head. "Oh, all writers do it," he says. "They use everybody. You should know that. One of my teachers at Vanderbilt once said that a good writer sells out everybody he knows, sooner or later."

She smiles at him. If she were to tell him now what Vista is about, what the fate of his masterpiece will be, what kind of "writer" he is, what kind of "editor" she is . . .

He moves his hand up her leg, grips her thigh.

"But I'm sorry I made you angry," he says. And then, looking down, "I'll go."

She makes no move to stop him, but watches him put on his coat, his shoes.

He stands in the middle of her room, face once again sad. "Can I call you?" he asks. "At home?"

She nods, realizing she feels a certain disappointment. Not, she thinks, because he's finally leaving, or because she's made up her mind not to sleep with him again, but because the questioning has stopped. Or maybe because the questioning had nothing to do with her, was for himself, his book.

She nods, feeling again like the child hiding in the dark basement, crouched on the cold linoleum behind an open door. The child who hears (her stomach dancing) the footsteps approaching, stopping nearby, turning, and then walking away, up the stairs to the light, to other, perhaps easier, discoveries. Feeling like the child in that minute when the hiding becomes being lost, forgotten.

"Yes," she says, nodding. "Call me. Please."

VI

$\mathcal{I}$T WAS AT A PARTY, SHE BEGAN.
I've told you the story, haven't I?

I said that she had, a long time ago, and then realized she had not asked the question to avoid repeating herself, but merely to determine what part of my own memory I would bring to the story as she told it, the way a recently returned traveler might ask: Have you ever seen this part of the world? with the lights already out and the slide projector humming beside him.

I told her I didn't remember it very well. We were on the beach, sitting on some large black rocks, a pale-blue comforter beneath us. It was where she liked to sit while it grew dark.

Betty had invited us. You remember poor Betty?

The *poor* was for a small patch of oil and rain that, six years before, had sent her car into a utility pole on Queens Boulevard as she drove from the beauty parlor to her semidetached ranch.

I said of course I remembered her. And remembered her again as heavy perfume and coats with fur collars and cuffs. As cigarette butts stained darkly with lipstick. As my mother's eternal "girlfriend." I remembered that she always clinked with bracelets and seemed unaware of the thin husband who followed her into our living room; that she had spent the last hour of her silly life under a hooded dryer, tales of the Lennon

Sisters on her lap, the tips of her small ears burning.

My mother pulled her legs to her chest, hugging her knees like an uncertain survivor. It was a girlish pose, made possible by her new thinness.

It was quite a party. Park Avenue, very posh.

I looked out over the slate-covered sand, the black water laced with foam, speckled with white gulls. I was, by then, already planning my steps once I got back to New York, and so, I suppose, with my own future once again imaginable I didn't mind letting her tell the story. She was full of stories that summer, stories about Ward's long devotion to his late mother, about some woman in town who'd had three husbands, about her childhood and mine—our past selves as useful as any third party in keeping us from discussing who and what we were now.

I sat slightly behind her and looked at her hair tangled around the thin rubber band, pulling from it, looping around it, a fine spray of gray sand, and wondered who and what now.

It was in a Park Avenue apartment with thick brocade furniture and rose-colored rugs. A skinny Irish woman passed around silver trays of caviar and thin toast. A slick-haired butler, just like you see in the movies, stood behind the long table that served as a bar. The room was smoke-filled, full of laughter, high and deep.

She sat on a couch in a far corner of the room, her two girlfriends on either side of her, and when an older man, balding and well dressed, crossed the room and sat in the chair beside them, the three seemed to ripple with attentiveness, like birds waking.

He found them cute, adorable, perched there on that couch like three little parakeets (he even made a joke about parakeets, since one of them, Dolores, my mother, wore a dress of powder blue) and sensing this, they answered all his questions pertly, precociously, chirping their names and the names of the companies they worked for, taking short drags on their cigarettes and quick sips from their martinis.

He promised them, if they were good and had not taken up with some young men by the end of the party, that he would take them all to Child's for an early breakfast.

"There's nothing," he said, winking at Betty, the blonde, who sat closest to him and because of her hair was always considered the most forward of the three, "like having pretty girls for breakfast." He patted the arm of his chair as if it were their collective knee.

When he walked back to the bar, Betty told them quickly, her hand over her mouth, that he was Samuel Southwick, the general manager, which meant that if he took them out for breakfast they would go in the company's limousine.

At this, Janet and Dolores laughed, although Betty, newly sophisticated since her boss had invited her to this party and asked her to bring her prettiest girlfriends, merely touched her bright hair.

My mother looked over her shoulder at me. The poor man died of a heart attack just a few weeks later, she added. He died on the floor of the men's room—the executive one of course —before anyone even got to him. It was a shame. But at least he was there that night.

As if his death was in some way redeemed by his presence at what was, for my mother, a fateful party. I remembered that she had included him in the story the last time, too.

Later, there was a commotion at the front door and four young men burst into the room, their faces flushed, ties pulled down and collars opened. One grabbed the skinny maid and kissed her on the lips. The thin toast slid from her silver tray. People laughed.

"Jerry Case," Betty whispered, her hand to her hair. "My boss's son."

The four men headed for the bar and the girls moved their

heads a little and leaned against one another, trying to see.

Suddenly, Betty drained her glass and turned to Dolores. "Do you want to go to the bar with me?" Her breath reeked of peppermint, and my mother marveled at how skillfully she had gotten the Lifesaver from her purse to her mouth without anyone noticing it. She laughed a little. "You can't just walk up there."

Betty looked at her a minute, considering, and then waved her hand. "Ask Janet."

But Janet's thin face was struck with horror at the mere suggestion. "You can't do that," she whispered.

Betty sighed, looked at her glass. "Then I'll go by myself," she said, touching her hair again, her talisman. But she made no move.

And then (here my mother's voice grew rich), then, like the waters of the Red Sea or the skies over Bethlehem, the crowd of guests parted and she saw the young men headed their way. She heard Janet take in her breath and she delicately tapped Betty's toe with her own. She could smell the three sweet odors of their perfumes rise into the air like an offering.

One sat in the chair beside Betty, another on the couch next to Janet, the third stood before them, and behind him the other. Dark hair and gray eyes, a trim mustache and a smile that was somehow pained, somehow lewd. A smile that seen alone, seen just as bright, slightly crooked teeth under a black mustache and a sharp nose could only be an evil smile, a nasty smile, but taken in with the whole face, especially the lovely, long-lashed eyes, was merely bemused.

A smile, I realized as I listened, no longer my father's, but Bill's, watching me from our bed, from across a table, from between my legs. Those blue eyes looking up, that smile—the teeth a little crooked, cruel, the sharp nose, the thick mustache —saying, Look what I can do to you. How I can change you, make you laugh, cry, scream.

The light out on the water was changing, playing silver to black to dark blue with each wave. I was tired of listening.

He stepped into the semicircle made by the couch and two chairs and fell on his knees before her. He took her hand from the lap of her pale-blue skirt and raised it to his mouth.

His teeth touched her skin and sent a chill up her neck, behind her ear.

"Madam," he said, still holding her hand close to his lips, raising only his eyes. "You are lovely." And his voice, soft, sincere, still British, was Ronald Colman's or Errol Flynn's, or even, her favorite, Walter Pidgeon's. (She told me once as we stayed up until three A.M. to watch *Madame Curie,* that during the war, before she married, while my father was overseas, she would cry each time she heard Walter Pidgeon's voice. She said she went to one of his movies nearly every night while my father was away. And she'd always cry.)

"You are so lovely," he went on, "that I know not what else to do but to kneel before you. Forever."

Here he swayed a little and his friends reached out to support him, laughing and saying, "Whoa!"

"I know not what else to do," he said again, apparently pleased with the phrase.

And then he looked up at her, placed his hand over his heart. "Marry me," he said.

And, hearing her two friends laughing on either side of her, feeling them nudging her, pinching her (it may have been a night's drunk for the men, my mother told me, but to the girls, a life hung in the balance), my mother said, quite softly and quite seriously, "All right."

And while the others cheered and declared this an official bachelor party, my father turned his secret smile on her again.

There was a line of bright blue at the horizon, above the darker blue that bled from ocean to sky and below the pale expanse that stretched above and behind us to wherever the sun was setting.

She'd told the story before, but when he was still alive, when his presence at the party that evening had seemed to me as miraculous as the sight of him at our dinner table on an ordinary school night. When I thought no past was irretrievable if he had been there then and was with us now, if I could see him clearly then and now. If, someday, I too would go to a party and he would fall on his knees.

A star appeared in the strip of blue, a royal blue now. First star. My mother stretched out her legs and said make a wish.

VII

WHEN ELIZABETH CAME TO VISTA
for her interview, after six weeks of sitting in employment
agencies and failing typing tests and sending résumés to box
numbers in the *Times* like so many anonymous letters to Santa
Claus, she told Mr. Owens that she wanted a career, not a job.
Thinking of Bill, she said she thought it was important for
every woman to have a career, something hers alone, something that would remain hers, that she could remain dedicated
to, despite the ups and downs, gains and losses, of her personal
life.

Mr. Owens had smiled over his fingertips and that evening
had called her to say she'd been hired. She was staying at
Joanne's house then, still looking for her own apartment, and
Joanne's parents, greatly impressed, had opened a bottle of
wine to celebrate. Even her own mother was taken aback by
the sound of it: "Editor-in-Chief of Vista Books," and a friend
from college quickly sent the news to their alumni bulletin. "At
least one of us is making it," wrote a former sorority sister who
had seen the item. She also asked if Elizabeth would mind
taking a look at her husband's nonfiction novel-in-progress.

Elizabeth, who had caught on by then, sent no reply.

When she did catch on to what Vista and her job there were
all about—and it took her only the first day, when Mr. Owens

beat the rhythm of her work onto her desk, the first week, when she met all her coworkers and heard them talk, laugh, about their jobs—she felt no real surprise and only slight disappointment. In fact, she told Joanne, there was a certain sense of relief. Not merely because the burden of "making it" as a real-life editor-in-chief had been lifted (she'd still spent many sleepless nights, in the beginning, wondering if she were up to even the reality of her title), nor because the demands on her time and her reading skills were suddenly so reduced, but because, she said, she was reassured that she had not, after all, as for one dizzy moment she had believed, somehow sprouted wings and brilliance and left the common ground for some vertiginous land of success. Her job was not what it seemed; therefore, despite appearances, she was still herself, still normal. It was, she said, a state that appealed to her, after Bill and her strange leaving, after a childhood spent in a middle-class neighborhood where achievement often implied exile, lonely worldliness and who-the-hell-does-she-think-she-is? Where, as a teenager, she overheard often enough other women call her mother "saintly," while using a fingertip to turn up a nose.

Perhaps, for a moment, she had believed the job to be something else, something grand (she *had*, after her interview, walked up to Saks and bought a suit of editor-gray tweed), but, she told Joanne, she'd always been suspicious of good fortune, and although she'd said nothing at the time, she began to think as soon as she was hired that her job couldn't possibly be what it seemed.

But there were compensations, she liked to point out.

There were, for instance, the bonuses. As Mr. Owens often reminded her, no other publisher, subsidy or otherwise (he refused to call Vista a vanity press, which may be what had misled her in the interview) so rewarded its editors. And when, after two weeks of work, she was able to afford a broker's fee and so finally move into her own apartment, she had to agree (as her mother and Mr. and Mrs. Paletti and Joanne agreed) that things being what they were, the money was a great advantage.

As was the job itself. For despite her early fears of incompetence, she soon discovered that the only talent she'd really developed in college—how to look as if you're listening and sound as if you've done all the reading—was the only talent required of her here, in what she'd once referred to as "the real world."

But the greatest compensation of all, she liked to say, was her initiation, at a time when she needed new friends, into the delightful secret society of Vista office workers. The den of thieves, as Ann now calls them, that consisted at the time of the guys in Production (many of them gone now), Marv in Publicity, Kevin the Art Director, Frieda the Copyeditor (now off writing comic books) and Jake, Ned's predecessor. (Ann herself came later, when Elizabeth had been at Vista for nearly six months. On *her* interview, she told Elizabeth that she was not a career secretary but a poet. She said she only hoped that a job in publishing would support her habit, give her incentive to write and, perhaps, a chance to make some contacts—a statement that is still a great source of amusement to them both.)

If Elizabeth had ever believed her psychology-major friends, who claimed that as an only child with a traveling father she would spend her life looking for siblings, family, she could have replied with great assurance that she'd found them in these people; the core of office workers who understood completely what Vista was all about; who winked at her over the heads of authors or culled for her favorite terrible sentences from each manuscript, or sent her facetious memos about the books she'd signed. (To Elizabeth, From Production, Re: *Tommy the Timid Toilet: A Fantastical Guide to Potty Training.* Book to be printed on 400 2-ply sheets. Strong, absorbent, squeezably soft. Pink, yellow or blue? Pls. advise.) The core of workers who kept one another laughing, kept the jokes rolling, as if this were not, in truth, a vanity publisher where real people spent real money to publish the books they'd spent years of their lives to write, but a half-hour situation comedy about a vanity publisher, where the authors were character actors or walk-ons or special guest stars and the regular cast of actor/workers vied each week for the best lines.

If she was not, in reality, an editor-in-chief at a large New York City publisher there was the compensation that she was at least a wry and well-loved co-star in this sophisticated and somewhat cynical comedy series. A buddy to her peers, normal to the rest of the world, and of course, to her authors, pure gold. If she had not scaled the heights of success, she had at least found a safe corner where the view was about the same; where there were enough people looking up to give her the illusion of looking down.

The authors, too, were some compensation (although this she did *not* say), for with each of them she became that glamorous, successful career woman she'd had in mind when she first recited her theories in Mr. Owens' office. Became, if only for a half an hour at a time, and if only behind her closed office door, that liaison between humble dreams and the glittering metropolis, that yea- or nay-sayer who could change lives; became, in short, everything she had, if only for a moment, imagined herself someday to be.

And how her authors believed in her! Because their own success was so wrapped up in hers, her brilliance so much a proof of their own, their awe of her—her position, her power —was completely guileless, utterly generous. They imagined for her none of the bitterness or disillusionment or private loneliness we like (hope) to bestow on one who has done so well at such an early age, and Elizabeth, when she was with them, was sometimes able to enjoy their admiration, enjoy the success her title implied, as if she was indeed an editor-in-chief and all their worship was indeed well-founded.

It was as if, with each author, alone in her office, she did sprout wings, take flight, but always within the safety of a dream. And always Ann's laugh or a wink from Jake or Bonnie's giggles and scowls could set her safely on the ground again; wake her in time to laugh softly at herself and to sigh, Ah, but it was a lovely dream.

With her apartment and her job, her new wealth and her new friends, all she needed to complete the picture (and she thought of it as a picture, much like the one she had successfully copied in decorating her apartment) was love.

Since coming to New York, she had tried to avoid thinking of Bill, tried to hold her thoughts of him aside the way she had seen mothers in supermarkets and shopping malls place a light hand on some screaming child's head and calmly, patiently, turn away, ignoring the screams and the demands, even the small fists that struck at her thigh. And yet, especially after a long weekend of eating alone, watching television, speaking so little that when she went into the office Monday morning her voice startled her, seemed loose and awkward like a limb just released from a cast, the thoughts came to her still, pummeled her with memories and regrets and a thousand futile comparisons.

So she began to go to bars with Ann and on Joanne-inspired blind dates. She brought men home. But she soon found there was little she could say to these strangers. If only because of all the hours of every day she heard it in her own voice, her ear had become finely attuned to falsehood, veiled indifference, and it frightened and disappointed her to hear it now, in the language of what she longed to call courtship. Testing some man, she would be evasive or coy, as flirtatious as a Southern belle or as full of *non sequiturs* as a politician, and he would simply smile, or look intense, or say something that might pass as a reply and then ask to take her to bed, just as she might say to an author, the preliminary compliments over, "Now, about the contract . . ."

And even in bed, during and after the love-making, the words would drop to her pillow like dull coins. ("Have you ever been in love?" was, she discovered, a favorite male question, usually asked while staring at the ceiling, cigarette in hand. "I'm not sure I even know what love is," she would say, testing. And he would nod, "Really.") Words exchanged like some cheap currency, one for another, no real value implied.

Had she spent any time with any of these men, she might, of course, have gotten beyond such hollow beginnings, but because even the most superficial conversation led her to something she would not carelessly divulge (the details of her job, her mother's lover, the way she'd spent the last year), she would always, having determined a young man's latent unconcern, grow silent or just silly and he in turn would grow awkward or bored.

She asked only for attention, she said, for something that at least resembled what she'd had before. Something that would not make her feel a traitor to her old self who had once believed, with Bill, that for the rest of her life every sexual act would be an act of love.

Joanne said she had simply become too picky. Ann said she should learn to laugh in bed, copulation wasn't that serious.

But she wanted to fall in love again and she could only think of love, real love, as a moment of consummate seriousness, consummate honesty. A moment when all the laughter stopped, when her life, which she admitted was only skimming along its surface now, would slow, stop, plunge her to a depth she had never before reached, that she could only equate with holiness or revelation or a cool, silent place where her past and future would meet like two fine sprays of water, meet and mingle and rise up like a geyser, burst forth like some miraculous spring or blessed fountain (a fountain of champagne, perhaps, because, had she thought about it, the place was not unlike a church and the sound of mingling waters not unlike that of whispered vows).

She wanted real love, she wanted true attention. She wanted, at least, to be gazed upon in the same way her authors gazed upon her, listened to in the way her authors listened to her. She wanted to find, in the real world, their kind of adoration, both to give and to receive, but mostly to show Bill someday in the future when they met again and, over lunch or a drink or in her dimly lit apartment she told the triumphant story of her life without him.

And so when she woke one morning, just a year since she'd started working at Vista, and about nine months since she'd started testing and discarding young men, and found a bearded stranger sleeping beside her with his mouth open and a line of dried saliva caked like salt along his mustache, saw her cluttered apartment and her twisted sheets, she swore: Not again until it means something, until there's care, love, worship. At least as much attention as her authors gave her.

Tupper Daniels, then, or someone just like him, was, of course, inevitable.

VIII

ANN LEANS INTO THE OFFICE, her pocketbook over her shoulder, her raincoat on, the tight belt making her waist seem false and arbitrary, as if a waist would appear wherever the belt were tied.

"Toodle-oo," she mouths, and Elizabeth waves.

"It was not mere coincidence, Elizabeth," the man on the phone is saying, his Southern accent thick and slick. "When I came down from the mountain and, as soon as I arrived, saw the newspaper on our coffee table opened to your ad, I knew I should call."

"Well, we're glad you did," she says, drawing daisies on her notepad. The typewriters outside are still. She can hear the front door opening and closing, people calling "Good night."

"And that's why I told your girl, 'I want the head man, the editor-in-chief, because I have good news that shall not be delayed by lesser employees.' "

She draws a smiling face and smiles into the phone. "I understand." Fifteen minutes ago, Ann had called her on the intercom and said, "There's a messenger of God on the phone and he wants to speak to you. It's also time to go home."

"And do you know, Elizabeth," he goes on, "When I heard your voice, something stirred within me. Something said, 'Ewell, this woman is a child of the Lord and she will serve you well.' Do you believe that, Elizabeth?"

"Certainly," she tells him, circling his name on her notepad. *Reverend Ewell Datz.* She wonders if it ever occurs to him that he sounds like a disc jockey imitating a preacher, a comedian doing Burt Lancaster as Elmer Gantry. A Billy Graham cliché. She wonders if he finds it reassuring—to be repeated and reproduced on all the major networks. "And we'll look forward to receiving your manuscript, Reverend Datz, if you'll just send it to my attention."

"I will do that, Elizabeth," he says softly, slowly. "But you are mistaken when you say *my* manuscript. It isn't my manuscript and let me tell you why."

She writes *mah ms.* across her pad. He seems to have moved away from the phone. She hears a chair scrape and pictures him getting down on his knees or clearing the floor for a song. Then his breath comes back.

"While I was on the mountain," he says in a new, low voice. "In that little cabin my daddy built, the one I was telling you about, I was filled one night with a terrible joy, like a great white light in my soul. And in this joy, I took up pen and paper and began to write. I wrote for seven days and seven nights and when I was finished, I had this book. Not *my* book, Elizabeth, but a book written by the Holy Spirit, through me."

Say Alleluia, she writes on the pad, surprised that she still remembers where all the *l*'s go. "I see," she says.

"That's why the cover of the book must say, '*How To Win With Jesus During the Coming Holocaust,* by the Holy Spirit.'" He pauses, as if to visualize it, and then adds, an aside, "I figure your people can do a nice representative drawing for the back, where they usually put the author's picture. You know, a sketch with a dove and light and all. Can you do that?"

"Yes, we can," she says slowly. Last month, she'd had a book by the prophet Elijah, and, just a few weeks ago, one by Sange 6-94, an extraterrestial being. Both times Ned had sarcastically asked her where they should send the royalty checks. "But, of course, the copyright will be in your name."

"In the name of the Holy Spirit," he says, as if repeating after her. "For He is the true author." He pauses. "As I mentioned, my congregation and I will defray the costs of publishing. I'm sure we'll be more than compensated by hardcover—and paperback—sales."

She sighs, deciding to argue about it when the contract has been signed. "Fine," she tells him, giving her voice that push-them-off-the-line tone. "Why don't you just send us your manuscript, *His* manuscript, and we'll work out the details then."

"I'll do that," he says. And then, whispering like a lover: "Elizabeth?"

"Yes, Reverend?"

"Do *you* accept Jesus Christ as your personal friend and saviour?"

She blushes—the comedian doing Elmer Gantry has suddenly called her up on stage. "Certainly," she says, in the same tone she uses when people ask if Vista is endorsed by the Better Business Bureau. "And thank you so much for calling, Reverend Datz." He starts to say something else but she coos, " 'Bye," and hangs up the phone.

It's nearly five-thirty and the office outside is in shadow. Only Mr. Owens is left and she can barely hear the quiet drone of his voice as he talks a letter into his dictaphone. She knows he is waiting for her to leave so he can make his daily inspection of everyone's desk and then go home himself.

She quickly types a memo to Production. Re: *How to Win With Jesus During the Coming Holocaust* by the Holy Spirit, Reverend Ewell Datz, editor. (Soon to be signed.) Author wants sketch of Holy Spirit on back jacket, i.e., dove and light, etc.

She recalls a time when she couldn't say Jesus without lowering her voice and bowing her head; when it was a word she said mostly to herself and only in prayer. Now it's on the lips of every TV preacher and country-and-western singer and left-over hippie—on bumper stickers and billboards. Like having the Coca-Cola Corporation for your personal friend and saviour.

Although she knows she shouldn't knock it; would-be gospel writers make Vista a lot of money.

She looks over the memo and then adds: Tell Kevin doves look just like pigeons.

She pulls the paper from her typewriter, puts it in the OUT box for Ann, straightens her desk. She's in no hurry to get home. Nearly two weeks and not a word from him. Joanne has stopped asking her to bring him over for dinner some Saturday night, Ann has stopped asking if he's called, the two of them, like sideline medics, ready to rush to her aid, to tell her he was a jerk anyway, as soon as she shows signs of giving up, being hurt.

They mean well, but she knows if she hadn't told them about him, the insult would now be hers alone, easier to ignore.

She wonders if she should send him one of her encourage-ment letters (Dear Mr., Mrs., Miss, Ms. _____, We thought we'd take this opportunity to write to remind you how anxious we are to place your book, _____, on our Fall/Spring/Sum-mer/Christmas list. Your book, it seems to us, is a timely/tasteful/touching account . . .), if, receiving it, he would remember that he'd slept with her, that she'd thrown him out. That she'd called her father a bigamist.

She picks up her pocketbook, looks at the phone. She could also call him at his hotel, pretending it was business, but Mr. Owens is waiting and he doesn't approve of after-hour calls. "Darling, you start treating them like gold, they get suspicious. Treat them like shit and they're impressed."

She's had enough of Southerners today anyway.

She turns off her light. Mr. Owens is standing in his doorway, his wide, compact body pressed nicely into his three-piece suit, his hairy fingers twirling a rubber band.

"Late," he says. The smile seems to drip from his long nose. It spreads across his face reluctantly, a thick fluid filling a narrow crevice.

"A call from Alabama. You know how slowly they speak."

He closes his eyes, raises his eyebrows, shrugs. "How'd you like to travel?" he asks, looking at the rubber band.

"For Vista?"

He doesn't raise his eyes. "Ellis is getting tired of the road. He wants to spend more time in the office." Ellis is the other editor-in-chief, the one who travels from city to city, preceded by large newspaper ads that herald the arrival of a major New York publisher and invite authors to stop by his temporary office at the Holiday Inn for a free reading. "You make a good appearance and Ellis is starting to get a fat ass. You might do better." He looks at her, or, like a blind person, at somewhere around her throat. "Not long trips, maybe a week or two—Boston, Washington, Miami. The old ones like you."

"Sounds fine to me," she says. She realizes he's not asking.

"All right. We'll talk more later." He finally looks her in the eye, making it clear he wants her to leave. " 'Night," he says.

"Good night."

As she walks down the corridor, she feels a quick pinch at the back of her heel. Startled, she turns. The rubber band is on the floor behind her. Mr. Owens is standing in front of her office, smiling.

She smiles back at him as if he has blown her a kiss and says, "Good night."

On the elevator, she thinks of traveling. Spending a few days at a Holiday Inn, eating breakfast in the restaurant, having a maid make her bed, going to the lounge to hear live, somewhat moth-eaten music, to drink gin and tonics. Moving on in the morning.

It appeals to her. She knows it's naïve, but business travel has always seemed to her the ultimate in sophistication. Packing, going to the airport, checking into a modern hotel. Seeing all those strange faces she will never in her life see again, maybe even getting to know some of them briefly. It reeks with adventure.

And yet, as she steps outside, onto the wet and darkening street where a large green trailer truck and a startlingly yellow taxi squeeze beside each other, horns blowing, voices shouting in what seems a perfect, grating illustration of hate, her enthusiasm snags. She suddenly feels a little repelled by her imaginings, even a little frightened, as if she'd been unwinding a fresh bolt of satin and suddenly came across a ringed spot of dried blood.

Perhaps it's just that talking to Mr. Owens always makes her feel somewhat cautious.

Or maybe because her father traveled. Died alone on the road.

He's at the corner, leaning against the building, hands in the pockets of his corduroy trousers. When he sees her, sees that she sees him, he doesn't straighten up, merely smiles a sly smile; even when she stops before him, he continues to lean, to look at her. She has a feeling he's about to say, "The jig is up."

"You look like Eliot Ness," she tells him, already adopting her on-the-road directness. "Smug."

His smile broadens and he pushes away from the building with his shoulders. "I was just thinking how great you look," he tells her, taking her arm, continuing her walk.

She wishes she were in love with him.

"Have you got plans for tonight?" he asks.

"No," she says, trying not to smile. Tomorrow she will tell Ann, call Joanne.

He pulls his head back, eyeing her. "What? No dinners with authors? No parties at Elaine's? Not even a tête-à-tête with Capote or Mailer?"

Her heart sinks into something hot, pebbly. So the jig *is* up. She stops. "Do you have something you want to say?" she asks, already rehearsing her reply, her defense: Vanity publishers perform a service and make no promises they don't keep. It's all in the contract. If they seem to promise more than they actually deliver, well, what company doesn't? What beer brewer or car dealer or international designer of blue jeans doesn't?

But her tone has surprised him. His smile loosens, sags. "No," he says, all innocence. "I just thought you'd probably be busy. I know your job must involve a lot of socializing."

She starts walking again, the way a dancer who has missed a step moves quickly on.

"How's the book coming?" she asks.

He shrugs. "Well, we haven't done much with it, have we?"

She looks at him walking beside her, that little bounce in his step. She wishes he were taller. "No, we haven't," she says.

A woman in a black coat and a matted orange wig approaches them, scraping along on clear plastic high heels. Except for her red eyes, shining like blood and rimmed in bright turquoise, her features are dark and indistinct, as if they'd been rubbed with a dirty eraser, smudged with a wet finger. "Have you got any money?" she asks, whining.

Elizabeth walks by her, but Tupper pauses, digs into his pocket. As he runs to rejoin Elizabeth, the woman screams back that he's a devil-fucker.

Elizabeth laughs. "Your just reward."

"But I gave her nearly a dollar," he says. "How much more should I have given her?"

She looks at him. He is blushing, truly embarrassed, and she laughs again. They are close enough to midtown now to be joined by other late workers heading home. "So I said 'Dammit,' " a young man in a shiny brown raincoat says to another in gray. " 'Dammit to hell,' I told him." Two young women, skirts and sweaters tight, figures perfect, knees bent slightly as they move over the rough sidewalk in their high, ankle-strapped heels, laugh together, licking vanilla cones. She thinks of a song about how New York is a wonderful place to be in love and then, as she hums it, remembers it's Paris.

"I came to ask you out to dinner," he says sorrowfully as they approach the subway. "I purposely came after work and waited for you outside. No business, all pleasure." He puts his hands in his pockets, bows his head, as if this offer too will be cursed. "Does that sound at all appealing to you?"

"Sure," she says, shrugging. "Sounds fine."

"Really?" He laughs, puts his arm around her waist. "Great. Do you want to go home first and freshen up?"

She pauses at the subway steps. "My home or yours?"

He grins. "Yours, of course."

She smiles coyly, settling in for another seduction. "Then this is my train." But as she starts down the stairs, he backs away, grimacing as if the steps were littered with dead cats. "Some things I cannot do," he calls to her, stepping into the street to hail a cab.

She has to dodge bodies like a linebacker to rejoin him.

Last Monday morning, over coffee and bagels in her office, Elizabeth had told Ann about Friday night. She'd said she hadn't made up her mind about what to do with Tupper Daniels next, and Ann had offered three suggestions.

First, she'd said, pulling her bagel apart with thumb and forefingers. "Keep seeing him until the contract is signed and the book goes into production. Then break up with him."

Elizabeth had smiled, taking her own bagel from the desk, tilting it to let the melted butter drip into the foil. For all her disillusionment and sophistication, Ann still uses terms like "break up" and "make out," as if she has relearned everything about sex except that first, formulative vocabulary.

"Breaking up is hard to do," she said, watching her own bagel.

"Just wait until he rolls over some night and says, 'What's this about my galleys being delayed by monsoons?' " They both laughed. One of Vista's typesetters is in India, where the cost of labor and paper are low, but where monsoons occasionally delay the mails. "You could have some very tacky bedroom scenes," Ann said.

Elizabeth nodded. "Yes we could."

"So don't see him again," she went on. "He's served his purpose."

"But he hasn't signed a contract."

Ann looked at her through half-closed eyes, assessing, and then shrugged. "Okay," leaning forward to dip the end of her bagel into a small container of purple jelly. "Here's what you do: You tell him you were just swept off your feet Friday night but now that you've had time to think about it"—she licked her finger—"you've decided it would be better business if you didn't sleep with him again. For his own good. Nothing personal."

"And then?"

"And then," she went on, chewing, "darling Tupperware will be so flattered that you succumbed to his charms in the first place, against your own better judgment, that he'll sign the contract out of pure conceit and, to save you from yourself, never make a pass at you again."

Elizabeth chewed her own bagel, considering. She knew it was a role that would suit him, and her—forswearing sex for the sake of business, for the higher good of his manuscript. "That's almost brilliant," she said.

Ann nodded. "It's a variation on the line Brian used to use

on all his little chickies in the typing pool. That's why he always went for the ambitious ones, they'd rather lose him than their jobs." She grinned. "Who said my marriage didn't teach me anything?"

Elizabeth stared at her, deadpan. "You just talked me out of it," she said. And Ann laughed. "I thought I would."

Just then the door slowly opened, and Bonnie slowly poked her head into the office, her eyes going immediately to the breakfast on the desk and then snapping away, as if she had looked down somebody's dress. A toothpick pierced the corner of her mouth and a single pink barrette pulled her hair back from her pimply forehead. "Mr. Owens just came in," she announced. "He's in his office. You told me to tell you."

Elizabeth thanked her and began to clear the desk. Ann moved on to point number three.

"You have to be careful you don't make too much of him," she said. "You might, after your long dry spell. I've seen the most sensible women fall madly in love, get married and everything, after a heavy dose of celibacy—as if marriage ever cured celibacy." She crumpled a brown-paper bag with small punches. "You'd better be careful."

Elizabeth tossed her hair, blithely. "No problem," she said.

It's the sexual part that's always puzzled her about marriage. Regular pleasure seems somehow a contradiction in terms. Passing that same freckle, kissing that same thigh, the same fine hairs on the same legs, the same slow movements of the same mouths: Ah, there's the way he blushes again, here's the way I like to turn; there's his cry, here's mine. Just like yesterday, last week, last year.

She's been told it puts sex in the proper perspective: regularity, monogamy, marriage. But it seems to her that proper perspective often verges on boredom, indifference; a way of disassembling all those angled and sloping and sharp-edged spirals of feeling that get in the way, slow you down. A way of making everything equally smooth, equally flat, as colorless as a desert, so the same shrug, the same laughter, can roll easily over it all.

She has her authors and all their sorry little books in the proper perspective. She has Jesus there, too. And her parents, perhaps.

She wonders if some things should remain without any perspective at all.

At least with Bill, she was never sure how she'd find him.

She gets up on her elbow, looks at him, at the blush fading from his chest. "Shall we go eat crêpes now? Just like last time?"

But he pulls her to him, holds her tightly. Without the excuse of passion, she feels awkward in his arms. She thinks of how both their chests are bare.

"I've missed you," he says into her hair.

Uncertain, she whispers, "Thank you."

"Did you miss me?"

"Yes," she says, improvising. It's as if the man in the projector room has put on the third reel before the second. She can only guess where they are now: friends? lovers? sex maniacs?

"I thought so much about you," he says, stroking her hair, then her back. She rolls away from him, leaving her hand on his stomach so he won't ask why.

"Have you been away?" This like an amnesia victim who's afraid she should know the answer.

"No," he says, putting his hand over hers.

"Working on the book?"

He shakes his head, turns to look at her. "But I've been thinking about it, though. I've got an idea for the ending."

"Good," she says. She decided in the cab that she'd take Ann's first piece of advice: sleep with him only until the book is finished and the contract signed, and then say good-by forever.

Already the decision is lending their relationship a sweetly fatal air, like *Love Story* the second time you read it.

"Do you want to tell me your idea?" she asks him.

He frowns. "I said all pleasure."

"I don't mind." She turns onto her stomach, tucking the pillow under her, cool side up. "Tell me." She is being very gallant.

He clears his throat. "Well, looking the book over, I realized there's not much in the way of background. Mostly because nobody where I grew up knew anything about Bailey's background either. He really did show up one day—just the way I have it in the book."

He pauses, and at first she thinks it's one of the many pauses that pepper his slow speech. But it lasts longer than most and so she says, "Go on."

"Well," he clears his throat again. "I thought maybe I could do something with that."

She looks at his profile. His neat, blond sideburn is oddly geometrical, a fine, square fuzz. "With what?"

"His past."

"But you just said you didn't know anything about his past."

He turns to face her. "I know," he says sadly.

He stares at the ceiling, she at the back of the couch, her headboard. Outside, a young boy's shrill voice cries *"Asshole!"* Another laughs.

"And don't you usually tell the past in the beginning?" she says slowly, watching the white threads of the couch moving in and out of one another, blurring into a whole. "Not at the end?"

"You think so?" His voice is humble. It reminds her that she's the expert. That she has no idea.

She wonders if she's trying to put off the inevitable. Only

until he finishes his book, until the stroke of midnight, until Jenny gets leukemia.

"Well," she says, conceding to fate, "I suppose you could end with the past."

He rolls onto his side, faces her. "That's what I was thinking," he says, enthused. "It could really be different. Like suddenly you see his past and you understand the whole book. Almost a touch of, oh, I don't know, Agatha Christie."

"Like Rosebud" she says, startling them both.

"What do you mean?" He looks at her keenly; they're brainstorming now.

She feels a little foolish but goes on. "I don't know if it applies, really," she says, "because I don't remember the movie that well, but wasn't it at the end of *Citizen Kane,* when they show you the sled burning, that you see it's named Rosebud? And that's how you know the way his past affected him?" She's sorry she mentioned it.

He shakes his head. "No," he says slowly, not wanting to offend her. "I don't think that's the same thing. I don't think this has ever been done before."

She turns to look at the couch again. None of them ever think it's been done before: coming of age during World War II as it's never been done before, the sexual liberation of a suburban housewife as it's never been done before, the Book of Revelation . . .

"All right," she says, feeling like a straight man. "What happened in his past that will make us understand the whole book? Why did he become a bigamist?" She realizes she's talking about *him* as if he were a real person.

He lies flat again, looks up at the ceiling. "That's what I don't know yet," he says. "That's where you have to help me."

"I see." She knows he is going to ask about her father again. Where did he go? What did he do? And, as if she knew all the answers, she smiles slyly. This time she will not get touchy.

Maybe she will even tell him, "My mother had theories." Watch his eyes shine.

But he merely turns to her, those nice blue eyes, the smooth skin. "Will you help me?" he asks, leaning to kiss her arm, her shoulder, her neck.

She smiles, puts her hand to his hair. "Of course I'll help you," she says slowly, Dorothy to the Tin Man, promising Oz and a heart. But all the while planning her own trip home. "I want to get this book finished too, don't I?"

On Tuesday of last week, Ann had come into her office to say, "You should probably get the Career Woman of the Year Award."

She looked up from yet another how-to-get-rich-quick manuscript. "Thank you. Why?"

"Well, the big problem for the working woman is how to combine a life at home and a life in the office. You know, a sex life and a professional life, right?"

"I guess so."

She folded her arms before her. "Well, you've managed to do both—beautifully!" She leaned forward, eyes bright. "You're screwing Tupper Daniels at home, and screwing him again when he comes in here. The perfect solution!" She laughed her laugh and Elizabeth smiled.

"I'll have to remember that," she said.

After dinner, Elizabeth insists there be a "decent interval" before they return to her apartment and her bed. He tells her she sounds like a reluctant nun, and as they walk toward the river he begins to recite every Catholic joke he knows. They're terrible jokes (What kind of meat do priests eat on Friday? Nun.), but she laughs at each of them—no hang-ups.

"That *is* my heritage you're talking about," she says as they reach East End Avenue and he runs out of jokes. "I should be offended."

He shakes his head. "It's not your heritage," he says. "You're English."

"And Irish."

He takes her arm, whispers in her ear. "That's a misfortune we needn't mention. And besides," getting louder, "I was under the impression you'd left all that mackerel-snatching stuff behind you."

"I have." She wonders if she's told him this or he's only presumed it. Presumed that a modern, sexually liberated young woman such as herself would be without religion. She wonders if the apostate isn't as easy to pick out as the preacher, and as much a cliché.

She steers him into the tiny dead-end street that leads to the promenade. "This is what I wanted to show you," she says. "It looks right over the river."

As they climb the steps and begin to stroll along the walk, she mentions all the movies that have been filmed here. He hasn't seen any of them and it somehow disappoints her, as if the significance of the place was suddenly lost, or there for her alone. Like watching a sunset with an atheist. She thinks of telling him this, but fears the tangle of logic behind it; fears it's an expression she learned from the nuns.

They pause to sit on one of the benches. The wind is getting stronger, colder. Without a word, he takes both her hands and puts them under his sweater, puts his hand over them. He pulls her close, until she has to bend her neck awkwardly to watch the tiny white and yellow lights of Roosevelt Island and the bridges.

"I'm beginning to love New York," he says. "The excitement, the glamour, the constant pace. Everyone's just so much more alive here than in the South." He lifts his hand off hers and points across the river. "Each one of those lights out there could be a person who lives in New York. Their lives glow just like that."

She wonders if he's being poetic and feels a little embarrassed for him. "That's Queens," she says, smiling, but he doesn't hear the contradiction.

"Look at you," he goes on. "If you lived in the South, you'd either be married by now with six kids or stuck in some boring job in an insurance office. I mean, I probably know a hundred, two hundred women back home, and not one of them has a job anywhere near as exciting as yours."

She sinks down on the bench, where she can only see the river from between the black bars of the railing. One hundred? Two hundred? "Don't you know any women who live in big cities, like Atlanta?"

He lets out a breath and she looks up at him. At the dark-blue silhouette of his jaw and nose. How many belles are waiting back home, waiting for this New York excursion to end, for Scott to return to his Zelda?

"Atlanta's not the same," he says, shaking his head. "No other city is the same. I guess you don't see it, having grown up here."

"On Long Island," she corrects him. But he is silent and she slowly leans her head against him, her ear against his soft sweater. She listens to the sound of his heart beating, thinking vaguely of all the movies that have been filmed here, all the movies that show the silhouette of a couple on a bench in a park, leaning together, looking at a river. She wonders if she is still playing the lover or becoming her.

He pulls away a little, squinting to see her in the darkness. "That must be weird," he whispers, "growing up in New York. Having it be your hometown. I don't think I'd like it. The city's so big. And it changes so much. I think I'd always wonder."

She frowns. "Wonder about what?"

"About the past, I guess." He pulls her closer. "If I grew up in the city, and my parents and grandparents and great-grand-parents grew up here, I think I'd always wonder, whenever I saw a new building going up or an old one coming down, if it had anything to do with my own past. You know, I'd wonder if this was the place where my grandfather once stood, if this was the same street he walked down when he was young. If this was where my great-grandparents' house used to be. Things change so quickly, it would be hard to have landmarks. I think I'd always wonder. Do you know what I mean?"

She shakes her head. He is leading to her father. Or his book. Or both. She has to admire his subtlety. "No," she says.

He clicks his tongue. "Well, say every morning when you walk to work, you pass by this high rise on your corner. You don't think anything of it, it's just one of many. But what if, where that high rise stands today, there had once been a house where your grandmother was born, or where your great-grand-father died, or was conceived—you may never know. That place would have real significance to your life and yet you'd probably never know."

"So?"

"So, it would always make me wonder. You could have ghosts anywhere."

She sits up to look at him, exaggerating the knit in her brows so he can see it in the dim light. "You Southerners do believe in ghosts, don't you?"

He laughs a little, pulls her close again. "I guess I'm not making myself very clear," he says, and she, on her own, puts her hands under his sweater, feels the steady rise and fall of his warm belly. "Try again," she whispers, leaning against him, giving him something, although, other than attention, she cannot say what it is.

He waits, breathes deeply. Between the bars, she can see the lights on the water, moving along the currents like bright ribbons. "At home," he says softly, "in our back garden, there's an iron bench. I tried to write about it once. It's worn down and kind of green, but you can see that it used to be pretty ornate. There's still some scrollwork on it and the feet are four animal claws. I used to pretend it was my horse when I was a kid. It's at an angle to the back of the house, actually facing the sunniest part of the garden, but if you sit in the far left corner and turn a little, so you almost have your feet up, you can look right up into the master bedroom."

He pauses as if to consider, and she smiles. She can see him trying to write about it. Childhood memories are as big at Vista as Jesus himself. My daddy's cabin, my grandpa's rocker, I remember Mama. Authors relating the bland details of their usual lives—their teddy bears, their backyards, their first loves —like breathless adventurers just out of the uncharted woods.

"When I was in my third year at Andover, I got called home because my grandfather was dying. It was spring. Still winter in New England, but spring in Tennessee, and, I don't know, but maybe that's why as soon as I got home I went out to the garden. And my father was there on the bench, looking up at the master bedroom, as if my grandfather were in there dying, not at the hospital thirty miles away. At first he didn't say anything, but then he told me, although I'd heard it a hundred times before, that this was where he'd sat the day I was being born, in that same hospital, because it was where his father had sat the day he was born upstairs in that bedroom. He said (and, of course, I knew this too) that until we started going to hospitals for all our entrances and exits, this was where all the men in the Daniels family had sat while their children were up there being born, and where their children—like the little figures in our Swiss clock, he said—had come out to sit while their fathers went in to die."

She hears the panting steps of a jogger passing behind them: an odd counterpoint.

"I thought it was a lovely image, a *kind* image of death, really," he goes on, "as if the children were born to relieve their parents' long vigil, their children born to relieve them. And I suppose what made it so kind was the continuity, the sense of sharing, that the iron bench provided. Each of them sat on that same bench; it was worn with the impressions that each of their bodies had made, and it had stood in that same spot for well over a hundred years." His voice grows softer, it can get no slower.

"I guess hospitals have made it into a mere ritual, but I'm romantic enough—maybe Southern enough—to know I'll be sitting there when my father dies and when my children are born. And I want my child sitting there when I die, even if I am in a hospital thirty miles away."

He draws in his breath, seems to hold it.

Yes, she thinks, ancestors too. Just that morning, she'd spent an hour with a large manuscript called *White Roots: One Hundred Years of the Armbrusters of Pinnington, Idaho.* It was an awful mess, typed by three or four different machines on a dozen different kinds of paper covered with penned-in notes and corrections. Between the pages there had been hundreds of photographs, each wrapped carefully in pale-pink tissue paper. Some were old, faded, formal portraits of plain, startled men and women with oddly glazed eyes. Others were grainy amateur photos—smudged families in front of large houses, couples in black clothes with gray faces. Still others were newer: men in uniforms hugging women with large flowers in their hair, wedding photos, color photos of families sitting on couches. The last was a studio portrait of a cute little blond girl with her fingers on her chin, wearing a dress printed with dancing poodles—as if one hundred years of the Armbrusters of Pinnington, Idaho, had produced only a vague imitation of a child star.

Orlee Armbruster, the little girl who had grown up to be the family historian, wanted Vista to contact ABC about making it into a mini-series. She suggested Robert Young or Lorne Greene play the patriarch. She was available for all talk shows.

A barge floats swiftly by, small clear lights along its flat deck, a pudgy tug on its side. He shifts a little on the bench. Wooden bench.

"All my ghosts are contained in that one object," he whispers, "that bench. It's clear and it sums up everything, and there's nothing in the world that can move me or comfort me or even frighten me the way it can—except, sometimes, the house itself. But here, things change so much, people move around so much, your ancestors could have lived and died in a hundred different places. You could have ghosts anywhere. Do you see what I mean?"

She shrugs. "People in the country stay put, people in the city move around." She hears her voice, petulant, contrary. Given a chance, she knows, these people will coat anything with poetry.

He shakes his head. "I don't know how to make you see."

She looks through the bars, out over the water, to the lights of Queens. Those people out there, she could tell him, don't live and die with the quaint, circular charm of figures in a Swiss clock, despite his daddy's homey metaphors. They're random, unattached, with a future that goes only to their retirement in Florida or Maine and a past that ends with Grandma in the spare room. They're like flash bulbs going off in a large, dark theater. That's how they glow, she could tell him, like quick, blinding flash bulbs.

"You're so Southern," she says instead, laughing. "All this stuff about ghosts and ancestors and monuments to the not-forgotten dead. Other people don't think like that."

He leans back, watching her. "Well, what do they think about then?" he asks. "What do the Irish think about, for instance?"

She laughs again. "I don't know—religion, leprechauns, beer. Not about ghosts."

He leans closer to her. His pale skin seems brighter than it should in this darkness. "What do you think leprechauns are?

And all those Catholic saints? They're ghosts."

She shakes her head. "But not ancestral ghosts. They're fictional ghosts, made up." She smiles at him to keep the conversation from getting too serious. "That's the difference. The Irish make up their ghosts. I mean, how can you turn homely Uncle Patrick with the big nose and the rotten teeth into any kind of respectable spirit? And who wants to remember him as an ancestor? Better to bury him and then throw a big party where you can get drunk enough to hallucinate someone more appealing—someone who's not going to burden your imagination with what he was really like."

He laughs and she laughs with him. "It's true!" she says. "You Southerners may want to sit on a bench with your ancestors and remember the dead, but there are other races who'd rather bury them and leave town. Good-by and good riddance."

She stops abruptly. She will not add, like my mother, like my father.

She looks at him and he is smiling, his eye bright in the darkness. He is waiting to hear her say it: Like my father. She hugs herself, rubbing her arms. "It's true," she says again, shivering a little, looking into the park behind them. "We'd better go before we get mugged."

He gets up, casually puts his arm around her shoulder. "I did have a valid point to make," he says after they've walked for a while. "I'll just have to write it down and then maybe you'll see what I'm trying to say." He stops, snaps his fingers. "The book," he cries. "The ending, using the past. That's it!"

She watches him, suddenly tired. If only he were normal, worked for the telephone company, talked politics and movies. "What's it?"

He begins to walk again, the little bounce a skip, his hand moving up and down as if he were leading a band. "I don't know yet," he says. "But what we were saying, it relates somehow. The past as an ending, it relates." He grins at her, all those lights behind him. "You see, you are helping me," he says.

And she laughs, takes his arm, tells him in that case, they should hurry home. The end is near.

IX

I RETURNED TO MAINE LAST SPRING,
flying this time, although whatever there had been to rush to
was already over. My mother had said, or Ward had told me
she'd said, that it would be silly to call me. Silly to have me be
there merely to steady her hand, waiting patiently, the way I
would help an old woman descend a curb.

Leukemia takes time and there had been some hope. She'd
thought it best that I not know until it was over; I had, she said,
better things to do.

Ward could not come to meet me. Carol, a large-faced
woman in her forties and Lillian, the old woman my mother
had met on the beach, were there instead, smiling like nurses,
oblivious to the chaos of the airport and the tangle of sullen
traffic outside, the stinking, slightly antiseptic haze over everything. At first I wondered why both women had come, but
when they put me in the back seat and immediately began
chatting about the weather and the news, I understood. It was
to allow me the opportunity of silence.

And I was silent. Not for any thoughts of my mother, but
because everything I thought to say to them, and I fashioned
and discarded a hundred sentences along the way, seemed a
lame variation of Blanche Dubois' "the kindness of strangers."

One of the most important days of my life and nothing
seemed original.

Ward's house had the sharp, wet odor of a recently doused fire. The two women brought me inside, and when Ward limped down the stairs they quickly went into the kitchen to make lunch. He seemed older. His face was drawn, his plaid shirt, though buttoned at the collar, barely brushed his thin throat; I wondered, with the quick, belated insight of those who have missed the point once before, just what slow illness his lean body held.

He shook my hand, awkwardly, his eyes filling and then quickly going dry, as if the tears had just lapped against them.

"I'm sorry," he said.

And I said, "Thank you. I'm sorry for you."

He shrugged a little, like a stranger at a bus stop who has also arrived too late, recognizing what by mere coincidence we appeared to share. The living room, the fireplace, the bay window, the old heavy furniture, so neat that even the worn threads of the cushions seemed recently combed, was filled with a mustard-colored light. The tea kettle out in the kitchen began to whistle.

"I'm sorry for *you,*" he repeated.

When Lillian came in with a rattling tray of sandwiches and teacups, she cried, "Sit down, sit down," as if we were up too soon after an operation.

I quickly sat on the couch. Ward on the chair opposite me. Carol then entered with the teapot and placed it on the coffee table between us. "Do you drink tea?" she asked, leaning to pour, and when I said I did, she went on about how her husband couldn't stand it. Lillian said it was just as well, it yellowed your teeth, although I, of course, had nothing to worry about, being so young and, she certainly hoped, free of dentures, what with flouride and flossing and all they have these days when she'd only had baking soda . . .

Ward seemed to retreat from the room as the women chatted, turning all his attention to the teacup and sandwich that balanced on his lap, absorbing himself in the careful progress of his spoon from saucer to coffee table to sugar bowl (his lips forming a small "o" as he scooped), back over the table and the carpet and his own knee. He stirred his tea with slow scrapes and clicks and kept his thumb and forefinger on the cup's delicate handle as he raised his sandwich and bent his head to meet it.

I wondered if my mother had ever grown impatient with this numbing care, or if she had found it sadly endearing.

He had called me at six-thirty the night before, Thursday, just as I bit into a limp strand of spaghetti and decided it was cooked. I turned off the burner under the pot, stirred the Ragú, and went into the living room to answer, thinking it was Joanne, or Peggy from downstairs. I had always imagined that such a call would come late at night—one of those screaming, hourless calls that wake you, heart pounding, fully prepared for whatever is terrible and unreal—and so when I heard the sputter of long distance and a man's hesitant, "Hello?" I felt only a mild curiousity.

As Ward began to speak, I had watched the silhouette in the high rise across the street moving around a kitchen, opening cabinets, carrying things to a table, standing, hands on hips, before what I imagined to be a stove, just, I thought, as I would be doing now if the phone hadn't rung. I noticed the traffic in the street had grown quiet. I longed for some loud noise to set my heart beating.

She had died at five o'clock. I remember thinking that if she had worked all her life, the hour might have had some significance.

After we'd eaten, and Lillian had poured us all a second cup of tea, Carol, who was sitting next to me, pushed her blue bandanna back on her head (her equivalent, I learned, of rolling up her sleeves) and took a small notepad from her pocketbook. Although she ran the local library, where she had met my mother, everything about her suggested a woman who shouted orders in the open air.

"Your mother," she began, "had certain requests for the funeral and I've already spoken to Father Lappen about them. It's all arranged, but he'd like to see you this afternoon. I'll take you down."

"Thank you." I sipped my tea, reminding myself that the ordeal was just beginning, and so was beginning to be over.

"The service will be at ten tomorrow. She asked that there be no viewing."

Lillian smiled at me from the other chair. "She said she didn't want any of us Yankees standing over her and saying, 'Ay-yup, thar she is.'"

Carol and Lillian laughed and Ward looked up at me, hopefully, I thought.

I smiled back at them. Last night, as I packed, I had realized I knew nothing of funeral arrangements and it frightened me. That dreamlike fright of walking into an exam unprepared. I suppose my mother had realized it too.

"She's asked to be cremated," Carol said softly. "I've cleared it with the Church for her." She raised her thick eyebrows slightly, as if this was my cue to approve. Her face was pitted, pale as concrete.

"All right," I said. My mother had chosen her well. It was clear that she was the type of woman who grew solid in difficulty, who became that retaining wall you trust you will eventually run into, no matter what the catastrophe. I felt myself flat against her now. "That's okay."

Ward leaned forward. "She thought"—he said, and then paused to clear his throat—"she thought it would save the complications of securing a plot here." He smiled; it was not a real smile, but that odd upward-turning of lips that people sometimes do when they're making a difficult point. "Or of bringing her back to Long Island."

I sipped my tea again and it was thick in my throat. "Sure."

"The cremation will take place after the service," Carol went on. "She said she wanted to be at the service." And then she placed her red hand solidly on my knee. "Would you like to see her, Elizabeth?"

I suppose I said, "No, I'd rather not," because the three of them bowed their heads and whispered that they understood.

Because I didn't see her.

There was the young, meaty priest that afternoon who took my hand to shake it and then held it, held it until my palm began to sweat and then held it still, as if to prove that nothing human repelled him, to offer this small sacrifice—the unflinching grasp on soaked flesh—to his Lord and Saviour. The priest who said that my mother, in death, had wished to be reconciled to the Church.

There was the mortician, who reminded me of the school photographer who came each year to take our pictures, placing each individual child on the same stool, in front of the same screen, saying the same words to get the same smile from this child unlike any other. The mortician too shook my hand, saying, "Yes, the daughter."

There was the plain coffin before the altar in the small church. The coffin covered with just a spray of lilacs from Ward's yard—another of her requests: No flowers, she'd told Lillian, nothing from a florist anyway, because she'd been walking into flower shops all her life and, no matter what she'd gone in for, had always come out thinking of funerals—the church filled with the people from town: the shopkeepers, the mailmen, the waitress from the coffee shop, the crossing guard, all the people a stranger would first befriend.

I was the daughter, Dolores' daughter from New York, and although I'd dressed carefully that morning, navy-blue suit, white lace blouse, good shoes, I felt somehow mistaken, inadequate, as if I were a new understudy taking on a role that had been played before, and much more effectively, by someone I alone had never seen.

She had asked that a rosary be said, and when the time came, I fumbled to find the pale-blue beads Ward had given me that morning. My mother's beads. I had a blind moment when I thought I had somehow lost them.

The priest came down from the altar, knelt in the pew across from mine, and began the prayers. When he announced the first Joyful Mystery, The Annunciation, he turned his flushed face to me, my cue.

I prayed: "Hail Mary, full of grace, the Lord is with thee." My voice trembled a little but with stage fright, not tears. "Blessed art thou among women and blessed is the fruit of thy womb, Jesus."

"Holy Mary, Mother of God," the others mumbled, the priest's voice clearest among them. "Pray for us sinners now and at the hour of our death. Amen."

"Hail Mary, full of grace, the Lord is with thee." Ten times I repeated the words, moving the beads between my fingers. The beads she had kept beneath her pillow, in the bed she had shared with my father, the bed I had shared with Bill.

Ward, a Methodist, began the next decade, his slow voice repeating the same words.

I remembered the nights my father was gone, when, frightened or sleepless or just bored, I would crawl into bed with her and, reaching under her pillow, feel the beads and her fingers upon them. I would ask, "Are you praying?" and she would finish whatever prayer she was thinking and answer, "Yes, I am." She would tell me where in the rosary she was so I could pray the rest with her; but silently, she would always insist, to myself.

I moved my fingers over those same beads now, repeating

the same words. If I could have rubbed some of that old belief from them, I would have. If I could have brought them to my lips and sucked from them anything other than the salt from my own fingers, any faith, any comfort, any of the old trust that the words truly meant something and that their meaning endures beyond all loss, I would have.

Carol was leading the prayers now. Holy Mary, Mother of God.

Because I wanted it all back. The eternal mother, the immortal confidence. The same prayers repeated. The feel of new clothes, the smell of my father's aftershave, the clean taste of a communion wafer on an empty stomach, repeated each Sunday for the rest of my life.

I looked at the familiar statue of the Blessed Mother on the side of the altar. Her white dress, her blue robes, her arms extended. Someone had placed a crown of flowers on her head. The wreath was a little too big and it dipped rakishly over one eye. The pinkie on her right hand was chipped, showing white plaster.

Father Lappen was leading the final prayer: "Hail, Holy Queen, Mother of Mercy, our life, our sweetness and our hope." His voice was high and nasal, as affected as a butler's. His hands were folded before his lips, the two fat index fingers raised to his nose, nearly plugging his nostrils. "To thee do we cry, poor banished children of Eve, to thee do we send up our sighs, mourning and weeping in this valley of tears."

I knew about conversions on battlefields and at gravesides. I knew that God had sprung from death and fear and loneliness and nostalgia in the first place. I knew why Jesus was big at Vista. I knew what I was asking.

The priest began the litany of Our Lady and I felt Ward's hand upon my back, felt him lean toward me and then lean away.

Our Lady of the Sorrows, pray for us.

Our Lady of Peace, pray for us.

Our Lady of Perpetual Help, pray for us.

I should have been crying for my mother, but I knew what I was asking.

I had planned to go back to New York that afternoon, but the luncheon at Ward's lingered until four, and as she was leaving Carol said she'd be by in the morning to take me to the airport. Lillian told me there was a dinner casserole in the refrigerator for Ward and me, and because accepting their help had already become habit, I merely smiled at them both and said thank you.

I stood at the door until their car pulled away.

The house, after all those visitors, had not quite settled itself. Although it showed no traces of the party (the women had seen to that) it seemed to resound with it in some way. Ward was in the kitchen, running water, clicking dishes, a loud bird was calling, cars passed by outside. The smell of perfume and food was still in the air. It was over but not yet past.

I went upstairs to change. The house had three bedrooms. One had been made into a den, the other, where I'd slept, was the room Ward's mother had lived in, and the third, Ward's room, was where my mother had slept during those long winter months. Although it occurred to me that she could have slept in this room too; that a mother or a lover might have suited Ward equally well. Ward, my mother's lover.

I took off my suit, put on jeans and a light sweater. Church clothes to playclothes. Someone had put the flowers on the night table beside my bed. They'd been delivered just as we got back from church—the florist, despite my mother's rejection, knowing just what time the service would end. Carol had brought them to me, grinning, and when I read the card out loud, "Sincerest Sympathy. We love you. Everyone at Vista," the people around me had smiled, as if reassured. Reassured that I wasn't completely alone and that, perhaps, indeed I *had*

had better things to do these past few months. Introducing me, they had all told one another that I was an editor.

I leaned to smell the flowers. My mother was right, you couldn't help but think of funerals and wakes. I breathed deeply.

I had read stories, novels, even manuscripts, seen movies on TV and in the theater, it's almost a cliché, but if cancer can be said to have any compensations, surely that is it: the final meetings, the wait together. The moment when the mother, while peeling potatoes or sorting clothes or setting her hair for the trip to the hospital, says some simple word or tells some new story and the daughter sees, for all of her life, what the love between them has been.

The days when the daughter, waiting at the hospital, reviews her own life, and taking her mother's frail hand, says, "Thank you" or "I'm sorry," or simply: "Mother, I'm here. Don't worry, I'm here."

If cancer can be said to have any compensations, surely it is in the cliché of time allowed. Time to say what can no longer wait to be discovered. Time when death is not merely a thought to put your teeth on edge, to be dismissed with a swallow, when life is marked clearly by beginnings and endings, by spoken words that mean something and change everything.

If she had called me, we might have said something, everything might have changed. If she had called me, I would have been delivered from all these past months of ordinary days.

I straightened up. I was descending a stair I couldn't see, couldn't trust, whose next step might disappear beneath my foot.

She hadn't called me, and whatever her dying had to give was given to Ward. I would think of her as I'd thought of my father: not here, someplace else—in Wisconsin, in Maine— apart from me voluntarily because we both had better things to do.

Ward was calling me. He was at the bottom of the stairs,

softly calling my name and he seemed a little surprised when I appeared, as if, like a child, he'd been calling for so long he'd forgotten the intent.

"Are you hungry?" he asked.

"No," I said. "But there's a casserole in the refrigerator."

"Yes. Margaret left it. The woman with the red hair. From the beauty parlor."

I nodded, staring down at him. The hours until I could leave seemed steep and ragged, impossible to overcome. I considered trying to get a taxi to Boston.

"I thought maybe you'd like to . . ." He smiled that strange smile again. "There are some things in your mother's house for you. Would you like to go out there with me?"

I shrugged, walked down the stairs, knowing it was ridiculous to think of farewell letters and revealing diaries. To think that when the two of us walked down the drive, through the chilled odor of daffodils and ocean salt, my mother would appear, the screen door slamming behind her.

The cottage seemed ready for new tenants, as if this month's occupant had only to make one more trip from house to packed car before the Labor Day group could move in. There were two brown cartons on the sofa bed, a gift box in a plastic bag from Barnes and Noble on the table by the window. The bed, except for a faded blue comforter, was stripped; the armoire, except for a few hangers, was empty. The kitchen was spotlessly clean.

"Your mother took care of everything before she went to the hospital the last time," Ward said, almost apologetically, as I searched the place. "She said everything you'd want, her good tea set, some photos, I don't know what else, would be right here. Her silver set is in my safe-deposit box in town, but of course that's yours too. And the rest of her savings."

I looked at the cartons. She had used them to move here from Long Island. Our old address and this one were written on them. The masking tape that had sealed them then had been sliced open but not removed. The tops were now neatly folded over.

I turned to Ward. I remembered from my last trip here that he'd had to stoop a little in this room to keep his hair from brushing the ceiling. He was stooping now, but seemed, still in his dark-gray suit, much smaller.

"How long had she been sick?" I might have asked the same question the night he called, but I couldn't remember the answer.

"I'm not sure," he said hoarsely. "She barely talked about it until the very end. She went off for her treatments by herself, at first." He shook his head. "I don't know."

I looked at the room, the floor swept, the corduroy cushions smoothed and tucked, a neat pile of magazines on top of the TV. My mother had straightened the room, set out the cartons and the bag and gone to the hospital. It occurred to me that she'd been there when we last spoke, two weeks ago now, although I'd presumed she was here, or at Ward's. It was Sunday, her usual day to call, and when I said she sounded tired, she told me she'd been sitting in front of the television all night, nodding off. We talked mostly about Joanne's upcoming wedding and what I should serve at the shower.

"I can't take this stuff back with me," I said suddenly. "I have my suitcase. I won't be able to manage everything by myself."

Ward rushed forward and pushed the cartons back on the couch, as if they'd been leaning on me. "Don't worry," he said calmly. "You can leave them here as long as you like. It's all right. I'll hold them for you."

I nodded like a spoiled child.

"I won't be renting this place again," he said. "Come up in the summer. Bring your friends. You're welcome to it. You can have it."

His eyes grew red, and I knew this was the moment I should

ask him. I heard myself urging me to ask him: Why didn't she call me? Why didn't she want me?

"The beach is right down the path," he said, going to the window to point it out: an anxious realtor. "It's lovely here in the summer. Bring your friends."

I smiled. "Thank you. Maybe I'll do that."

We carried the cartons and the bag back to his house, and lined them up against the wall in his dining room. As he put on the casserole and made the salad, he told me what he knew about my mother's illness, explaining the difference between chronic and acute, lymphocytic and granulocytic, describing what she wore to the hospital, what she ate there, what her doctor looked like, as if detail alone were sufficient, all I needed to know.

"Everyone said she was fortunate. She didn't linger. But she always had her own way of doing things." He was setting the table. He had not changed his suit, but had taken off the jacket and tie and rolled up his sleeves. The hair on his arms was still thick and yellow, and I could tell by the way he moved around the kitchen, set out the place mats, folded the napkins, checked the oven and mixed the salad dressing, that he was used to doing those things, used to doing them for another, a woman.

Although I'd asked him twice if I could help, I was sure that I couldn't.

"When things got bad, she simply said, 'That's enough.' I stayed with her then because I knew she'd made up her mind."

He put the salad on the table, slowly dished out the casserole.

As he sat down, I said, "I'm glad you were with her," not sure I meant it, but wanting him to believe I did.

He shook his head. "I didn't do any good." He looked at me and I felt again what we shared: not a knowledge but an omission. "I wanted to call you," he said. "She wouldn't hear of it. It was as if she wanted to keep the whole thing to herself."

And then he told me, not as if he were recalling it but cautiously inventing as he went along, that, at the end, she had called my father's name. She had struggled up out of the illness and the drugs and all the years she'd been without him and said his name—clearly, stubbornly—said it and then pulled it back into herself with a breath so sharp and so deep that he had leaned closer, believing she would say more, but receiving only the shallow death rattle, a sound like an echo, a sound receding, its source already far away.

He looked at me, pursed his lips. "It surprised me," he said. "I must say it surprised me. After everything. I mean, the way your father was."

I could have asked him then, *How* was he, what stories had my mother told him? but I didn't think of it. I thought only of how she had called his name. Of how, after everything, he alone had figured in the drama of her death.

Melodrama, I decided on the plane the next morning, calling his name on her deathbed when, after he died, she'd barely mentioned him, had kept no picture of him around the house. When it hadn't even occurred to her to be buried at his side. When it wasn't until she moved to Maine and met Ward that the pictures reappeared, and the old bedspread and the sweet stories of their first meeting.

Stories whose meanings, if they had meanings, were recited like prayer, silently, to herself.

Joanne and her parents met me at La Guardia. Her mother gathered me in her fleshy arms as soon as I stepped through the gate. She cried openly. Joanne patted my hair. On the way to the city, she and her father argued loudly about whether to take the Triboro or the Queensborough and when we got to my apartment, they bustled me inside with a plate of lasagne and a bucket of meatball soup. They left a mass card on my table and pleaded that I call them for anything, anytime, even just to talk. Mrs. Paletti sobbed again as they left and although Joanne rolled her eyes and said, *"Ma!,"* she too cried when she hugged me. Mr. Paletti rocked me like a tall baby.

At six, the phone began ringing, cautious voices asking how I was. I let them convince me I was fine and I returned to work early Monday morning. It proved to be an ordinary day.

X

KEVIN SENDS WORD THROUGH
Bonnie that Elizabeth should come to his office. That a matter
of utmost seriousness has to be discussed. Bonnie cracks her
gum. "He wouldn't even tell me what it was," she says. "He
is so weird sometimes." She shakes her head. She has braided
her hair, small, wiry braids secured with thick rubber bands,
and each time she moves, they fall across her cheeks and
spotted forehead like strangled worms. "He wouldn't even talk
to me. He just wrote down, 'Go tell Elizabeth I must see her.
A matter of utmost seriousness.' He wouldn't even *talk* to me."

Elizabeth laughs. "That's Kevin," she says, but Bonnie continues to shake her head, disgusted. "Fucking weird," she mut-
ters, with a bitterness that Elizabeth thinks must be either
typical or very rare in a twenty-year-old.

Kevin is bent over his drawing board, his thin legs wrapped
around the base of the tall stool, his bowling shirt (*Oddballs*
written in white thread across his back) taut between the two
sharp lumps of his shoulder blades. She knows if she could see
his face he'd be biting his lower lip, like a child with a dull,
unwieldly crayon.

"Give me a minute," he mumbles without looking up. She
stands behind him, studying the prints and color charts and
elaborate pencil sketches he has hung on his wall. His cubicle

is damper than her own office, infected by the draughts and cold concrete of the stockroom, and only about twice the size of his drawing board, but still she always likes it. No authors are allowed in here—the only outside visitors are the half-dozen freelance artists (interesting-looking women in long skirts and paint-spattered young men with lovely hands) who stop by every few weeks to drop off and pick up their assignments—and, by Kevin's decree, nothing that happens in this room is allowed to be taken seriously. Kevin's real life, he insists, is his own work, and Vista is only a place he comes to for comic relief.

Elizabeth admires him for this, for having such a well-defined "real life," the life of an artist, although she often wonders why the admiration is mutual. They are known as particular allies around the office.

"This is what I wanted to show you," he whispers, head still down. She looks over his shoulder and sees that he is perfecting a pen-and-ink sketch of a pretty woman looking into a series of progressively smaller mirrors, smiling. The title of the book, in fancy script just above the woman's head is, *Reflections of My Mind.*

"I remember that one," she says. "It's pretty incoherent, isn't it?"

Kevin blows on the drawing and then sits back, rubbing his thighs, grinning. "It's not only incoherent," he says. His pale skin glows beneath the web of freckles. His short, greased hair, meant to be stylish, is more butch than punk, more Dennis the Menace than David Bowie.

"It's another secret masterpiece." His eyebrows dance. "Can you see it?"

She laughs and bends down to look carefully at the sketch. Whenever Kevin gets fed up with an author or a book or Vista itself, he draws a jacket illustration that subtly reflects his disapproval. For a book called *Lots of Laughs,* he drew a jacket full of small, laughing clown faces, three of which, when the cover was viewed upside down, became screaming women with red tears running down their faces. (The book, called an exposé, was a series of cruel, intimate jokes about the author's three former wives.) For another, a children's book, he had drawn a long curving line of elephants joined trunk to tail, growing smaller and smaller and finally fading off into the distance, but not until one of the smallest, most distant elephants had shoved his trunk up the ass of the even smaller one in front of him. He'd had to use a magnifying glass to point this out to her and he said he'd done it because the book was heavily phallic (the elephants were always poking their trunks into tight places) and he thought the author looked like Anita Bryant. The title of the book was *The Elephants Are Coming.*

Elizabeth steps back from the illustration, pointing to the smaller mirror images of the smiling woman. "I bet you did something to those," she says. "They look a little strange."

Kevin laughs. "Ah, you know my style." He reaches for the set of galleys beside him. "But let me show you why I did it. This woman is too much. Look what she wrote here."

On the first page of the galleys, an ambitious copy editor had underlined three long sentences and written in the margin, "Au.: sense?" Under the question, the author had neatly printed, "Thank you. It's a theory I've long held, and my mother lived her life according to it. It does make good sense."

Elizabeth laughs. "That's great."

"But there's more," Kevin says, flipping through the galleys, reading: " 'Author: facts correct?' And the woman writes, 'That's true, but facts alone aren't enough. As I always tell my children, we need faith in God and all his wonders.' " He opens his mouth and lets out a single laugh, like a bubble bursting. "Is she too much?"

Elizabeth admits that she is and looks at the drawing again. "So what did you do?"

He glances over his shoulder and then turns back to her, whispering. "You know this is just between us. If Ned finds out he'll have my nuts."

She nods and Kevin reaches for the magnifying glass. "It's another miniature," he whispers, his breath smelling slightly of licorice. "See these smaller reflections?"

She looks carefully and gradually notices how the reflections of the pretty women slowly become more and more deranged-looking. It's very subtle. The eyes become only slightly crossed, just a tip of the tongue shows through the teeth, the smile becomes a grimace, the hair a bit disheveled, the neck longer, thinner, as if it contained a scream.

She steps away. "Kevin, you're out of your mind. She'll see that."

He frowns, looks at the drawing. "No she won't," he says slowly. "Look how pretty the first few reflections are. That's all she'll see. She'll show the book to all her friends and say"—he bounces from side to side, makes his voice high—" 'There I am, aren't I pretty?' " He smiles.

She leans to look at the drawing again, imagining the woman showing off her book, pointing to the pretty pictures and saying proudly, "There I am," the terrible faces staring back.

"Look," he says, touching her arm. "You're too close to it. Move away." She does and looks again. The faces seem fine.

"You've got to have a certain distance in these matters," he says, raising his eyebrows. His smile breaks on the word, *"Distance* is very important in this place."

She looks at him and he winks. "I get your meaning," she says, smiling, although some part of her has just touched down at Heathrow and remembered the water is still running in the bathtub in New York. Some part of her is slapping a forehead and sinking into a seat. She wonders if her face (eyes crossed?) will appear in miniature somewhere on Tupper Daniels' book jacket.

Kevin is smiling at his drawing. He blows on the sketch, gently flicks something from the far corner.

"Did Ann tell you about him?" she asks, feeling herself blushing. "About Tupper Daniels?" She thinks of adding, the one I'm having an affair with, but the word always makes her feel like a Connecticut housewife screwing her dentist.

Kevin looks up, squinting. "An author?"

Ann has told him nothing.

She laughs. "Never mind." Looks at the sketch again. "Distance," she says, with a determination that makes it sound like *Onward!*

He closes his eyes and nods. "Exactly. And mum's the word."

She smiles. "As always."

But distance, she thinks much later that day, must have been easier when she was on the Pill, when there wasn't any touring of the scene the morning after. In college, when the Health Center was handing out the Pill more readily than aspirin, she could sleep with someone she didn't particularly care for, and then, as soon as he was gone, never think about him again. She could treat her vagina like a hungover roommate: I don't care what you did last night, I'm going to the library.

At least, that's how she remembers it.

But these days, she must reach into herself the morning after, slide out the warm diaphragm, rinse off the white cream, the bit of mucus, hers or his. These days, she can't help but think it's appropriate to feel something, if only that vague Catholic guilt of temples violated, treasures dissipated, gifts lost.

A guilt she tries to assuage, no doubt, by promising herself love, next time it will be for love. The thud of love, love, love not unlike that of a fist against a breast, her own silent *mea culpa*.

Not unlike Bill's name, invoked each time, as if he were a grace once earned. A plenary indulgence.

Tupper Daniels walks naked from her bathroom to her kitchen, his shoulders slightly slouched, his face a little dumb, like a man alone. He comes out of the kitchen with two bottles of beer.

She wonders if she even remembers what a plenary indulgence is.

"Think about bigamy," Tupper says, handing her a cold green bottle and climbing back into the bed. "Polygamy. The concept."

"All right." She wonders if she hadn't, in a way, been thinking about it already.

"Think about what it implies: not a man who has affairs, who sleeps with his secretary or a mistress or some woman he met on the street or in a bar, but a man who loves and marries, loves and marries. A man who is, ironically, incapable of having an affair. A man who must always, always sanctify his love with marriage, who must establish a home for himself and any woman he loves and then must return to that home whenever he can. A man of great nobility, I think. A truly romantic, heroic character."

He turns to adjust the pillows behind him, and then crosses his legs again, cupping his hand over his penis and moving it gently, the way an adolescent girl might absent-mindedly arrange her hair on her shoulders, nearly draping it. He rests the bottle on his thigh.

"Compared to him," he goes on, "the monogamist is a bore. Without imagination or energy or passion. A coward whose loyalty is merely an excuse. He's one of those men who considers sex a function and marriage a duty. Who wears a ball and chain or a noose around his neck to his own bachelor party, and believes in everything it symbolizes."

He raises the bottle, drinks slowly. She wonders if he is

speaking extemporaneously or again reciting from his book; if she should reply or merely cite the page number. She wonders if he's testing her.

She lowers her eyes, as she might have to avoid being called on in school, and drinks too.

On her stereo, a woman is singing, "I-Want-Your-Love," over and over, letting the emphasis fall on a different word each time, as if she can't get it right. Her voice is whiny and passionless, full of a dull kind of longing.

"Did it surprise you?" he asks, "When you read the book and discovered that Beale, the bigamist, was actually portrayed as a good man, a hero? Did you feel some of your own values were being turned upside down?"

She pulls the bottle from her lips, swallows. "A little," she says.

He nods, pleased. "Most people do. Bigamy equals villainy for most people, like the townspeople in the book. But you have to know how to look at it." He presses his lips together. "When Bailey was found to be a bigamist, in Gallatin, everyone acted like he was the devil himself. But I said, 'Hold on, he's no villain, think about it.'" He pauses, thinking. "Of course, no one did. But *I* did." He drops his voice and raises his colorless eyebrows. "I discovered," he says, "that Bailey was the stuff of great literature."

She smiles. They have been sitting side by side, leaning against the back of her couch, but now she moves away from him, to the center of the bed, and pulls her legs up in front of her, crossing her ankles, pressing her thighs to her breasts. He watches her movements carefully and then smiles too, as if he has read some meaning into them; a meaning he knows she is unaware of and so refuses to share.

She rests her chin on her raised knee and says, "Go on," to make it clear she will not ask why he's smiling. The lamp beside him makes his hair seem white, his face powdery.

He leans his head back against the couch, looks up at the prints hanging just above him, as if he were trying to read what was written behind them. The light falls over his taut throat. "A man who loves and marries," he says to the ceiling. "Loves and marries." Without moving his head, he looks down at her, making his eyes seem shifty. "But why? Why does he marry when he could just have affairs? When extramarital sex—as we've just proven—is as good, if not better, than marital, and certainly, even forty years ago, nearly as available." He looks up again. "Why indeed?"

She waits, wondering if he expects her to answer, wishing she hadn't been so willing to think about bigamy. "Why?" she asks softly.

He lets out a long sigh: Is it disappointment?

"In a way," he says, "it's for the ceremony. The way it can bind the woman to him, not through the vows, really, but through the religious, mystical, almost dreamlike aura of it. The sense of fate, of fulfillment of prophecy, that it must give a woman." He lifts his head. The light falls on his face again. "Remember Joy? The fat wife? The one the townspeople call Joy in sorrow?" He says *sorra*. "Joy in longing?"

"Yes," she says.

"Remember her wedding scene?" He raises his free hand, two curved fingers, as if he were about to make a shadow-bunny, and scratches two marks in the air. *"Joy looked at him through her tulle veil,"* he recites, his voice suddenly low, formal, as if he were on the telephone, *"the bride-veil that even now was being flecked with black from the inside, from her heavily mascared lashes."* He moves his raised hand gently, humming the words, wafting a tune toward her. *"She smelled the warm, turbid odor of orchids, a smell close and hot like that of an animal, trapped, panting, and knew this was not merely a dream, this body perspiring in its bride-white dress not merely the trick of some heavy guilt or a supper eaten too quickly, too*

*soon before bedtime, this man before her saying yes and making
it both an affirmation and her name, the word itself her name,
not merely the ascension of her waking hopes into somnabulant
dream, but knew instead that this was the beginning of her life;
the secret life that had, since her birth, been spinning itself at
her core."*

He closes his eyes, smiles softly. Another woman is now
singing that if you're a girl from New York City, you know love
is like a Broadway show. Opens them again. "Remember?"

It occurs to her that he could be leading her into a trap,
getting her to say, yes, yes, I remember and then crying, Aha!
I never wrote such a thing!

"Yes," she says.

"The ceremony itself is important to Beale," he goes on,
"because of the way it binds the woman to him. But the
repetition of the ceremony, the ceremony taking place again
and again is important to him too—although one is never any
more important than the other."

He scratches the air again. *"First second third would mean
nothing to a man whose life was without progression, was only
a series of rhythmical stops and starts, each as impossible and
as fruitless to rank or distinguish as the rhythmical stops and
starts of a heartbeat."* He brings down the hand. "Did that
stand out for you, the image of each wife as one of many
heartbeats?"

I never wrote such a thing, he could cry, which proves you
never read my book. You're no real editor!

"Yes," she says.

He leans forward, holds up one finger. "Well, that's another
reason why he marries. The women sustain him, just as the
townspeople do when they talk about him, meet on porches,
*in the thick, turbid odor of wisteria and breathe into his ubiqui-
tous ghost those stories and speculations that would sustain him
all the time he was away.* He is a man whose life is without

progression, who loves and marries, loves and marries. Beginning after beginning, but"—he waves his hand like a magician —"no end."

She nods. "I see."

"Which may be why I'm having such trouble with the ending," he says. "*Any* kind of ending undermines one of my basic themes—Beale's immortality."

Elizabeth agrees. A man's voice on the other side of the wall yells, "Carol," as if it were a warning. Or maybe, Elizabeth thinks, it was "careful." More appropriate.

"But the most important reason why he marries," Tupper says, "is because he loves. Because, despite appearances, he is a good man, incapable of having affairs. A man of great integrity. Infinitely moral." He points at her, seems to suppress a smile. "Quickly," he says, "what comes to mind when you think of a bigamist?"

She frowns, slowly, resisting the game. Or the trap. "I don't know," she says: A man with a raised collar and a lowered hat brim, a guilty walk? Edmond O'Brien portraying a bigamist in a cheap, black-and-white movie, shown very late on TV, the dialogue trailing the film by only a few seconds so the words seemed dubbed? A joke about two women wanting to screw the same man? Woman crying? Ward's voice?

"Your book," she says finally. But he only rolls his eyes.

"Before that."

She shrugs. What comes to mind is that her mother alone was not quite sufficient for him, that the one quick ceremony was not quite enough. They were married right after the war, her mother always said, as if her father had arrived at the ceremony in stained khaki, covered with dust, a green helmet under his arm. They were married in a rectory in Brooklyn. Her mother wore a suit but no corsage.

"Don't you think of a villain?" Tupper asks, impatiently. "A cruel, selfish man? Or else a stupid one, forced to the altar against his own will? A man who has let his love life get ridiculously out of hand?"

She smiles, searching for her editor's voice. "I suppose so." They lived alone together for nine, nearly ten years before she was born. Their time without her, they called it. "B.E."

"Would you have ever—before you read my book—ever have thought of a bigamist as a moral man? A man of integrity?"

"No," she says. And now she is living her time without them.

He slaps his palm on the mattress. "And that's my point," he says. "That's one of the things that's so unique about this book. Bailey was no villain, nor is Beale. Despite our standard ideas of bigamy as villainy, selfishness or stupidity, they're heroes, they're good men." He quickly gulps some beer, like a marathon runner slowing only to grab a cup of water and spill it over his mouth, never losing his pace. "I want this book to show that values are meaningless in themselves," he goes on, "fragile as glass and useless as dust. I want it to show that value depends only on how you look at things, there are no absolutes. One man's meat, the eye of the beholder." He drinks again. "Morality is point of view."

She rests her head on her knee, letting him run on. She thinks vaguely of the *Reflections of My Mind* book jacket and how much depends on how you look at it. She wishes she could tell him about it, make him laugh, change the subject. Also of a poem Ann showed her once, called "Prayer to Orion." Ann had written it, she said, after a ski weekend in Vermont when Brian had announced that he wanted to marry one of his company's vice presidents. "She's her own woman," was the way he'd described the attraction. She was also three months pregnant.

In the poem, Ann described how she'd gone out that night, alone, limping (she was not used to skiing) and crying a little, catching cold, had looked up to see the constellation. It told of how she began to imagine the male body ("blue black winter night skin/Cold") around and between the stars that formed his girdle and shoulders and sword; how she began to imagine the details of his face and arms and waist. How, standing there in the cold, looking up, a salty phlegm running down her throat, she began to feel strangely aroused, and reassured. How she knew somehow that she would love again; that she would some day again be satisfied by a man.

The professor she was then studying poetry with at The New School had given her an A on the poem and had written on the side, "Cosmic Fellatio!!" Pointing this out, Ann told Elizabeth that he had missed her point. "But," she said, laughing, "maybe he's right. Maybe all I really wanted to do was to suck off the Milky Way. I suppose it all depends on how you read it."

Was her mother alone not sufficient for him? Or was her father merely spreading the wealth?

"Let me put it another way," Tupper Daniels is saying, drawing up his knees. "A man falls in love, gets married, falls out of love, divorces, falls in love again and remarries—we say, fine, happens all the time, right? The man's done nothing wrong."

She nods.

"But another man falls in love, marries, stays in love, but then falls in love—equally in love—with someone else and so he marries her too. And then we cry bigamy! Villainy! But, really, who's the better man, the more loyal, more loving, more true-to-his-word?" His little round eyes are stretched open.

She tries to laugh. "There's got to be something wrong with your logic." Spreading the wealth? Blessing other women with his sudden homecomings?

He throws up his hand. "What's wrong, except the way we're used to looking at love and marriage, and divorce? Except our obsolete sense of values."

She looks at her beer, picks at the gold foil around its neck. And if her father had called them that morning, said he was in Wisconsin with his other wife, would they have said, How lovely, how loyal? "But he lies," she says slowly. "He doesn't tell one wife about the other." She realizes she's talking about his book and quickly adds, "Does he?"

Tupper leans back, like a man sitting exhausted under a tree. "No," he says, "that's true. But I think, somehow, they know. He doesn't need to tell them. I think they're all in a kind of conspiracy of silence."

She continues to play with the label, scraping gold flecks onto her sheets. Her mother had theories.

"They say nothing—and, you probably noticed, asked him few questions—because they understand, somehow, the delicate balance he has established between them. And because they know the other wives don't imply he loves them less. In fact, each time he returns to one of them, it's a confirmation of his love. That's why I named one of the wives, the blonde with the painted toes, Penelope—'Penelope, after Ulysses' wife, who waited those many years, who was beset by suitors yet ever-assured, ever-faithful.' " He nods a little, as if to say, You know the rest.

She nods back: Yes, I do.

"Ulysses, after all, had Circe while away, and still he returned to Penelope. And I don't think there can be any doubt of his love for her." His hand is splayed over his stomach. He strokes himself gently. "This is what I mean in the book when I call him the Magician and talk about the spell he casts over the women when he marries them. It's a spell that keeps them from questioning him, but also keeps them assured that he'll always return." He smiles at her. "So he doesn't lie to them, he merely accepts their silence."

She shrugs a little, as if to concede the point. Perhaps, if her father had called that morning and said he was in Wisconsin with his other wife, she and her mother would have shrugged, said nothing, waited for him still. Perhaps she would have believed he was merely spreading the wealth—for what magic did her plump, plain mother have except that she was the woman her father had chosen, the one he came home to?

She presses her lips to her knee, recalls a night, the night of the East Coast blackout. She and her mother were in the kitchen, making dinner. The back door opened and her father appeared just as all the lights went out; instead of his usual greeting, there was a wild clamor for flashlight and candle, their movements through the dark made more frantic, no doubt, by his sudden presence beside them, slapping his pockets for matches, advising they try a different drawer. As soon as the flashlight was found, he went down to the basement to check the fuse and she and her mother stood side by side in the kitchen, in the hollow blue light of the gas flames under the pots on the stove, staring at the open cellar door like wives outside the black mouth of a mine.

They said nothing, exchanged no look. The only sound was the muffled tattoo of boiling water, and Elizabeth was suddenly filled with the fear that her father would never emerge. That she and her mother had shared an illusion in that single moment before the flickering lights died, in the first few minutes of darkness, that they were sharing some strange unconsciousness now. She feared that any look, any touch, any word exchanged between them would break that unconsciousness, throw the lights back on, return them to the ordinary evening they'd been living just moments ago.

And then the faint round moon of light, so faint that at first she didn't trust it, moving in soft loops toward the basement wall, and her father's voice, "They're out all over," the solid footsteps on the wooden stairs. She and her mother moving toward him, simultaneously.

His face was cold as she kissed it and he smelled of alcohol, either a shot of whiskey or a slap of aftershave (he kept a bottle of each in his glove compartment) and when the candlelight caught his eyes, they were small, sparkling, bright as silver. He joked all night about his exquisite timing.

"So the bigamist is a hero," she says softly, her lips touching her bare knee.

"Yes," he whispers. He has slid closer to her. "If you look at him the right way."

She looks down at him. He is watching her intently, smiling. There are specks of gold around her feet. A woman sings about her last chance for romance.

She laughs. "No," she says, shaking her head, refusing it. "There has to be something wrong with your logic."

XI

MARGARET ALICE GREER, AUTHOR of *Gouged of Womanhood: Poems of Two Mastectomies*, wants T-shirts. Her book is due to be published in June, and the woman feels that T-shirts printed with the title will help attract beach readers.

Elizabeth smiles at her across the desk, careful to keep her eyes on the woman's face. "I'll mention it to our publicity department," she says. Hard drops of rain hit the window behind her.

Margaret Alice leans forward, puts one white hand on the desk, tentatively, long fingers open, like a bad actress pretending to be nervous. She is tall, homely as Lincoln, forty-nine, according to her bio. Recently divorced. Fading orange lipstick and long feet in flat black shoes. The collar of her navy-blue dress is lacy with dandruff. "It's important that it sell well," she says seriously, almost sternly. "I want it to be well read."

Elizabeth holds her smile. She could say, flicking an ash like Groucho, Then send it to college, but instead she pushes the contract across the desk. "I'm sure it will be. Your work is very powerful. I especially like the recurrent images of fruits and flowers." She makes her eyes wide, her handiest false gesture. "It's very exciting."

The woman closes her fingers, catching the words, and

obediently pulls the contract toward her. There is a fogged place on the steel where her hand has rested, like breath on cold glass. On the floor beside her there is a lump of wet dry-cleaner's bags, the color of phlegm. When she came in, she'd had them wrapped like gauze around her manuscript; had the manuscript clutched to her gouged chest like a rescued child. Now she reads the contract carefully, her head down, her elbow on the desk, her fingers moving through her thin bangs, shaking white scales onto each official page. Because of the clouds outside, the light in the office seems yellow and close.

Elizabeth flips through the manuscript once again. Titles like "Empty Cups," "Treasure Chest," "A Plucked Rose." Ned will ask: Is this supposed to be funny? And she'll tell him that the woman believes the poems have "clothed her suffering with nobility." Ned, no doubt, will mention a certain naked king who also believed he was clothed in nobility, arrayed in gold. Pure gold.

The pages of the manuscript smell like Band-Aids.

When she looks up, the woman is writing out a check, smiling smugly. Now I know why it happened to me.

Despite herself, her eyes go to the woman's chest, the two slight yet false breasts. She imagines the poor body beneath them (And why not? Margaret Alice would not be her first naked author.), imagines the chest, gouged, torn, shiny with scars, as if the woman has embraced a burning meteor. Lifted her face and stretched out her arms to declare it a beautiful day and found herself a target. A victim of chance, circumstance, some gross practical joke.

Why me, Oh Lord? Why me?

Elizabeth leans forward, checking her own soft breasts against the edge of her desk.

"I have endorsements for the jacket too," Margaret Alice says as Elizabeth takes the contract and the damp check that shows a field of yellow daisies and a blue sky. She leans down, searches through her rain-drenched pocketbook, pulls out a piece of paper folded into quarters. "These should help sales."

The first line reads, Patricia Marie Randall, poetess, English teacher, Cayuga High: *If Edna St. Vincent Millay had had two mastectomies, she would have written poems like these.*

Another, Linda Eli, A.A., B.A.: *I laughed, I cried. These poems chart Everywoman's triumph over pain.*

She attaches the paper to the manuscript. It occurs to her that anyone could do her job—Everywoman. If you can lie, giving assurance is no chore. "I'm sure they'll be very useful," she says, smiling still. She wonders if she has mentioned that the poems are powerful.

At the door, Margaret Alice grabs Elizabeth's wrist and presses a moist piece of paper into her hand. It is, she explains, a wide smile thoroughly corrugating her cheeks, contracting her small black eyes, a poem to Vista Books, composed that very morning while she sat in the waiting room. Elizabeth thanks her for it, waves good-by and then hands the poem ("Vista, vision of all my dreams/From your summit, I view my heart's desires.") to Bonnie. "A present for you," she says.

Bonnie looks up, reeking of grape gum. There is a cold sore above her lip, just under her nose, and it makes her mouth seem grossly bowed, or puckered for a kiss. "Thanks a lot," she says.

As Elizabeth walks back to Marv's office she passes the conference room, where Ann is leaning over a manuscript with a fat, melon-faced man—Walter Merkill, author of *My Life and It Could Have Been Verse.*

"I see it," she hears Ann cry. She could be looking through a telescope. "I see exactly what you mean. It's a beautiful image."

"You think so?" the man says, grateful, awed. She has spotted his very soul. "Really?"

Last night, while she was with Tupper, Ann had been at her favorite bar. She told Elizabeth this morning that she met a man there who looked like Marlon Brando and claimed to be a feminist. She said she knew it was a line, but brought him home anyway—to give him credit for being innovative. She's been in a wonderful mood all day.

Outside Marv's office there are piles of books in soft brown mailing bags. They remind her of sand bunkers from World War II movies. Each is addressed to the book editor of a major newspaper or magazine and each is marked, by that editor, RETURN TO SENDER. As publicity director, Marv sends free books to every major reviewer (as per contract) and stacks them up as they come back, unopened and unread.

She thinks of Tupper Daniels, waiting in Sardi's until morning.

Inside the office there are more books, wrapped and unwrapped, forming a real bunker around the desk and around Marv himself. She must peer over them to see that he is sitting with his back to the door, his feet on the windowsill, reading a copy of Andy Warhol's *Interview* and drinking his jasmine tea. The wall behind his desk is filled with the autographed glossies he and his friends have collected from celebrities.

"Gouged of Womanhood," she says and he looks up over his shoulder, under his short white bangs, as bored as Greta Garbo. *"Poems of Two Mastectomies* by Margaret Alice Greer. She wants you to send out T-shirts with the title on them, for beach promotion."

"Did you tell her it would cost her?"

Elizabeth laughs. "Are you kidding? You'd do it?"

He blinks slowly. "Sure, if she wants to pay for it." Marv is not known for his wild sense of humor, only his complete, unflagging disdain, which is also very funny.

"But it's so tasteless," she says.

He sighs. "Tell me about it." He reaches behind him. *"Walk This Way,* by Lou Herman." He holds the letter away from him and moves his tongue and mouth as if the tastelessness were literal. "Legless Vietnam vet turned literary wit, Woody Allen style. Wants us to get him on the Gong Show so he can mention the book. Free air time he calls it. He wants us to book him as a 'sit-down comic.'"

"Why do they do these things to themselves?" she asks, her voice louder than she'd intended. "I don't care if they write their goddamn books, but why do they have to humiliate themselves in public? Why can't they just write the books and leave it at that?"

Marv's eyes flicker over her and she throws up her hands dramatically, trying to make it into a joke. "Where's their pride? Their self-respect?"

He puts the letter down and turns back to his magazine. "When you're after fame," he says to a picture of Liza Minnelli, "there's no such thing." And then, to Elizabeth, "Send me a memo on the T-shirts, will you, Babe?"

"Sure"—and if Tupper Daniels could be content that his book was written, although never read, her ass would be covered. She'd be gold to him forever.

Ann follows her into her office. "So you're going to travel and I'm going to be stuck with Ellis the pear," she says, continuing the conversation they were having before Margaret Alice and Walter showed up.

Elizabeth picks up the wet plastic, stuffs it into her wastepaper basket. Takes a tissue and wipes the remaining flakes of dandruff from her desk. "It looks that way," she says. "Owens said this morning that I'll do Ellis's next trip, through New England."

Ann rolls her eyes. "That's great. That's just great."

Bonnie walks in with the afternoon's mail, barking, "Mail," sullenly, as if it is her excuse for entering where she herself would rather not be. Elizabeth takes it from her, nods thank you, and, oddly, Bonnie smiles a little, the blister cracking almost audibly. As she leaves, Elizabeth notices that the cuffs of her pants are wet and spattered with mud, that her heavy thighs make the tight beige slacks seem pock-marked.

Ann is saying, "If that asshole feminist calls me, I think I'll marry him and stay home and have babies. It would be better than putting up with stinky Ellis."

Elizabeth laughs, leaning against her desk, the steel cold under her palms. She knows once she says it she'll have to go through with it, and so she takes a deep breath, anxious to get it said.

"I'm going to ask Owens to give you a raise and make you an official assistant editor. I don't think he realizes how many authors you see now. If he agrees, you'll still have to work for Ellis, but you can do your own work, too. Make some commissions."

Ann stares at her. Her graying curls have turned to steel wool in the rain. Her loose beige dress seems to touch her body only at the two soft mounds of her breasts, and there the material shines, as if with wear. As if, Elizabeth thinks, she has comforted too many greasy heads. The feminist, of course, was married. But seeking divorce.

Margaret Alice Greer's husband divorced her before the second breast had gone.

Ann puts her hands on her hips and looks up at the ceiling. Sends an exasperated breath in the same direction. "This job," she says, her voice loud. "This job is getting to be more and more like my marriage every day. I know it's dishonest. I know I'm being ripped off. It's not what I wanted. But, hell, the people are so nice and the alternatives are so bleak." She lets her arms fall straight to her sides. A small puff of air chugs through her dress. "Thanks. It's really nice of you." She smiles quickly, somewhat painfully, showing all the dry lines around her eyes. "But I'd really rather you wouldn't. I couldn't do your job."

Elizabeth feels for a moment as if she has passed through a

warm spot in a cold lake. She wonders if she's blushing. "Of course you could do it," she says lightly. "You practically do it now. You'd just get paid for it."

Ann raises her shoulders, rubs her arms, smiles again. "No. That's okay." Her eyes are on Elizabeth's desk. "I don't want to get paid for it."

Elizabeth frowns, feels her palms growing warm. "What are you?" she says, imitating Owens, keeping it light. "Made of money?"

Ann laughs. "I wish." And then, suddenly, almost insistently, as if she fears Elizabeth won't believe her, "They just depress me sometimes. Our so-called authors. Sometimes they depress the hell out of me." She points toward the conference room. "Walter Merkill just depressed the hell out of me. He had this poem"—she rolls her eyes—"in the middle of his autobiography, he writes a poem." She swallows, shakes her head. "It was about his little granddaughter, his only grandchild, who died, hit by a car. He said he wanted it to be a tribute to her." She looks toward the ceiling again. "And it was *so* awful. Little angels with golden curls skipping along the New Jersey Turnpike." She looks at Elizabeth. "It was embarrassing. Just the worst thing you've ever read."

Elizabeth shrugs. "I doubt it."

"And he put so much into it," Ann goes on, leaning toward her. "He tried so hard." She slips her hands into her pockets, lowers her voice. "They all try so goddamn hard, that's what depresses me. The way they blow their material." She takes a deep breath, preparing to explain it to her. "They absolutely rack their lives," she says, "give it all they've got, squeeze out every little thing they've ever felt, and what pops out but a bad version of a fucking Hallmark card." She sighs, her body seems to heave. "It makes me lose faith in humanity." Bows her head. "Not to mention poetry."

Elizabeth laughs, expecting Ann to, and when she doesn't, she straightens up and walks around the desk. "Some people like Hallmark cards," she says, sitting, wanting instead to say I know how you feel sometimes, the tastelessness, the desperation, but fearing what her admission would imply. She picks up a letter, throws it into her OUT box. "But if you really hate dealing with them . . ." Pushes the stapler to the front of her desk. "I won't make you see them anymore."

Ann is fingering something in one of her pockets, a coin or a Lifesaver. "No," she says. "I'll see them, when you're busy. I don't mind doing it if I'm helping you out. I just don't want to get paid for it. I don't want to get any more mired in it than I already am."

Now Elizabeth knows she is blushing. She can feel the blood throbbing in the small capillaries just under her skin, feel it banging from wall to wall like a drunk in a fun house. "All right," she says coolly. "No problem." Is she then, *mired?*

There's an awkward silence. "Sorry I'm so irrational," Ann says finally. She pulls her hands out from her sides, making the dress taut against her belly. Looking as if she might curtsey. "You know how stupid women are about money."

"No problem," Elizabeth says again, realizing that she will not, after all, have to ask Owens for the raise, trying to let the realization calm her.

"It must be the poet in me," Ann says. She tosses her head back, flutters her eyes. "I too," she says, putting her fingertips to her throat, "am a poetess, you know."

Elizabeth laughs, but only reflexively, only because she always laughs when Ann calls herself a poetess. Because, like her own, "We are the editor-in-chief, aren't we?" it is a phrase, a pose, that Ann dons for her, like glasses and a fake nose, whenever a laugh is needed. Whenever one of them is taking herself too seriously.

Until now, it never occurred to her that Ann, still, might be taking herself seriously. "I know," she says smiling, "you're a poetess."

As Ann turns to leave, they notice Bonnie standing in the

doorway, partially hidden, watching them with only one eye, like a bad detective. She disappears.

Elizabeth looks at Ann and shrugs. Ann shrugs back. "Normal," she says. And then, "If my feminist friend calls me, I may marry him anyway. Let him take me away from all this."

Elizabeth smiles, getting back to work. "See if he has a friend for me," she calls.

With Ann gone, she goes through her mail: pleas, prayers, expressions of gratitude. She puts the letters down and pushes away from her desk. Gets up and goes to the pile of manuscript behind her. They seem damp, as if they gave off their own wet breath, moist pleas, prayers. *Deliver us from our daily bread, our daily boredom.*

And she can do it; she does it every day. Yet Ann would not trade places with her.

She glances out her window. The cars are there, beaded with rain, a small river flows along the gutter, moving papers and plastic cups, small pieces of garbage, gently, almost gracefully. She tilts her head a little to look toward midtown, where the buildings are like cardboard against the overcast sky, a badly drawn stage set. Radio City Music Hall presents . . . She imagines Rockettes, in brightly colored raincoats and umbrellas, kicking down the rain-drenched streets.

She smiles. She could have told Ann: What profit it a woman if she gain the whole world, if all the world's a stage? What profit and what harm? Morality is point-of-view. If we didn't take their money, someone else would. Hope springs. Like a Jack-in-the-box.

In the street, a car horn blares.

This morning, when she woke beside him, the rain had just begun and her room, in the dim brown light, looked like a tent. The ceiling seemed to sag, the walls to billow, even the floor, covered with their shoes and socks and two pillows from the couch, seemed as soft and as lumpy as a public beach. The noise from the street—the rain, a truck, a sound like the crack of a baseball bat—seemed to fill the room easily, as if it had traveled across an empty space, passed through walls made only of canvas.

She'd looked at his wide back and tried to keep herself from thinking by smiling and telling herself, "Well, now you're even sleeping with them." But the joke had lacked irony, acted not as a stop but a wedge; a wedge that split the laughter, the perspective, from her real life like flesh from a bone.

Her bed was a tent and she had pitched it among them, in the desert of their dry hopes. And now she too had hopes, vain hopes.

When she saw he was awake, she moved to kiss him, both their mouths parched with sleep.

A man in soaked T-shirt and jeans wheels a rack of green and red dresses, swathed in plastic, across the street and into her building. If all the world's a stage, better keep your costumes dry. Poet costume, artist costume. Husband and father. Feminist. Even Hector in the stockroom is, on the outside, a king of the discos. He told her once that he hoped, someday, to be taken seriously as a dancer.

If no real editor, Tupper Daniels would surely ask her, what are you?

She turns, picks up a manuscript and carries it to her desk. Even *Time* magazine says casual sex isn't as simple as it used to be. We're all looking for meaning. We're all getting older.

"Dear Mrs. Connelly, Editor-In-Chief," the cover letter begins.

"What does a woman do when she is so trapped in her own home that a prisoner in a Nazi camp would feel the same way?

"Lucinda Brookefield, the plucky heroine of my enclosed novel, *The Last Kiss of Love,* is just such a woman. What she does is cry and pray. And then a brave man, who happens to be her boss in the frozen food factory where she works (for fear of libel, I have not mentioned the company's name), teaches her what freedom and love is. Only to have it snatched away from her again by the greedy hands of her lawful husband.

"Interested? Read on.

"Lucinda Brookefield is twenty-six years old, voluptuous of figure and golden-haired. Because of her early development, she married her husband when she was sixteen and he was eight years her elder. She loved him very much, not having a mother and father who cared for her, one of nine children. When he beat her black and blue three days after their wedding, she forgave him and stayed with him. After their first child was born, she was afraid to sleep with him right away and so he tied her hands and feet and left her that way without blankets all night. She next had twins and another little boy. Her fifth baby was lost when he beat her and kicked her stomach when she fell to the ground at six months. She bore all her tragedies like a saint and became a stronger person for them.

"Right after that, a large file cabinet fell on his head at work and he was out of a job for a long time. So she had to get a job at the aforementioned frozen food factory. There she met Randolph Wisk, her supervisor. At first he didn't pay any attention to her, for he was very business like and could not be persuaded by a pretty face, but then he saw in her sad eyes that she had been through alot for her age and that she was mature beyond her years. And one special night, when she stayed late to work, he took her into his strong arms. . . ."

Her eyes go to the last paragraph.

"Alot of this is true. My husband is back at work now and I have secretly saved some money. Your brochure says some authors know their books are worth investing in and mine is alot like the books they sell in all the supermarkets and my friends pay $2.50 for. Only mine is modern and not set in history, but if you want me to, I will change the dates and make it all seem older.

"I look forward to your reply and thank you in advance for your time and consideration.

"Sincerely yours, Ellen Belster. P.S. Please don't think I've done what I said I did with my boss. He is very respectable. I just made that part up. My husband is a good man, basically."

Elizabeth flips through the neat manuscript. Always, she thinks, the troubles are real, the solutions imagined.

She could, of course, reject Mrs. Belster, tell Owens the book was pornographic. But no doubt the woman will send it off to another vanity press, and Owens, checking her list of rejections against their rivals' lists of publications, will want to know why.

She could make the contract very cheap, say $2,000, $3,000, forget her commission and tell Owens the woman obviously couldn't have afforded more. Make Mrs. Belster's dreams come true, for a while.

Or she could make the cost of the contract so high that the woman will have to abandon her plans to publish. One more stroke of bad luck for poor Lucinda.

She could write a normal Congratulations letter, charge the normal price for a book this size and let the chips fall where they may. Crawl out of bed with her. Gain some distance. She can't, after all, let each author become a moral issue. It would depress her.

She nods, turns to the typewriter. It's out of her hands.

The phones all over the office begin ringing.

She turns again and sees the five lights on her phone flashing wildly. When she picks up the receiver, she hears a dozen angry voices shouting, "Hello? Hello?"

She goes into the corridor. Marv is standing there, his plastic cup of tea in one hand, a copy of *People* in the other. "Bonnie's not there," he says calmly.

Mr. Owens pulls open his door. "What the fuck?" he says, patiently, as if it were a sensible question. "Where's Bonnie?"

Elizabeth walks past them both, into the front office. The switchboard at Bonnie's desk is blinking like a dazed robot. Connie and Maguerite, the tiny, pastel-colored grandmothers from the file room, are watching it, wringing their hands, looking frightened.

"Where the hell is everybody?" Elizabeth says.

They cower and shrug.

She picks up the receiver. The board has been flung wide open. There's an oozing tube of Blixtex beside it. She punches buttons, passes a few calls through. Disconnects a few more. The mouthpiece smells like sulfur. "Vista Books, good afternoon." Dead air. Punches another button. "Vista Books, good afternoon." For Marv. "Vista Books. Ms. Connelly is in conference right now. May I take a message?" As she copies the number, she notices the poem, on the wall above the switchboard, below the reception window, carefully flattened and framed in tape.

Vista, vision of all my dreams,
From your summit, I view my heart's desires.
Through you, I silence all my midnight screams
And quench the hopes that come of earthly fires.
No more for me the pain that longing brings,
Only the peace that suffering inspires.
Through you, I rise, as if on angel's wings,
And know my poor heart, though set apart,
Now laughs again and sings!

Someone behind her says Bonnie is in the bathroom and won't come out. Someone else is laughing.

XII

SHE WAS NOT SURE WHAT WOKE her that morning: a dream, the low rumble of a truck driving past their house, her father's voice, muffled, low. Maybe when her father was home, she always slept lightly, slept listening.

But whatever the reason, she tells him, she woke that morning when her room was pale gray and the door and the furniture—even the foot of her own bed—a darker, shapeless gray, and heard her father's voice. He seemed to be asking a series of dull questions, his voice unmodulated until the end of each phrase, when it rose a little and then paused. Perhaps for her mother to answer. She heard him laugh once and then begin the series of questioning phrases again, a faint drumming of sounds, and she may have fallen asleep concentrating on the rhythm of them.

If she did sleep, she woke again to the sound of a door, or maybe just the creak of the stairs. A car drove by outside. The room was still dim. She knew he was leaving again.

Suddenly, she was up, in the dark hallway, running down the stairs. She punched through the coats in the hall closet, pulling them from their hangers until she finally found her pale-blue ski jacket. She slipped her feet into the rubber boots she found at the bottom of the closet and pulled open the front door. It must have been very early; the air was sharp.

She ran down the steps to the garage, sure she would see him there. But the garage door was closed.

She then ran to the corner, expecting now to see him just halfway down the block, on foot, his back to her, but there were only the gray lawns, the silent houses. She ran farther. Her rubber boots stuck to the bottoms of her feet and made a hollow sound against the sidewalk. Her coat was open and she began to perspire under her pajamas. In one corner of the sky, just above the chimneys and TV antennas, there was a pale bit of pink, flesh-colored, like a tear in gray flannel. The houses lining the street seemed flat and blind.

At the next corner, a weak outdoor light glowed at the end of someone's driveway, growing dimmer as she watched it. The sidewalk, narrow and bone-pale, seemed to go on forever, and she was sure that somewhere on it, up ahead, she would turn a corner and see her father's back, walking slowly away from her.

She decided to go after him.

But then, across the street, a front door opened, a bald man in a white T-shirt peered out, scratching his stomach, and turned away. A light went on in his living room, behind white blinds and gauze curtains. She turned and walked home, her boots slapping foolishly against her bare ankles.

He pours more wine into her glass, watching her. "That's interesting," he says lightly, treading carefully. "Probably significant."

She lifts her glass, holds it before her chin. "When I got home, my father was in the shower. I could hear him singing. My mother was asleep in the middle of their bed."

She smiles at him but he smiles back with only one side of his mouth, and she suddenly feels like a woman in a low-cut dress, leaning playfully, straightening up just in time. He hadn't asked her to talk about her father. They'd merely been exchanging childhood anecdotes and she'd told him how she woke, heard her father's voice, as if it were one of them. As if she didn't know it would lead to this. "So it's not significant at all. He hadn't gone anywhere. They probably just woke up and made love. Like any normal couple."

He sips his wine. They are in a small restaurant named after a romantic cliché. Each tiny table is partially surrounded by Oriental screens or curtains of long black beads, lit only by a candle-shaped bulb and the red lights of the entrance and exit signs. Like a subdivided brothel, she'd said. He'd called it a place where they could talk.

"It still has significance," he says now, in a tone he might use to tell the bending and straightening woman, *I saw them anyway.* "You chased after him. You wanted to go with him."

She shrugs. Behind him, through a veil of beads, she can see the profile of another couple bent over their electric flame, foreheads nearly touching. They make her think of scientists, Pierre and Marie Curie looking for radium. She hears a woman's voice behind her saying, "You don't know how I react to him."

"Sometimes I think the whole thing was a dream," she tells Tupper. "It doesn't make sense that I could have left the house like that without my parents hearing." *Scarlett O'Hara,* Bill had said when she told him the story. He'd pointed out that Scarlett O'Hara also ran after someone—although through fog, not at dawn—at the end of *Gone With the Wind,* and that scene, more than anything else, was probably the source of her own recollections. He'd said she often had trouble distinguishing what she'd seen and read from what she'd actually experienced. As if she'd ever seen or read anything that could have turned that monotonous neighborhood into the frightening, fantastic place it had seemed to her that morning.

"Even if it is a dream," Tupper says, cutting a piece of cheese from the board between them. "It's significant."

She laughs. Behind her, the man is saying, "But if you'd stayed with him, you wouldn't have come to New York. We wouldn't have met."

The woman says, "We'd have met. Sooner or later."

Elizabeth thinks of Reverend Datz: It was not mere coincidence.

"What about your mother?" Tupper Daniels asks, leaning back and hooking his finger in his belt like a country lawyer. "Was it hard on her, your father being away so much?"

She picks up a cracker and bites one tiny corner, not for the taste, but the gesture, like an actress in a soap opera who must have her mouth clear for lines. "We were both used to it," she says. "It was no big deal."

He leans forward, puts his hand under his chin. *"She cried like a wife for a husband,"* he says in his recitation voice. *"Like part of some lugubrious tradition. Like women at train stations and airports, on docks and balconies and homely porches. Women crying with hands raised and a particular name on their lips, although before them there is only the curving earth or sea, the general, ubiquitous mist."* He winks. "Chapter Fifteen."

She studies her glass.

"I'm learning when to change the subject," he says finally. "You get kind of arrogant and pouty, like you've got a wonderful secret and you're afraid no one's going to ask you to tell it."

She smiles, shrugs, wonders if it's true.

"So I'll change the subject," he says. "Tell me something else about your past. Tell me about your lovers. All your other lovers."

She raises her eyebrows at the *other*, but knows there is no sense denying it. They are lovers now, just like all the other couples in this tacky, overpriced restaurant ("Come in and fall in love," says a sign in a glass case by the door, where other restaurants might suggest, "Come in and try our roast duck."), just like all the other lovers, leaning over small lights, peering into each other, searching for the significant, the special, the glowing, never-before-seen compound buried in all that grimy, indistinguishable pitchblende.

Tell me about your parents, your childhood, your other lovers. Tell me how you came to be mine. For it was no coincidence.

It occurs to her that what lovers do for each other, Vista does for each author: passes through their dull lives and comes out crying *Eureka!* There *is* meaning, there is an equation!

She looks at his blue eyes lit by the yellow bulb. They're nice eyes, but then most eyes are.

"Faces without eyes," she tells him, "would all look alike. Like potatoes. Or rocks."

"Or clay before the sculptor gets to it."

"Or elbows."

He laughs, reaches for her hand. "Tell me about your other lovers," he says again. "I want to know everything about you."

Behind him, Pierre and Marie have their fingers on each other's faces. Blind men trying to recognize a stranger.

"In my memory," she says. "They're all a bunch of elbows."

He sighs. "You're being evasive. You're a very evasive person, Elizabeth. You're full of secrets."

She bows her head as if he has complimented some small exquisite detail of her dress. *How good of you to notice.*

When she went to the bathroom to get Bonnie, she had felt an odd, Hitchcock kind of trepidation. She felt it was very possible that she'd open the door and see dangling legs, the shadow of a rope. Or Bonnie crouched upon the sinks, chattering in a man's voice.

But she was merely washing her hands and idly studying her cold sore in the mirror.

"There's no one at the board," Elizabeth said, trying to sound pleasant. Suzanne, the office manager, was supposed to handle these things. She could yell at Bonnie when she got back from the dentist.

"No?" Bonnie said, pumping more slimy green soap into her palm, creating another lather.

"No," Elizabeth said. She noticed that the girl was leaning her stomach against the sink, getting her blouse wet. She walked past her, into one of the cubicles, hoping that when she came out, Bonnie would be gone and back at her post.

The cubicle had that close, human smell. The seat was warm. She tried not to think of Bonnie sitting there, and found herself thinking instead of what Bonnie, surely a virgin, must look like inside: matted, gummy? The pubic hairs woven into a coarse, impenetrable net? Or fine, untouched, as fresh and moist as the core of a peach?

She pushed the imagining away. She'd been undressing people all afternoon.

When she came out of the toilet, Bonnie was still there, washing her hands. Elizabeth washed hers too and then, taking a coarse sheet of paper towel, said, "I closed all the lines for you. But you'd better get out there."

Bonnie turned to look at her and then turned off the water and shook her hands.

"You don't have a boyfriend, do you?" she said, eyeing her.

Elizabeth laughed, startled. She had an impulse to lie. "No," she said. "I don't."

Bonnie reached for a towel, dried her hands, and then held the crumpled paper, just as Elizabeth was holding hers.

"I don't either," she said, shrugging, raising her chin to show she didn't care. The tiny grosgrain ribbon tied into a bow at the neck of her blouse seemed ridiculous under her large face. Like a butterfly on a bulldog. Her small eyes, brown and set close, seemed to poke at Elizabeth's clothes and hair.

She leaned forward to throw her towel in the basket. Bonnie followed.

"What kind of make-up do you use?" the girl asked, trying to seem casual.

Elizabeth moved to the door. "Revlon."

"I use Maybelline," Bonnie said. She seemed intent on this girl-talk burlesque.

Elizabeth put her hand to the door. "You'd better get out there," she said.

"What else do you do?" Bonnie asked, quickly following after her, raising her own hand to the door, or to Elizabeth's face. "Besides work here? What do you do? Like on weekends?"

Elizabeth pushed the door open. Laughed. "Not much."

"Me neither." Her face came closer, the lips swollen, blurred with salve. "I've worked here for as long as you have." She seemed to smile.

"There's no one at the board," Elizabeth told her again.

"If you could show me what you do, I could probably do it too. *I* could be an assistant editor. I wouldn't get depressed. I could handle these creeps just like you do."

Elizabeth smiled. "We'll see." Stepped through the door and heard it swing closed behind her. Heard it swing open again.

Bonnie was on her heels. "I've watched you," she said. "Please. I could do it too, just like you do. Please."

Elizabeth turned a corner, took the long way back to her office. "We'll see," she said over her shoulder. And behind her she heard Bonnie cry, "I'm as good as you."

"I'm beginning to put you together," he whispers, later that night, when they are lying in the orange-tinted darkness of her room.

She is drifting to sleep, her mind mechanically reciting Congratulations letters, her limbs tired, her pulse dragging after the slow movement of his fingers. She feels she needs to be put together.

"You're a pseudocynic. A hesitant daredevil. You run to the

water's edge and run back, the same way you ran after your father and then ran back."

She feels her pulse quicken although his hand is still.

"You want to pretend your father was just an ordinary man with a job that made him travel, but inside you believe something else."

She keeps her eyes closed, keeps silent.

"You want to say the past doesn't mean anything, except to romantic Southerners, and yet you know otherwise. You remember the past vividly."

Her body is tense. It is sexual, sensual, this slow unveiling, slow revealing. This strange man unraveling her life like a gypsy fortuneteller, an ancient oracle, giving it meaning, coating it with gold light. And what else do you see? What other wondrous thing am I? What wondrous thing that poor souls like Bonnie would fear to aspire to, if they only knew the truth? That women like Ann, if they only knew, would long to become.

"You think you're tough," he says. "The hard-boiled editor. But inside, you just want love. Like everyone else."

She moves her head into her pillow, smiles, turns it into a laugh. Put me together and I'm just like everyone else. She laughs, softly, breathlessly, as if she has swallowed too much common air.

Misunderstanding, he comforts her.

XIII

---

*A*LL HER OTHER LOVERS.

God was first, of course. He was Zeus, Merlin, the Handsome Prince in all her fairy tales. Every night, her mother would read to her from a book called *Lives of the Saints,* concentrating—as she herself would do when she learned to read—on the female saints, not because they were to provide her with role models (her mother would have known nothing of the term), but because their stories were so much more romantic and dramatic than the males'. Because the woman saints were so much more given to grand gestures and heartbreaking miracles, to throwing themselves at the feet of the Lord—the quintessential Lover, Father, Husband, Knight.

There was the story of young Saint Agnes, a mere child, whom the Romans tried three times to burn at the stake, but whose lovely skin God would not allow to be harmed. (Eventually, they chopped off her head, her complexion preserved.)

There was Saint Lucy, so adamant about saving herself for the Lord that she plucked out her eyes and handed them to the young prince who, while trying to seduce her, had told her they were beautiful.

There was Saint Theresa of the Little Flower, a young orphan raised in a convent who wanted so much to receive the body and blood of Christ in Holy Communion, that God, like an indulgent father, ignored the opinion of the humorless nuns who felt she was still too young to receive and made a floating host appear before her during mass. A girl whose body was rained with rose petals from heaven when she died.

And then, of course, there was her patron saint, Elizabeth, the cousin of Mary and the mother of John the Baptist, who conceived her son in her old age, not with the help of her husband, the priest Zachariah (who, having doubted God's word, was struck dumb throughout her pregnancy), but through the will of God himself.

The story goes that Mary, after hearing that she was to be the mother of Jesus, packed her bags and went to visit Elizabeth, who was six months pregnant herself. There was a painting in the vestibule of the Connelly's parish church, St. Elizabeth's, depicting the scene: Mary, young and blond, in her perennial blue robes, greeting the gray-haired (and still slim) Elizabeth outside her home in Judaea. Elizabeth is reaching out to touch Mary's arm, and Mary is smiling, her eyes and one white hand raised toward heaven, the other reaching for Elizabeth. The skirts of their long robes are spread out and seem to be rustling, as if the two women had run toward each other, and Mary's pale, sandaled foot peaks out from under her hem. Both women have golden haloes around their heads and their faces are bright, beautiful.

Under the picture, in a yellowing glass frame, were the words of their greeting: Elizabeth's, "Blessed art thou among women," and Mary's, "My soul doth magnify the Lord. And my spirit hath rejoiced in God my Saviour . . . for behold from henceforth all generations shall call me blessed. Because he that is mighty hath done great things to me."

It was for her the most romantic, most human, even most miraculous scene in the Bible: The young virgin and the old barren woman rejoicing in their pregnancies, and God alone—God the Prince, Father, Husband, Lover, Knight, was its sponsor. Elizabeth's husband after all was old, struck speechless, lacking even the imagination to accept the miracle without question or doubt. Mary's fiancé was puzzled, unsure, back home in Nazareth with his wood and his tools. One a mere priest, one a mere carpenter. No match for the virile God whose will alone could fill their wombs: The God who was the hero of all her dreams and fairy tales and prayers throughout the first decade of her life; through the years when she, as every Catholic schoolgirl must at some time do, planned to be a nun and played at being a mother.

The exact transition is unclear, but after God, there were the Beatles. Their importance should not be underestimated. They established in her and, she sometimes likes to believe, in her entire generation, a quality of devotion that to this day endures, if only to fill her with a sweet nostalgia when faced with the concept of undying and unrequited love. If only to keep her believing, as all women are said to believe, that the imported male is always more desirable than the domestic.

For two years (eleven to thirteen? twelve to fourteen?), she lived and breathed the Beatles, wrote their names all over her notebooks at school, plastered her bedroom walls with their pictures, studied their lives. At the time, she and her friends were too young to be allowed to actually go see them in concert, and so they went to their first movie and, imitating the audiences they had seen on Ed Sullivan, screamed at the images on the film, crying, reaching out, calling names and secret messages. When the movie ended, they hugged one another, their own Paul, George, John and Ringo surrogates.

She was just beginning to hear about the details of sex then, and although she found the concept of it somewhat repulsive and certainly humiliating, she decided (recalling St. Lucy?) that, for the love of Paul McCartney, she could bear it.

With the right man, she was sure, all things were possible. It shouldn't be surprising that she spent her teenage years in a state of what might be called push-me pull-me virginity.

On the one hand, there were the nuns at Blessed Virgin who couldn't say enough about the sacredness of sex—as if, having hooked the Almighty, they were anxious to prove that they were not scornful of those who had to settle for lesser mates. They constantly assured their students that "secular" marriage too was a divine union and the marriage act (what the girls were then calling "doing it") quite nearly a religious experience. (A ceremony of Holy Orders for lay people, Sister Barbara had called it in Elizabeth's junior year, coining a phrase.) And, ironically, it was their approbation of marriage and the marriage act and all the wonders it entailed, impressed upon her in religion class, during retreats, in her senior-year marriage course, and even in Home Ec, that brought her to the conclusion that the right man would be second only to the nuns' Mate Himself, and that, as with Saint Theresa, once he appeared, all nit-picking details should be put aside and their consummation be immediate and miraculous.

On the other hand, there were the boys.

At the time, all the boys she knew she'd met at dances given by the all-male Catholic high schools in the area, and, later, at bars where everyone had phony proof and drank sloe gin fizzes or whiskey sours. They were typical Catholic high school boys, boys who tended to travel in groups, who often poked each other, slapped each other, held each other in headlocks and half Nelsons. Boys who threw up between cars and popped pimples while they danced. Who were without theories about love and sex and the role of women in their lives; who wanted only to know if you would or you wouldn't (and how their voices lacked—was it only a British accent?) because they had to get up early on Sunday to play basketball.

Often, she said she would.

Crushed up against a car door, believing the miracle of the act would somehow transform him, she'd hold her breath and whisper *yes,* trying to recall all the things she liked about this particular young man—the way a martyr must recall past favors in order to face the rack—trying to remember why she'd noticed him at the dance, the bar, why she'd been so happy he'd called and asked her out, praying he'd say some magic word that would make the moment perfect. But then, five well-bitten fingernails would be shoved down her pants or a penis would appear like the groping head of a curious one-eyed turtle, and she'd have to admit that she'd changed her mind.

("You've gone too far," she'd say, meaning, of course, that he'd gotten too close.)

And a week later, ever hopeful, she'd find herself in the same position, with the same or another boy, saying yes again. Then no again.

She chalked up her hesitation—and the dissatisfaction of her friends, who were one by one losing their virginity and assuring her that it was no big deal—to her theory of the right man. She, and they, simply hadn't met the right man, or if she had met him, he hadn't, like Rosemary Hart's brother or Mr. McKinney, the basketball coach at one of the boys' schools, been available to work that miracle that would change her life.

Gradually, like many of the bored or dateless girls in her school, she began to turn the bulk of her romantic energy toward a more appealing, more worldly, and, because of the upper middle class's penchant for college deferments, an even more incorporeal set of knights: the boys in Vietnam.

No one she knew knew one personally. But still they watched them on TV and saw them in magazines and history-class documentaries, and every once in a while a girl would come to school with the story of someone's brother's friend's friend who was blown up a week before he was to return, or someone's older sister's boyfriend who came back without a leg, and they would all shake their heads and let their eyes fill with tears. They prayed for them in homeroom every morning, drew peace signs on their notebooks, cut bloody pictures out of *Life* magazine and hung them on their bulletin boards.

They sandwiched tear-filled arguments about our boys in the swamps between discussions of prom decorations and who had just had an abortion. They were, once again, too young to actually participate in marches on Washington and takeovers of administration buildings, but they looked forward to college, when they would have that kind of freedom, and she began, as her senior year came to a close and her virginity was still upon her, to associate the romance of protest with other sorts of romance as well.

But by the time she started college, Kent State was old news and the war was "winding down." Her visions of herself as a red-faced college student screaming her anger and crying her love on the barricades would have gone entirely unrealized if it hadn't been for one demonstration, organized early in her freshman year: The last demonstration the college, which had been surrounded by the National Guard four separate times during the sixties, would ever see.

They walked through town on a warm fall day, in single file, chanting like acolytes and feeling very smug when men in bars or gas stations called them hippies and gave them the finger, and then, in the center of Main Street, they came to a halt. One of their leaders, the word went around, was to run down the line like a MIG fighter plane, and as he passed them, they were to scream and fall to the ground, as if they'd been shot. They were to lie in the road like that, blocking traffic and representing the many civilians killed in the war, until the featured speaker had completed his address.

They nodded solemnly to one another, and then, from the front of the line, a fat boy with long, thinning hair came running toward them, his arms stretched, his cheeks puffed, his pale belly peeking out from under his American flag T-shirt and his fat, corduroyed thighs chafing each other with a soft, farting sound. As he passed them, he showed his teeth and screamed rat-tat-tat, and they fell like dominoes, clutching their hearts, screaming too. On the ground, she carefully rested her head on the thigh of the boy behind her—everyone was making pillows of everyone else—and prepared to listen closely to the bald, one-armed Vietnam vet who was the guest of honor. But just as the speech started ("Where have all the flowers gone?" the vet began), she felt a twitch beneath her head. At first it was just a slight ripple, but as the speech continued, it grew stronger and stronger, until she was sure her head was literally bouncing up and down. Behind her, the boy who owned the leg was giggling—holding his breath as if to stop, whining a little, and then giggling again. She caught it, her head bouncing, and started giggling too, and the boy in front of her, who had his arm across her stomach and his nose to the road, started whispering, "I'm going to pee. Stop it, you're gonna make me pee," which started the person in front of him giggling, and so on.

When the speech finally ended ("When will they ever learn? When will they *ever* learn?"), about a dozen of them lay immobile in the street, tears streaming down their faces. Two had actually peed.

That night, she went out with the boy whose leg she'd been on. They drank beer until they'd convinced each other that they really were very concerned about the war, very serious about life in general, and then she went back to his dorm room with him to prove just how serious she could be.

First, they smoked some hash and discussed what was about to occur. ("Talk strategy," he'd said, as if they were about to run a three-legged race together.) She told him she was on the Pill, although she wasn't. And that she'd done this many times before, although she hadn't.

He said he didn't believe in commitment and thought sex was just a basic human need, like food and air and water.

Being an antiwar activist, she agreed.

He said he only thought they should be honest with each other.

She said, "We can ask no more."

It took six minutes, by the clock, and the only perfect thing about it was the way he lit two cigarettes afterward, both at the same time, and handed one to her. The gesture made her believe she loved him for nearly six months.

Her next two years were occupied with a succession of boys who, with their plaid shirts and beer drunks and worn Cheech and Chong imitations, all seemed alike. (As, she is sure, she, with her uncertain major in social science and her crush on her anthropology professor and her dilemma of to pledge or not to pledge, must have seemed to them like every other girl.) Boys who were worth more to her as stories she could tell Sunday morning back at the dorm or apartment (or, for a semester, the sorority house) than as companions in bed or bar. Boys whom she often told, when drunk or high enough to be able to deny it in the morning, that she loved.

Early in her senior year she saw Bill for the first time, and thought of the height and breadth and depth that her soul had yet to reach. Like Saint Paul on the road to Damascus, she was struck, reprimanded, enlisted. She knew her life would never again be the same.

A year later, he spoke to her.

Tupper Daniels travels her body and returns with reports of spices and silks, strange seas, small treasures, deposits of pure gold. He details the pleasure she gives him.

There is, he tells her, a small bone or tendon near the skin inside her thigh, that rises or tightens under his tongue, creating a deep hollow in the flesh around it. A hollow that could, he is sure, catch rain.

There is, at the small of her back, a slight dimple like a gentle thumbprint. When he puts his thumb to it, she moves her hips. Always toward him. (He says this seriously, uncertainly, as if he himself believes it too good to be true.)

At the back of her neck, under her dark hair, there is a

tapering line of lighter, finer hair, fading down into the shadow of her spine. If his fingers follow it, he thinks of fur, quick bones moving underneath. If he reaches around to her soft stomach, he feels he has suddenly lost his footing, as in a dream. Like a sailor who has suddenly considered the depth of the ocean beneath him.

He lies beside her, whispering: She tastes of rain—the way the heavy air tastes just before a thunderstorm, or just after. Of sea salt. He licks his lips in the dark, puts her hand to his mouth to taste her again.

He sometimes asks that they leave the light on. He loves the way her mouth seems to turn into itself at its corners, as if, he says, her lips, having given the world enough pleasure, quickly and demurely meet to withdraw.

Her bottom lashes are unusually long, did she know that? They seem to move together, forming points like small petals.

Her hair, he tells her as they are walking, takes on a different odor in bed. It loses its perfume, has a humid, grassy smell, much better. It feels cool when it brushes his chest.

One morning, he proudly shows her where she has bitten him, dug her nails into his flesh. He laughs when she apologizes and says she was unaware. He tells her they are his first tattoos. Gained while on adventure in a foreign land.

Alone, she studies herself, remembering his fantastic reports. She lifts her hair, watches her thighs, doubts him. Begins to believe.

He offers to photograph her.

She laughs, "But no one's ever mentioned it before."

He's a writer, he tells her. The first thing he learned at Vanderbilt was to be specific.

She studies herself again. If he is no writer, what can be said for his writer's eye?

XIV

*T*HE SIMPLEST QUESTIONS, THE
most ordinary responsibilities, are the ones that throw her. She
can explain to any author, without hesitation, how eight pages
added to a manuscript will mean adding another signature,
which will mean increasing the size of the binding and the
jacket, which will, of course, add considerably to the cost of
production, and thus the contract itself. But let the same
author ask her (after having eliminated the extra pages or paid
her for them) how to get to Columbus Circle by subway, and
her mouth will go dry, her heart will sink.

It's as if the fine web of lies and illusions with which she gets
through her day is penetrable only by those small, definite
questions. Factual questions that can't be faked, that slip like
pebbles through the weave of her various poses and strike at
what she fears is her raw stupidity.

How, after all, can a bright young editor at a large New York
publishing house not know the difference between IRT and
IND, between ounces and pints, between affect and effect?

And so, that Saturday afternoon, as she and Tupper Daniels
pull out of her street in a rented Firebird and he says, "Which
way?" the name of every road on Long Island—the Expressway, Grand Central Parkway, Southern State, Meadowbrook,
Northern State, Cross Island—meet and fuse in her mind,

becoming, for her, one long stretch of featureless concrete.

"Take the Tunnel," she says, trying to buy more time in the city, where names and numbers are predictable. "The Midtown Tunnel."

He smiles, looking like a pale pervert in his flashing sunglasses. Though it's late October, the day is warm and bright. He has a deep red sweater tied around his neck—it is blinding against the car's white interior. "I take it then I have to go toward midtown."

"That's right," and before she can adjust her seat belt he has cut west, through scornful pedestrians and changing lights, and turned onto Fifth Avenue.

She laughs. "Not this far midtown. The Tunnel's on the East Side."

He shrugs. "So we'll go down Fifth. It's prettier."

Stopped for a light, he puts his hand on the seat beside him and races the engine. He only needs, she thinks, a can of beer and a wad of gum.

"You look right at home behind the wheel," she says.

"I was *born* behind the wheel." A teenage hillbilly grinning over his hot rod. She notices that he *is* chewing gum. When the light changes, he pulls out in front and cuts off two cabs, swearing he'll make every light to Thirty-fourth Street. They're stopped at the Plaza and in front of St. Patrick's, and again at Forty-second Street, but he slips under each light going crosstown and veers into the Tunnel like a barnstormer.

She laughs. It's a silly, peacock display, but it's been a long time since she's ridden in a car with a man, and not terribly long since such displays truly thrilled her (like Ann, there are parts of her adolescence she'll never shake). And there is, she thinks, something about a man's hands on the steering wheel—thick knuckles, strong wrists—something about the casual slump of his body in the seat, the easy, screeching turns and clever shifts of gear, the absolute male confidence on the road, that makes her feel lucky, taken care of. Dad's in his bucket, all's right with the world.

She remembers breaking up with a boy in college because he sat stiffly behind the wheel and bit his nails as he drove.

In Wisconsin, her father had been killed by the other guy. Although the police had pointed out that her father, too, had been drinking.

As they come out of the Tunnel and go through the toll-booth, Tupper looks up at the signs and asks, "Do I want the Long Island Expressway?"

She says, "Yes," although she means *If you say so,* and tries to force her mind to remember what comes next. She can only be sure of Montauk.

"How long do I stay on here?" he asks, getting into the fast lane.

"I'll let you know," she says. "It's a ways."

He glances at her, then in his rearview mirror. "Well, just give me fair warning. I hate it when women give directions like, 'Make a right. Back there.' "

She smiles. "I'll let you know." And now even the names of the roads slip from her mind. Of course, it's women. Women will get wet when you drive fast and look pretty beside you, but you sure as hell can't depend on them for intelligence, much less directions. They'll giggle and say, "Make a right. Back there."

She gives up the idea of giggling and saying, "We'd better ask at a gas station."

"What a beautiful Ferrari," she says instead, casually, trying to sound like one of the boys, although she has to squint to read the car's name. She considers saying something crude about the blonde driving it. *Dumb bitch, probably lost.*

Tupper turns his head to look at the car. "Nice," he says.

They drive silently, past the sloping lawns of Calvary Cemetery, where gray and beige and bright white tombstones crowd together like pedestrians on Fifth Avenue at lunchtime—although the cemetery has placed these New Yorkers in what seems an incongruous kind of order, as if, at their point, order mattered—and, weaving quickly through the traffic, follow the road through Queens.

They pass a sign for a street that she knows would lead them to her old apartment in Flushing, where she lived until she moved up with Bill, but she'd spent her year there without a car, being chauffeured by Bill or Joanne or the MTA, and all but the location of her own building and her apartment within it is a blank to her now. She could have spent that year as a murmuring recluse.

"I used to live around here," she tells Tupper, although she suspects she is lying.

She'd found the apartment the day after her mother had announced she was leaving for Maine. Found it quickly, in a cold sort of fury—the pathetic girl-child flung from the nest— and she moved in before her mother had even begun packing, determined to prove that she too had plans for her own life and was anxious to get on with them, but hoping, she is sure now, that such a swift, startling first flight would frighten her mother into bringing her home again.

Instead, her mother had said, "What luck!" and offered her the good furniture from their living room. Elizabeth refused it, tightly telling her she could make do with the stuff from the basement, playing the martyr but also fearing to see the pieces from her own home huddled in that ugly apartment like flood victims in a school cafeteria.

She did, however, accept the double bed from her mother's room, feeling that if her mother was making a statement by offering it to her, she would make a statement by accepting it. Although just what either of them might have been stating remained unclear.

"Have you known this girl a long time?" Tupper asks suddenly.

"Joanne?" She wonders if the driving has made him forget to say woman. "Since grammar school."

"What's her last name?" The car has increased his accent too.

"Paletti. Or it was. Now it's Paletti-Hanson."

"Sounds like a machine gun," he says. "The Paletti-Hanson 244."

She smiles. Short rows of stores whizz by. A place where she and Joanne used to stop for bagels after bar-hopping in the city, still decorated, as it was then, with its multicolored grand-opening flags and a spindly fluorescent sign that says HOT. She calms down a little. This must be the right way.

"What does she know about me?"

She looks at him. His jaw, reflecting the red sweater, moves slowly.

"Just that you're a friend."

He nods. What she'd really said was that he was an author she'd met at work, so don't ask what ridiculous things have happened at Vista lately. Joanne, who has always been more interested in romance than ethics, had said only, "Who cares what he does. Is he cute?"

"What does *her* husband do?" He emphasizes the "her" as if he were comparing hers to yours.

"Tommy's a lawyer." She sees a sign for the Cross Island Parkway, and so, because it's two miles ahead, says calmly, "We take the Cross Island. It's up here about two miles."

He nods and looks over his shoulder to change lanes. She feels her heart pounding. Cross Island goes where?

"What time are they expecting us?"

"Between six and seven. But I told her you wanted to drive out to the beach first."

"Here?" he says, slowing for the exit.

"Yes," she says, having no idea. She's reading signs desperately now, wondering how long she can keep him lost before he realizes it.

"You almost sound worried about meeting them," she says,

still looking out the window, trying to sound calm.

He shrugs. The road is narrow. Cars seem to squeeze in on all sides. "Well, this is the first time you've introduced me to any of your friends. I feel you're finally letting me get past your professional life." She wonders if he considers sleeping with him part of her professional life. He takes one hand from the wheel and puts it over hers, which is perspiring on the white seat. "I feel I'm finally getting close to you."

He looks at her, smiling, squeezing her hand, and she smiles back at him, still glancing at the fleeting signs. He will make this evening significant despite her.

She has invited him, she thinks, because Joanne asked her to. Or, no, because he suggested renting a car and taking a drive and Joanne provided them with a destination. Because she had promised Joanne she'd come out and he could save her the trouble of the train.

They go quickly through an underpass that blocks the sun and her ears.

She has invited him because she feared, has been fearing since the wedding, to go to Joanne's newlywed apartment celibate and unattached, like a pathetic old aunt. Because she feared Tommy's exuberant graciousness as he carefully avoided touching Joanne or discussing their affection in front of her, the way one might avoid references to color and light when your only guest is blind. Because she feared Joanne's pity and optimism—"Oh, you'll meet someone. It always happens when you least expect it"—dished out in her cozy living room, in her lucky marriage.

She invited him because she needed someone, some man, to hold up beside Joanne's: Joanne's man, Joanne's love, Joanne's happiness.

And yet, Joanne has claimed she's not happy. Maybe, she thinks, she needed someone to hold up beside that too. If you're out, I'm out.

They pass a sign naming a familiar road.

"The next exit," she says, hoping, once they're off the Parkway, that her memory will clear.

"Are you sure?" he says. "I thought you could go straight highway."

"You can, but this is more scenic. The trees are so pretty."

Saying it, she notices them for the first time. Brown, gold, yellow, red, lining the highway. Autumn again.

"You're the native," he says, turning off.

"That's true." But as they drive down a wide road, past 7-11's and Burger Kings and body repair shops flanked by weary trees with bright leaves that are as pathetic as all final efforts, she knows she is lost.

"Where now?"

"Keep going." She is the native. She lived on this island for eighteen years. You'd think she would remember.

And then she sees the white bank with the turquoise clock. It is a clothing store now.

"How'd you like to take a detour?" She tries to make it sound bright, impulsive.

"Where to?"

"To the town where I grew up. I can get us to the beach from there as well as from here." She can get them to the beach if the A&P where you're supposed to make the turn is still there.

He grins at her, squeezes her hand. "I'd love to, Elizabeth." This too he will make significant. "Just point the way."

"The street we want is up here," she says, hoping it is, and twenty minutes later the tangle of streets and towns and highways that is Long Island falls simply and orderly into the neat lawns and straight sidewalks and shaded avenues named for flowers that is her home.

"There's where I went to kindergarten," she says, turning in her seat. The old house is a day-care center now. "And that's where Paul Schuster lived, the kid who always tried to kiss me at the bus stop." She laughs. "You wouldn't think a seven-year-old could have such bad breath."

Tupper laughs. He has slowed to a tour bus's pace and is looking eagerly around. *How did you come to be mine?*

"Up here is St. Elizabeth's, where I went to grammar school."

The sun is slanting through the old trees now, falling on red leaves and green lawns and sidewalks littered with Big Wheels and bicycles.

The houses, except for various colors and additions, flower gardens and shrubs, are all alike, all covered with smooth aluminum siding now rather than the wooden shingles they'd had when she lived here. It makes them all look falsely young, like middle-aged men with crew cuts. Like the now-aging vets they'd first been built for.

"Does everything look smaller?" he says.

"Kind of crushed."

"It always does. Where's your house?"

She fears for a moment that she has lost her voice. "The other side." She clears her throat. "Out of the way."

They drive slowly past the back of the school, where two little boys in puffed baseball jackets are shooting basketballs into a netless hoop. The school building is a flat rectangle. Two stories of orange brick turned gaudy by the setting sun. The windows are filled with construction-paper ghosts and witches and lopsided orange pumpkins. She sees a white nun with skinny legs walk quickly from the school to the convent and imagines she is going in for a glass of ginger ale or a weak cup of tea.

"The church is around front," she says. "We have to turn past it." Obligingly, he slowly moves the car around the corner. But the church, which had also been built of white shingles, its entrance marked by a long green awning and steep brick steps, is now the same bright orange as the school. Is now flat and round with eight sides and eight entrances, like a sturdy circus tent.

"Modern," Tupper says.

"It's new." She remembers hearing that it was being built. It was why Joanne had had to be married in Tommy's parish. She is oddly disappointed. Where there had been grass and a grotto filled with votive candles (and where she often feared the statue of the Blessed Virgin would come alive and speak to her), there is now only a parking lot, bordered by a chain link fence and the cemetery.

"Is your father buried there?" Tupper whispers.

"Yeah. You want to make a left at the corner."

But he makes an immediate right and pulls into the parking lot, pulls up until his headlights are facing the first row of stones. "I thought you'd want to check on him," he says when he's turned the engine off. "I'll wait here." His smile is kind, understanding.

She has never before wanted so much to spit at someone.

But she grips the handle, pulls it. She cannot say, "No, never mind, I don't feel like it today," not when she's this close and has avoided coming here for so long. Not when, by mere coincidence, she got him lost and brought him here, and he, for his own reasons, and again by mere coincidence, wants her to see her father's grave.

She gets out of the car without a word, thinking that the vision of her father materializing in some dark bedroom has not yet left her. That she is still Irish enough and Catholic enough to be waiting for a message from him.

The air is sharp, full of autumn, burning leaves and the edge of snow. The time of day when a sweater becomes too light, when, going home for something warmer, you find your play-time has prematurely run out. Dinner's almost ready, since you're here you might as well stay. Trapped by your own eagerness to be well.

She wishes the gate to be closed, but it isn't. She knows lying about it won't help.

This path, she remembers. Down the center, three rows to the left. The cemetery is not large and seems nearly at capacity. Most of the grassy spaces are between stones or just before them. They'll have to dig up the parking lot when the baby boom starts turning over.

She and her mother had walked solemnly down this path with no tears, and later everyone said, "Just like Jacqueline Kennedy," as if her mother's reserve was a mere imitation, as adoptable and faddish as a pillbox hat. But not long after, Jackie married Onassis and the award for tasteful widowhood went to her mother alone. For widows were only admirable when dry-eyed and celibate. Ever-assured and ever-faithful, like Penelope.

She wonders what their old neighbors would say if they knew about Ward.

His stone has nothing to distinguish it but a small hedge, not even a foot tall, planted on one side. She wonders if that was where her mother was supposed to have gone. If the church put the bushes there just in case she changed her mind.

There are a few dead leaves gathered at the base of the stone and she nudges them with her foot. And then, awkwardly, squats down to pull them away. She remains squatting, as if to read the inscription (there is only the name and the date, *beloved father, beloved husband*), until her leg falls asleep, and then she straightens up again. In front of her there is a line of trees; behind them, the convent and school parking lot. To her right there is the remaining side of the cemetery, the high chain fence, a road, and, across it, a Shop Rite, a pizza parlor, a car stereo shop. To her left there is the rest of the church parking lot, where four teenagers are riding skateboards, oblivious to the terrible sounds they make, and beyond them more homes, each with its own chain-link fence or hedge.

She reads the inscription again, but there's no message in it. At least, she thinks, some of the Italians have pictures on their tombstones, something to remind you that the person once smiled and looked over his shoulder and wore his shirts open at the neck. Maybe even to remind you that you both have the same eyes or nose or mouth. You and this person gone.

She looks across the street to the Shop Rite, where families are coming and going, pushing steel carts full of grocery bags, opening car doors, dragging children.

All right. She can remember her father doing that. Going shopping with them, driving the car, sitting at the dinner table. She remembers chasing after him one morning and hearing him sing in the shower. She remembers his laugh, a silent, swallowed laugh that always came when his head was bowed. His homecomings, his sudden departures. His eyes that only after his death she learned to call "piercing." And now he is here, in a town where he had only occasionally spent his life, deserted by the women he'd spent his life coming home to. All right. So what? Put it all together and it says what?

She walks back to the center path. Down toward the car. Something more compelling, Ward said. He'd left each time for something more compelling.

She opens the gate and it shuts behind her with a cold ring. She wishes it were true. Wishes it was something damn compelling. Another life, a thousand of them.

Tupper is leaning against the car, talking to a midget in a crash helmet, orange foam rings wrapped around his every joint.

"Hiya!" Tupper says as she approaches, suddenly Andy of Mayberry. "My friend here says we can pick up the Parkway just past the A&P."

"I know," she says, but the kid points his skateboard and explains it to her anyway.

"I know," she tells him again. "I used to live around here."

She sees the boy and Tupper shrug, exchanging a look that says, *As if that mattered.*

He was fifteen when he came over from London. One of seven children, but the aunt had sent for him alone, and his parents—the father a beefeater at the Tower, the mother an immigrant, English in everything, he used to say, except her guilt about no longer being Irish—gave him up gladly.

They put him on the boat with ten pounds and a list of other relatives they had in the States, just in case the aunt, his mother's sister, proved unreliable. He said he'd sold the list, and all the details of his own life, to an Irishman he met on the way over, and, as far as he knew, the Irishman presented himself to some or all of the names on the list and was taken in as Lizzie's son from London.

It's possible that the man goes by her father's name even still.

His uncle, the aunt's husband, met him in New York. He was a broad, flat-faced, serious man. A Dutchman whose family had owned and farmed the land on Long Island's east end for four generations. Who believed in a just, tyrannical God and a hard life and the ghosts of his ancestors that stirred in his attic and called him, late on dark nights, to the small cemetery in one lonely corner of his farm. Who was slightly bewildered to find himself, well past middle age, no longer a bachelor, and now, no longer a quiet man with a childless wife.

They rode out to the Island together in silence although the uncle often glanced at him with a look both startled and afraid, as if he'd lost his senses at an auction and raised his hand for the boy.

His wife had said her nephew would be the child they never had.

His first morning, the uncle woke him early, handed him large fishing boots and a crooked, whittled walking stick, and set off with him for a tour of the farm. They went through the back hedge, which was still wet with dew and full of pale cobwebs, across a field of soft brown dirt, along a country road and another field of sharp brambles, and then, with a sudden dropping of the land, to the beach and the sea itself.

He was out of breath by then, spent by his uncle's pace and the expanse of the farm, which, although not really large, seemed to him, after his cramped home in London, as vast as America, but the sight and the smell of the sea crashing itself against the sand (as if, he said, it too was trying to get somewhere, and not merely content to let others ride on its back) made him laugh wildly and scramble to climb the highest dune along the shore.

And when he shouted down to his uncle—the first question he dared ask him—"Where does it end?" the uncle, misunderstanding, had raised his own walking stick to the line of the horizon and said, "Where you came from, boy. England."

But my father shook his head, and, watching from his height the ocean throw itself again and again upon the slowly yielding sand, said, "No, it never ends. It goes on and on and on."

She stops, feeling the foolishness. A gull cries above them.

"There are always new places to go," Tupper says softly.

She looks at him. The wind is whipping his blond hair over his forehead, into his eyes. He could be discussing his own life, his face is that still, that serious.

She looks out over the beach, squinting to keep her own hair from her eyes, pulling strands of it like seaweed from her mouth. The concession stand behind them is closed, the other steel picnic tables around them deserted. She can't distinguish the sound of the wind from the sound of the waves.

"Can you use it?" she says and even she can hear the hope in her voice. Like an old woman passing out her life's souvenirs to reluctant nieces and nephews. Can you use this scarf, this jewelry box, this initialed beer mug?

Once, a grateful, childless author gave her a Kewpie doll, won in Coney Island in 1957. Won for her by her late husband. It had smelled of cheap perfume and she'd dropped it off at a church rummage sale on her way home.

He rests his elbows on the table behind him. "Don't know," he says softly, musing. He shakes his head. "What made your father tell you about it in the first place? What was *his* point?"

She tries to remember. When did he tell it? Where were they? How much of the story has she imagined herself? "I think he was trying to explain why the uncle liked him. He died only about a year after my father arrived, but in his will he asked that all his money and property go to my father."

"The son he never had."

"I guess so."

He raises his warm hand to her cheek, brushes the hair from her face. The wind blows it back again.

"Do you want me to use it, Elizabeth? Do you want it to be in my book?"

She thinks of their books, life stories told again and again, printed on cheap paper, piled in damp stockrooms, returned to sender.

She said she didn't blame them for writing the books. Lovers do it for each other. Making sense isn't such a bad dream. It's the clamoring for fame and fortune that makes them ridiculous, the way they blow their material.

She'd told herself that she wanted only to believe he'd had a thousand other lives.

She looks at Tupper Daniels' serious face, as pale as sand, at the darkening sky behind him. His eyes are on hers and won't leave them. She loves him. Soon she'll be traveling.

"I only want you to get your book finished," she says. "Whatever it takes."

XV

M Y MOTHER SAID, "HE SOLD that land for a song," as if she meant it literally.

We were at her kitchen table in Maine, my last night with her. We'd had a late dinner and a walk along the beach and we were sharing a bowl of blueberries before going to bed. The bowl was between us on the table, the lamplight shining in its pale blue dregs of sugar and milk. Occasionally, a moth would strike the window screen beside us or the wind would rise, lifting the leaves on the trees and making me believe I could still hear the sea.

I was tracing lines into the yellow oilcloth with the edge of my spoon.

"It was a lovely, large piece of land," she said, smiling just enough to darken those deep lines around her mouth. "It was where he'd grown up, and if he'd kept it, he could have given it to you. It would have been your inheritance. But he sold it for a song." As if she had been there and he had, literally, asked only for a song. As if he had heard some strolling minstrel or itinerant tenor singing sweetly to the ocean or the fields and like a touched, impetuous king had said, *My land for a song, just another song!*

"You would have thought he had a hundred other plots just like it," she said.

She folded her arms over her slight breasts. The sweater she was wearing was Ward's, a long brown cardigan with suede patches on its sleeves. She'd thrown it on when the two of us went out for our walk, but had not taken it off on our return.

"He was like that," she said, her thin white hand moving slowly from her elbow to her shoulder, up and down the dark sweater. "He came home with the cash from the sale and a hundred little boxes filled with, oh"—she closed her eyes briefly—"silly things. Scarves and stockings and that little crystal bird I used to have in the china cabinet. And some beautiful wine, just for me; he wasn't drinking then." She tilted her head, only slightly, almost sadly, rounding her lips for the words as if there were more pleasure in the sound of them than in their memory. "And some tins of strange teas," she said. "And English toffee. And a box of green tomatoes. Just things he'd picked up on the way home—stopping for one thing and then another, all the way across the island—to appease me for the loss of the land."

She looked at me in the dull light of the small, milk-glass lamp, smiling as if I, too, should be appeased by this tale of his charming eccentricities. Reconciled to the loss by the lovely story it made.

"That's what he did," she said, and there was something about her mouth, some movement in the shadows that framed it or in the long thin set of her lips that made me think she was going to cry. But I'd never seen her cry for my father. "That and a thousand other things. Since you've asked."

She stood and picked up the bowl, brought it to the sink.

"I meant on his trips away," I said, nearly shouting over the running water, refusing to be appeased. "On all his trips away."

She turned, as she had turned that day in our own kitchen when I had sat on my father's lap to share his morning beer and had asked him, too, what he did. "Government work," she said over her shoulder. "You know that."

Then she asked if I'd mind driving down to Boston alone tomorrow. That is, alone with Ward.

I said I didn't mind, and just a few hours later I watched from his car as she turned back to her cottage, a small woman with a ponytail, rolling up her sleeves.

XVI

JOANNE SCREAMS, AS IF SURPRISED to see them, throws her arms around Elizabeth and says "Hi" to Tupper with a laugh that would make anyone suspicious.

She pulls Elizabeth through the narrow hallway ("Tommy wanted to put a bar in here, but I said, 'Let people get in the door before you make them a drink.' ") and into the living room where Tommy is getting up slowly, smiling his shy smile. He kisses Elizabeth on the cheek and firmly shakes hands with Tupper. ("Tupper?" "As in Tupperware—no relation.") She and Joanne smile at their fair men.

"This is beautiful," Elizabeth says, looking around the living room. "What a gorgeous color."

Joanne laughs, wrings her hands. "Do you like it? Everyone's showing so much beige, I thought this was different. It's coral."

"It's almost pink."

She bends with her laugh this time, like a rubber stick being shaken. "Don't say that! It's coral."

"It's pink," Tommy says, matter-of-factly. They've had this discussion before.

"Well, it's very pale," Tupper adds.

"This wall is nearly pink." Joanne holds her open palm to the far wall. "You see? Every wall is a slightly different shade."

Elizabeth and Tupper study each wall.

"I got the idea from *Apartment Life.*"

"Her bible," says Tommy.

"And the carpet is called Palest Misty Rose."

"Pale is big," Tommy says, like a man who has lost his temper in furniture stores.

"Well, the whole effect is very beigey," Elizabeth says. "Only warmer."

Tupper agrees.

"Pink," Tommy says again, and then, slapping his hands together, "Enough talk, how about a drink?" It is, she is sure, the way his father, a burly fire chief, gets a party moving.

She and Tupper say "Of course," and follow Joanne through the rest of the apartment while Tommy clinks glasses in the kitchen. In the small bedroom—dark-blue carpeting, dark-blue spread, towering oak headboard and bureau—there is an 8 × 10 of Tommy and Joanne on their wedding day smiling from the vanity.

It surprises, even disappoints her. You'll get over it. Everyone gets over it. She wonders if she would have preferred Joanne not to—preferred her to have spent the rest of her life refusing to admit that her wedding actually took place. Like some reverse Miss Havisham.

She looks at the picture and smiles meaningfully at Joanne. But Joanne doesn't catch it.

In the living room, Tommy is placing drinks on the coffee table, beside platters of cheese and crackers and melon wrapped in prosciutto. She notices that he is built much like Tupper, short, broad, though a bit more stocky, a bit wider around the waist. In a few years, he'll probably be fat. Even now, his corduroy pants look as if they could be hiked a little.

She and Tupper sit on the edge of the coral-colored couch, Tommy and Joanne on the coral-colored chairs opposite them. All four lean into their laps a little to reach the coffee table. It makes them all look like children trying to hold it in.

She wonders if they'll eventually have fun.

"So, Joanne tells me you're a writer," Tommy says.

"Yes," Tupper answers easily. "I'm just finishing my first book."

Tommy nods. He is colorful—edible-looking, Elizabeth has often thought. Even in midwinter, his complexion is a somewhat transparent red, and the freckles across his nose always remind her of berries pressed in red Jell-O. His eyes are grape-green, his hair the color of canned peaches. "What's your book about?" he asks and his voice, which is perhaps a little too high, is full of catches and bumps, the texture of a grainy pear.

"It's a novel," Tupper says. "About a man in my hometown who was a bigamist."

Joanne laughs.

"Nonfiction?" Tommy asks, leaning to pick up a speared melon. "Help yourself."

Tupper does. "No, a novel," he says, and Elizabeth detects a certain disdain in his voice. "Novels are fiction."

Tommy puts the toothpick on the arm of his chair, chews and smiles. "Some of them are, I guess. But personally, I'd rather read books that don't pretend to be made-up." He shifts a little. "It seems to me that fiction is just so much self-centered autobiography."

Tupper bows his head, the perfect Southern gentleman. "You're entitled to your opinion." He need only add, "Suh."

"How's the lawyer business?" Elizabeth asks casually, also reaching for some food and heading off Tommy's happy approach to a full-blown argument. He has a bachelor's in philosophy and seems to think an evening is a failure if he hasn't slammed his fist on something and shouted, "That's exactly my point."

Often—in bars and at parties, and once in the parking lot of a shopping mall—she has seen Joanne soothing friends and strangers by saying, "He doesn't mean it personally, he just loves to argue," the way a woman might pull at the leash of a barking dog and swear he's just being friendly.

"Being a lawyer is great," he pronounces, apparently content with his second-favorite line of conversation. "Especially the money. Every week, when I run out of money, they give me more. And when that's gone, more. They can't give me enough of it."

"They don't give you enough of it," Joanne says, her fingers over her mouth.

He laughs a little and seems to blush, although it's hard to tell. "Well," he says, "I'm still paying off loans."

"Where is it you work?" Tupper asks.

"Sayville."

"Here on Long Island," Elizabeth explains.

"Yeah." Tommy looks at his glass. "It's a small firm, just five lawyers, including me, but it's a good place to start. The pay isn't fantastic, but I'm learning a lot."

Something's wrong, Elizabeth thinks, watching him lean back casually, legs crossed, beige shirt a little tight around his belly.

"We do a lot of malpractice stuff," he goes on. "Some of it would scare the crap out of you. We're handling this one case . . ."

She looks at Joanne, who is still sitting up over her lap, one arm draped across her knee, one under her chin. Her dark brow is slightly lowered, as if she too senses something wrong but can't quite spot it.

"The lawyer I work for said it was like the surgeon cut into her with a broken Coke bottle."

She looks behind him to the pale-pink wall, softly lighted, the curtains of Palest Misty Rose, a feathery green fern, Georgia O'Keeffe's seashells and flowers framed in silver. Joanne's done a nice job. You'd never know her mother's house is all turquoise and gold, couches, chairs and lampshades covered with thick plastic.

"Of course, we asked for the most ridiculous settlement. As far as we're concerned, there are only three kinds of settlements: ridiculous, more ridiculous and most ridiculous. You ask for the most ridiculous sum and usually end up with just ridiculous or more ridiculous, as a compromise."

Tupper laughs and Elizabeth looks at Tommy again. The effect is startling. His red face, his strawberry-blond hair, his orange freckles, the pale pink behind him. He clashes! Clashes horribly with the entire room.

She sips her drink and glances at Joanne. She would love to tell her. Years ago, it was the kind of remark that would keep them laughing for hours. (Joanne would scream, make her eyes wide, touch her fingertips to Elizabeth's arm. "He *does!*" she'd cry, surprised, delighted.) But she knows there are certain things you just can't tell a woman about her husband. Not even your best friend.

She looks at Tommy again and sips her drink to keep from smiling. He is simply the wrong color. When Joanne quietly gets up and goes to the kitchen, she says, "I'll help," and follows her.

Tommy is still telling his story of the Coke-bottle doctor and Tupper is listening closely. Material?

With her and Joanne gone, she knows, Tommy will work the conversation around to Kant or Hegel, the British empiricists or the Christian existentialists, explaining first all their ideas and arguments, and then—always—how philosophy is meaningless to the real world. Every new person he meets sooner or later hears it. Like a rejected lover, Tommy seems compelled to tell, over and over again, why he spent so many years passionately involved with the subject and why he is not with it now, why he never really liked it anyway.

Pretending to be worldly, he will claim that he went into law for the money ("big bucks," he'll call it), but Joanne has told her that Tommy went into law because he feared philosophy would make him foolish. Feared, as his father might have put it, that he would spend his life in an ivory tower, asking questions with no answers, the real world snickering below.

Joanne told Elizabeth this, but added that Tommy didn't know it, and Elizabeth often imagines that he will show up at Vista someday with a philosophical treatise and an assumed name.

Joanne is at the sparkling counter, feeding carrots to her food processor. "Can I help?" Elizabeth asks over the terrible hum and Joanne answers, "He *is* cute. And I just love his Southern accent."

She holds a carrot in the air and raises her dark eyes.

"Oh no," Elizabeth says. She knows what's coming.

" 'I had malaria fever all that spring,' " Joanne recites in a soft, Long Island version of a drawl. " 'The change of climate from East Tennessee to the Delta—weakened resistance—' " She puts her thin fingers to her forehead. " 'I had a little temperature all the time—not enough to be serious—just enough to make me restless and giddy!' " She sashays slowly. " 'Invitations poured in—parties all over the Delta!—"Stay in bed," said Mother, "you have fever!"—but I just wouldn't— I took quinine but kept on going, going!—Evenings, dances! —Afternoons, long, long rides! Picnics—lovely!—So lovely, that country in May.—All lacy with dogwood, literally flooded with jonquils!' " She pauses, looks meaningfully at the refrigerator, smiling. " 'That was the spring I had the craze for jonquils. Jonquils became an absolute obsession. Mother said, "Honey, there's no more room for jonquils." And still I kept on bringing in more jonquils. Whenever, wherever I saw them, I'd say, "Stop! Stop! I see jonquils!" I made the young men help me gather the jonquils! Finally there were no more vases to hold them, every available space was filled with jonquils. No vases to hold them? All right, I'll hold them myself!' "

She brings her eyes to the carrot, smiles at it as if it were a jonquil. " 'And then I—met your father! Malaria fever and jonquils and then—this—boy. . . .' "

The two of them lean together toward the Formica counter, laughing. "I can't believe you still remember all that."

"It was my stage debut!" Joanne laughs. "Remember when I started going out with the guy who played the gentleman caller, Frank O'Murphy, and my mother thought he must be half Italian with a name like Franco?"

Elizabeth nods. "I remember hearing about it. I was up at school."

Joanne sips her drink and then grimaces, swallowing hard. "I hope I don't start imitating Tupper. You know how I get when I drink."

Elizabeth laughs, lowers her voice. "You should really recite your speech for him at dinner. He'll think you're very literary. Even poetic."

Joanne lowers her voice too. "Can you imagine? I'll just turn to him at dinner and say, 'Tell me, Mr. Daniels, have you ever had malaria fever?' "

They laugh again, girlfriends, until Tommy comes out and moves the bottle of gin away from them. "I knew you two would be giggling out here," he says fondly. "We're going to have another drink, but maybe I'd better cut you ladies off." Spoken like a buddy bartender.

Joanne puts her glass in front of him and wipes one corner of her eye. "We haven't even started yet," she says, shoving the jonquil/carrot into the machine. "We're gonna take quinine and keep on going, going!"

When Tommy hands her the drink, he leans to kiss her forehead. She smiles up at him, eyes huge.

"He's sweet," Elizabeth says, after he has returned to the living room. ("So," they hear him, "what was your major in college, Tupper?") She is not sure why she says it, except that, as if she'd been shown a newborn baby, a compliment seemed appropriate.

Joanne smiles. "He's my honey. Whenever I get sick of being married, I think of how sweet he is."

Elizabeth recalls Ann's "The people were so nice." It hadn't occurred to her that she'd meant Brian.

"And he really puts up with me." She dumps the sliced carrots into a wooden bowl already filled with lettuce and tomatoes and cucumbers. "I've been making him take me out on *dates* the last few weekends. You know, waiting for me in the living room and everything." She makes a face to show how silly she is.

"That's good," Elizabeth says.

She shakes her head, tossing the salad with her hands. "How can you have a date with someone who was sitting on the toilet with the newspaper when you stepped out of the shower?"

They both laugh and Joanne says suddenly, "Do you remember the time I went to the Xavier prom and the guy—Larry —showed up in a top hat and tails? He had a cane and gloves and everything."

"Senior year?"

They both nod.

"Well, you can't have surprises like that when you're married. You see too much of each other." She turns to put the salad into the refrigerator. Unlike when they met in Penn Station, she doesn't seem to be protesting this—merely passing the information on, an old married lady advising the virgin bride.

Elizabeth decides not to bring up the wedding pictures.

"But you're happy?" she says and realizes she has, in a way, brought them up.

Joanne wipes the wet counter and unplugs the processor. "Oh, yeah. Really. Tommy's so great." She rinses the sponge and smiles at Elizabeth over her shoulder. "You like the apartment?"

"Beautiful." She can't possibly say, *Everything matches but Tommy.*

Joanne leans against the counter, drink in hand. Tucks the

other under her arm. She is braless and her plaid shirt is thin. There's a deep shadow where the buttons open at her throat. Even without a bra, Elizabeth thinks, admiring the achievement, she has cleavage. Her denim skirt is straight and perhaps a little too large. "I'm not happy with this room," she says. "I may repaper it. Use brighter colors. Although I'm kind of stuck with avocado green."

Elizabeth looks around the crowded kitchen. The appliances are avocado, the food processor, the tea kettle, the electric can opener, the coffee maker, the blender behind the bottles of vodka and gin. Also the pinstripe in the ruffled curtains they'd picked out together in Macy's, the clock, the juice squeezer, the popcorn maker, the canisters for sugar and flour and tea. Even the handles on her utensils and the labels on the spice jars.

She laughs. "Well, you asked for it." At the engagement party, the shower, the wedding, on the bridal registry in Bloomingdale's where the long list of kitchen items that could be bought for the bride was headed: avocado green.

Joanne shrugs. "And the bathroom is all wrong. It was Tommy's idea to use the kiddie wallpaper. It doesn't work."

"Oh, I like it. It's cute."

She shakes her head, takes a long drink. "It's too cute," she says. She slips her hand into a green mit and pulls open the oven door. Elizabeth can feel the warm gust of air, smell the oregano. "We're just having lasagne," Joanne says. "I hope it's all right."

"Fine."

She closes the door. "I didn't know what to make." She leans back, throws the glove on the table. She seems distracted. "Are you hungry?"

"Just a little."

"Good. I'm not hungry at all. Let's get drunk. We never get drunk together anymore."

They laugh and touch glasses, both remembering all those nights they spent in bars together, meeting boys, all those nights Joanne would stay at Elizabeth's apartment in Flushing (her father calling three and four times a night and once showing up at the door at six A.M. just to make sure she was really there), the two of them lying side by side on the double bed, drinking wine and telling each other stories, love stories, war stories, fish stories, about boys.

"You remember Mark Leibowitz?" Joanne asks.

"The Mark you dated?"

She nods. "He called me. Or called my mother. He's getting a divorce."

"Why'd he want to talk to you?"

"To go out. He didn't know I was married." She picks up a stray piece of carrot and pops it into her mouth. "And know what my mother said?"

Elizabeth shakes her head.

"She said, 'She married a lawyer. He's not Italian, but at least he's a Catholic. I guess you never heard of a Catholic lawyer.'"

"You're kidding!"

She rolls her brown eyes, flutters her hands. "My mother? That surprises you? I'm surprised she didn't say worse." She takes Elizabeth's glass and makes them both another drink, the smell of lime suddenly overpowering the lasagne. "So, anyway," plopping ice into each glass, "I've been trying to call him. To apologize. He hasn't been home."

She hands Elizabeth her drink. "Maybe I'll have lunch with him or something. I'd like to see him again."

Mark had been the love of Joanne's life when Elizabeth was in Buffalo. She never met him, but somehow the possibility of Joanne seeing him again disturbs her. She had considered him long gone. Like Bill.

"What about Tommy?"

Joanne laughs. "He knows I've had other gentlemen callers—" She picks up the accent, " 'Why, sometimes there weren't enough chairs to accommodate them all.' " Drops it. "And besides, if I have lunch with him in the city, Tommy will never have to know."

Elizabeth frowns, but before she can say anything, Joanne takes a quick step forward, touches her arm. "Oh, I'm only kidding. I wouldn't sneak out on Tommy." She looks at her glass. "He's my husband, not my father."

Elizabeth smiles, wondering whose side she's on anyway. "It would probably be fun to see Mark again," she says. "Is he a doctor now?"

Joanne looks up, brightening. "I guess so. I'd love to know what happened to his wife. They were only married about a year." She shrugs. "I'm just curious about him. That's all. Don't you ever wonder about Bill?"

Their nights together in her Flushing apartment had ended when Elizabeth met Bill. Better to share your bed with.

"You mean, do I wonder who's kissing him now?"

She laughs. "Something like that."

Elizabeth nods and then closes her eyes, nonchalantly, like Mr. Owens. "I wonder. You can't help but wonder, really. After you've lived with someone."

All that's happened to him since she left has carved a hollow space into everything that has happened to her.

Joanne purses her lips. "Or even just been in love with someone," she says lightly. They both sip their drinks.

In the living room, there is a sudden dull thud and they hear Tommy shout, "No, I insist. Literature is secondary." Tupper's voice follows it, lower, calmer.

The two women glance at each other. Slowly, they smile.

"Honey," Joanne says in her Amanda Wingfield voice. "A little education is a dangerous thing in a man."

"I feel I haven't seen you all evening," Tupper says as they drive home.

She has her head back, her eyes closed against the lights.

"You and Joanne must have spent half the night in the kitchen. That surprised me. I didn't think you were like that."

Like some lugubrious tradition, his book says. "Like what?"

"Segregationists."

Like some lugubrious tradition, she thinks. Not the waving good-by at thin air that he wrote about, but the hiding, the need to be away from them. The long, sad tradition of two women huddled in a kitchen, whispering about their life behind their life with a man.

"We wanted to talk," she says.

"Well, it must have been about us and it must have been nasty if you had to be so secretive."

She has not raised her head. He and Tommy are now us. Versus them. "We weren't being secretive. We were just being polite. It was a lot of gossip you two wouldn't have been interested in."

Some lugubrious tradition. Shall we retire to the drawing room and let the men smoke their cigars? Shall we go up to bed while the men finish their whiskey? Shall we knit together as they plan their war? Shall we drink our coffee in my kitchen while they work, golf, hunt?

She smiles. He's right to be suspicious. Only a very blind despot would fail to notice how his subjects gather when his back is turned. Only a very stupid one would fail to fear some whispered revolution.

She lifts her head and opens her eyes. Tupper's face is pale blue. The lights seem to crack over his forehead, sink down his cheeks, break over his forehead again. He seems young and pale, and it occurs to her that he is a long way from home, on unfamiliar ground. That he is, except for her, alone.

She reaches over and pats his warm thigh. Was it Lenin who said a revolutionary must be without pity?

"I guess you didn't have a very good time."

He smiles at her. "No, it was fine. I just wish I'd seen more of you."

She slides her hand up between his legs. He is soft, warm. And just what whispered female revolution is she thinking of anyway? She herself decided tonight, in the warm glow of wine and candlelight and Joanne's beautiful china, in the soft pink living room, in the moment when, leaving the apartment, she turned to wave good-by again and saw Joanne wrap her arms around Tommy's neck, saw Tommy move his chin against her hair, that she still wanted it, still believed in it: marriage, eternal love. The silverware I'll pass on to my favorite grand-daughter, the dear first apartment we'll remember all our lives, the sweet solid sound of *husband:* This is my husband.

Given that, her own decision, what whispered female revolution is she thinking of?

She clicks her tongue, laughs to herself. A little feminism is a dangerous thing.

He shifts slightly in his seat and she removes her hand. She wonders if Tommy and Joanne are making love. She imagines Tommy would be very gentle, nearly polite.

"I guess I'll never feel I see enough of you," Tupper says.

"Well, you can see all you want of me when we get home. No holes barred."

He laughs, eyes on the road. "That's vulgar!"

She smiles. A little feminism, she thinks, merely makes you suspicious. Makes you kick at all those pretty pink rocks of romanticism, exposing their wormy undersides, but doesn't make you lift them up and toss them out completely. Doesn't keep you from pity and hope and seeing his side of it. From those old longings for husband, beloved husband buried forever at your side.

She looks out the cool window. Through the dark trees that line the highway she can see the yellow lights of dens and living rooms and bedrooms, each with a blue television light within it like the heart of a flame, or the iris of a jaundiced eye.

She tries to think of feminism again, whispering in kitchens, kicking at rocks, but it all flicks away, comes to her in parts, as if someone were spinning the dial, finding nothing to watch.

She read somewhere that children raised on television have problems with attention spans. And job satisfaction.

She leans back against the door, facing him. "I'm drunk."

He glances at her. "Good. I want to ask you something."

She places a hand on the dashboard, elbow straight. "Shoot."

He moves his head to see her, faces front again. "Let's go away together. Next weekend. Just the two of us. I'll rent the car again and we can just take off."

"Where to?"

"I don't know. Maybe out on Long Island, where your father was from. You said it's pretty."

She studies his profile, but the passing lights are like a strobe. He could be smiling, frowning, or alternately doing both.

"Why?"

He faces her briefly. "I want to have you to myself. I want to get out of the city. You said you liked it out there."

She smiles. They will go to the land of her father and there she will discover her birthright. Her white roots.

"And you talked to me today," he says. "I won't deny it. I want you to talk to me more. I want you to tell me everything you know."

"For your book?"

"For us, too. For you."

They will go to the land of her father and there they will be bound forever by the discoveries she makes. Bound hand and foot. Bound to be disappointed.

"I doubt that we'll dig up any artifacts," she says.

He reaches out to touch her. "We'll be alone. We'll create our own artifacts."

And what if, out there, just a hundred miles from where he spent his life with her and her mother, there is a family by the same name in a small house, also waiting for the father/husband to return, waiting these many years. In the house she'd said he sold for a song.

"All right," she says. "We'll go if you like." And what would the wife, or even the daughter, have to tell her, whispering in the kitchen about the father/husband so long and so far away? Your mother has worried, has theories. What life behind the life in the stories she told?

At dinner, Joanne had said, "Do you know the one about the Italian weatherman predicting fog—a biga mist." It is not, in this age and time, a word to be taken seriously.

Any family by the same name would, she is sure, merely be a descendant of the Irishman who bought her father's list.

But later, as they reach the city, where the small orange lights of buildings and streets make the sky above it rosy, make the darkness beyond it starless, impossible to imagine, she asks him, casually, "Do you know the play *The Glass Menagerie?*"

"Of course," he answers. "Tennessee Williams." And then adds, "The father was a telephone man who fell in love with long distances."

He looks at her, significantly, and she nods, accepting it. She cannot deny that it is the stuff of great literature.

XVII

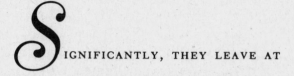

Significantly, they leave at dawn.

The city seems drained at this hour, and the sickly bit of orange-pink rising just over Queens only adds to its pallor, a misleading trace of color on a clearly doomed face. A bit of false hope. A bruise, not a blush.

The red car, which Tupper Daniels picked up last night, is still where he parked it, its silver bumpers locked coldly between two others, a wet brown leaf plastered to its windshield like a violent drop of blood.

She rubs her arms as she watches him skip around the car and let himself in on the other side. The street is empty, eerie, somehow too wide and too close, or just too much a city street at dawn, too set with large but perfect details—a fire hydrant, a row of brown stoops, a grouping of black garbage cans—to be real.

"All set?" he asks, turning on the ignition.

She nods.

Only coffee shops and delis are open on the avenue, and even these seem uninhabited. A man in a white shirt and apron stands in one window, looking out over two upright tins of pale muffins, waiting. A paneled delivery truck turns a corner and stops, a man in gray hops out, his breath visible, his footsteps silent. Two bent and ragged bums solemnly shake hands at a corner, a dawn farewell.

Tupper has had the people at Hertz draw a red line across his map, tracing the route from Manhattan to the end of the Island, and so this time he asks her no questions as they cross the Queensborough Bridge, the steel girders and, on the other side, the shadow of the el blocking from moment to moment what light there is. He only hums, smiling to himself. She sits quietly with her hands in her lap, like a pregnant woman being driven to the delivery room.

It is, without a doubt, the beginning of a trip. Up before everyone else, moving swiftly. Everything behind and on either side falling away, while whatever is ahead, whatever destination, remains round and hollow and as ready to be filled as a ringing silver bowl. It's a kind of suspension, she thinks, this traveling, stepping in at one place and out at another.

"Sleepy?" he says, his voice soft and faraway.

"No. Just thinking."

And her father traveled. Left again and again. Sailed off the edge of the earth, stepped into the clouds, passed through the looking-glass. Arrived again at the home of a family just like the one he'd left. Arrived, perhaps, to wake in yet another woman's bed, to receive yet another celebration from another family for another homecoming. Arrived to repeat himself over and over, all the same gestures, the long kiss for the mother, the lift and twirl for the child, the loosening of the tie, the kicking off of the shoes. The sinking into the couch with his arms spread out across its back, a huge embrace for all he sees, repeated again and again from one trip to another, so that the past becomes the future and the present and the past again, all indistinguishable, concurrent, never-ending. She remembers there being so much noise in the house when he came home, as if she and her mother had waited for him in silence, in a kind of suspension.

"Thinking what?" Tupper says.

She opens her eyes. Already the sun has cleared the highway and most of the trees. Briefly, as they pass, she can see it fully —made small and round and moonlike by the haze.

"Just thinking." It's become their game. He will ask her to elaborate.

"About our trip?"

"About our trip." The strangeness of the morning makes her daring. "About the dawn. About my father."

He merely says, "Yes."

Soon, pockets of suburbia go by. Trees growing bare. A reservoir, that at first she mistakes for a lake, mist rising from it.

"Should we stop somewhere for breakfast?"

She shakes her head. She realizes she is hungry but is not sure she could eat anything. Or, if she were to eat, taste anything. Perhaps it is the hour, or this odd anticipation she feels, but, whatever the reason, she imagines that anything she eats will have the plain, papery taste of a communion wafer. She recalls the stories the nuns used to tell of Crusaders going into battle after having knelt before the altar all night. Holy Communion their only breakfast, victory or heaven assured.

It had always seemed to her an exquisite gesture.

"Let's not stop," she says. "Let's keep going until we get there." She pulls down the visor as the sun begins to shine in her eyes.

"When we get there," he says, after they have driven a while in silence, "can we see the house where your father lived? Do you know where it is?"

She shrugs. "No. I've never seen it. He sold it before I was born." *B.E.* "He sold it for a song," she adds, trying to make him sound cavalier.

Tupper looks at her. He is wearing a loose fisherman's sweater, a turtleneck that makes him hold his chin high. "We could probably find it if we looked, did a little research. Wouldn't you like to see it?"

"Sure, if you want to." She has a picture of it in her mind. Small, two stories and a slanting roof. Weathered shingles. A long porch across the front, its roof supported by white wooden beams. A smell like old pine, like an attic, like her father's closet at home that was filled with gray suits and silk ties and white cotton shirts that were starched and pressed so carefully, their creased arms seemed paper-thin, slightly bent at the elbows. A closet filled with more clothes than a traveling man should leave behind.

"Do you know the uncle's last name?"

"Neilson." She tries to remember. "Nevelson. Nelson. I don't know, something like that."

He glances at her, smiling a little. "It would help if we knew for sure."

She folds her arms before her. "My father always referred to them as his aunt and uncle." Points of his own personal history, not hers. His past, which could have been another life. Which should have been her inheritance.

Tupper sighs. "What else do you know about him?"

"He was a Dutchman. A fire-and-brimstone Dutchman, my father said. And he married very late in life. And he had a farm."

"And there was something about your father," Tupper adds, slowly, staring ahead, "that appealed to him so much, he left him everything he had."

"Yes," she says, watching him. "Even though my father had lived there only about a year." There was something about her father, some intrigue, some charm, some story to tell her grandchildren: He was no ordinary man.

Tupper looks at her, says, "It's interesting," as if he is developing a theory. He takes her hand. "I'm glad we decided to make this trip."

"Yes," she says.

They drive silently. The houses that line the highway have gradually disappeared. First there was one house after the other, then large clumps of houses interspersed with small, then only one or two, and now just the occasional, irregular home or shopping center or farmhouse and roadside stand. The trees along the road have grown sparse, the fields appear more frequently, the Island seems to be flattening out before them, shaking itself of the city and the suburbs and the last fifty years, becoming more of what it was when her father lived here.

Of course she has been out this way before, years ago, in high school and college, on those summer weekends when she and her friends would take off from their jobs as salesgirls and waitresses and nurse's aids and head for the Hamptons, but she is not sure that she ever thought of her father then. Thought that this, perhaps, was the road he took that first day with his uncle or this the town where he lived those first ten years, or this the road he took back again, into the city, riding this time with Jerry Case and the other sons of the wealthy summer people whom he had also somehow charmed, somehow befriended (riding in drunkenly, impulsively, like Gatsby and Nick and Jordan and Daisy and Tom), on his way to meet, for the first time, her mother.

She has no recollection that she ever thought these things, or, if she did think of them, the recollection has been obscured by her own, primary memories of those weekends: the crowded motel rooms or cottages littered with nightgowns and beer bottles and electric curlers, with opened bags of potato chips and popcorn and a dozen damp pieces of bathing suits that hung from shower curtains and curtain rods and chair backs and faucets like bright, broken balloons. The drunken rush for the shower when she and her girlfriends came home from a day on the beach and a four-to-seven happy hour; the various formulas for getting a second wind (ice on the face, a brisk walk, a Pepsi, a nap, a joint), and then, all of them sunburned and shampooed, piling into cars and heading into town again, where the boys would be standing on tables in bars and shouting in hoarse voices, spilling beers and starting fights and pulling down their pants. The waking to find those same boys, or ones just like them, asleep in the living room or in cars outside the door or on the bed or floor or sleeping bag next to her.

Memories that now are without meaning—or, as memories, have no more meaning than they had as events.

And yet, all along, through it all, whatever this place had to tell her about her father had been there. All along, if she had just driven past the bars and the discos and the desperate, nearly crazed struggle to have fun, if she had just gotten alone and driven a little further out onto the Island, she could have found the house where her father once lived. She could have, perhaps, watched it quietly from across the street, from behind a tree or inside a car, until sooner or later the screen door opened and slammed behind a girl much like herself, with her father's gray eyes and sharp nose and dark hair, who would step barefoot from the shaded porch to the grassy lawn, a whittled walking stick in her hand.

She looks at Tupper Daniels. His profile is perfect, without irregularities. It moves perfectly into the collar of his white sweater, his smooth chest, his loose corduroy slacks which are the palest, softest gray. His gray suede bucks. *Gentleman's Quarterly* might call it the casual look for fall, perfect for an autumn weekend in the Hamptons. He has a sense of what's appropriate, she'll have to admit that. He does know how to put things together.

"I *am* glad you talked me into this," she says.

He pats her hand, returns his to the wheel. "I'm glad I did too." And once again, there is in his voice, in the way he moves his mouth and raises his chin, that sense of quiet, subtle sagacity: He knows more than he's telling. Yet now she finds it not threatening, but assuring, exciting. Soon, he will let her in on it.

"I can't wait to get there," she says.

The road ahead is straight and empty and he seems to accelerate as a reply. Clouds have begun to gather over the sun, like dawn coming back, or refusing to leave. She opens her window and smells a cold trace of the sea, and with the gray road beneath them and the flat fields on either side, and the wind blowing in her face, she can almost imagine she has set out upon it.

It's raining by the time they reach the town. It's a light rain, seen more easily in the town pond than on the windshield or in the air, but it gives everything a sodden, somewhat unsubstantial look that she finds appealing. The reds and browns and golds of the trees seem ready to drip from their branches like wet dye.

On Main Street, there are a few shoppers covered in plastic raincoats and umbrellas, but they, and the small shops themselves, seem somehow aware that their season is over and the first of the other three already well begun. They move languidly, almost sadly, like a hostess in her bathrobe emptying ashtrays on Sunday morning.

"I've done a little research already," Tupper says as they pass through town. "There's a motel just down the road somewhere."

"Oh?" she says. She hadn't considered staying at a motel and as it appears before them, pink and blue, white arches over the office and the ice machines, she knows why.

"It's not," she says when he pulls up the drive, "Quite what I'd had in mind."

Without a pause, he pulls out again, onto the road. "What did you have in mind?" he asks patiently, carefully, as if he fears he has made some gross error.

"Something with a little more atmosphere."

He nods, pulling smoothly into a gas station. "Atmosphere," he says, opening his door.

The two men inside the station watch him carefully as he walks toward them through the rain. Inside, his head is obscured by a poster advertising snow tires, but she can see that his arms are straight at his side. The men, who are both sitting at a large desk, one with his feet up, slowly smile. Tupper raises his two arms and one of the men glances out the window to her. The other stretches out his arm and points behind him. The other man points too. Finally, Tupper points in the same direction. The two men laugh heartily and Tupper, smiling, is out the door.

"Not much atmosphere to choose from this time of year," he says when he gets in beside her. "But they said there's a place off the road somewhere. A place with little cottages or something."

The two men are standing at the window as they pull out. They are still smiling. Immediately, he turns off the main road onto one that is narrow and tree-lined, bordered by fallen leaves that have been crushed shiny and dark brown. The houses they pass vary from shingled cottages to sprawling ranches to old Victorian mansions, but mostly, it seems, there are trees and lawns. The air is wet and fragrant, and despite the rain she has her window wide open.

At first glance, she thinks it is merely a name above a mailbox, but as they pass it, it occurs to her.

"Stop!" she says.

"Why?" He slows down.

She turns around. "Back there. Go back."

He stops, puts the car into reverse. "What am I looking for?"

"Stop," she says again. She reads the sign over the white mailbox, dark blue painted on gray: "Overnight Guests." The house, behind a long green lawn and a split-rail fence is a tall, somewhat crooked-looking old home with dark cedar shingles and black shutters. Behind it, there seems to be a barn and a chicken coop and a small white corral.

"Your uncle's house?" he whispers.

She turns to him, smiling. "No, but let's stay here."

He is bending to look at the house through her window, frowning. "Why?"

"It's different, it's unique. Hell, maybe it's even the uncle's house, who knows?" He doesn't stop frowning and she pulls out her editorial voice. "And I don't particularly want to stay someplace recommended by the neighborhood service station."

He looks at her, sighs, straightens up and shifts gears.

The driveway is covered with white gravel that crackles under the slow wheels and sounds to her like every arrival. A dog barks somewhere behind or inside the house and the slamming car doors echo. She sees a reddish-colored horse peering from the back barn.

The front door opens before they have mounted both steps of the small porch.

"Hello," a woman cries warmly, stepping out to meet them. She is tall and freckled and her short red hair stands up straight over her forehead, a cigarette dangles from the corner of her mouth and she squints through the smoke. "Welcome."

"We'd like to see a room," Tupper says, very formally, and the woman says, her voice dry and husky, smoke-filled, "Wonderful."

The house smells of cats, and, Tupper insists, turpentine, but the room is large with dark floral curtains and a thick floral comforter and a working fireplace already stocked with wood, and Elizabeth insists that it's perfect. Their view is to the back, the barn, the corral, a blasted flower garden and then a hill of grass and a line of thick trees, and Mrs. Carpenter—Hedda, she said they must call her—had made them stand silently in the room, their noses in the air, until they all agreed that they could, indeed, hear the sea.

"It's fabulous," Elizabeth says again, standing in the middle of the room, hands on her hips. Hedda has left them to make their decision. "It's like something out of a movie."

"Sure is," Tupper says, examining a large black-and-white sketch that seems to be of two sleeping cats. He turns to her. "And just what you were looking for."

It is something Bill might say, sarcastically, but when she meets his eyes, he is smiling, fondly.

Hedda calls to them from the kitchen as they hit the last step, and they follow her voice down a hallway, past a bathroom and what seems to be a small library. The kitchen is a large room, the entire back width of the house, with a long continuous line of small windows, like those of a railroad car, splitting each of the three outside walls. She is standing by the sink, drying her hands on a checkered dishtowel. Elizabeth had at first put her at forty, but realizes now she could be fifty, or thirty. There seems to be some gray in her dull-red hair, but no lines in her dark, pleasant face. She is slim, and over her jeans she wears a man's long white shirt. It covers what might be any telltale sign of age in her stomach or her breasts or backside.

"It's a wonderful room," Elizabeth tells her. "We'll take it."

She smiles. "Good." As if she had no doubt that they would. "Have some coffee." She points to the cloth-covered wicker basket on the table across the room. "I just took those muffins out of the oven."

They sit at the table, under a small, tin-shaded light, Sears Roebuck Colonial, its bulb burning. Outside, the sky has grown darker, the rain visible. On the window ledge beside them is a Cheshire-like cat with dark ivy growing from his back.

Hedda puts two mugs of coffee before them and pulls out a chair to sit down. "That's strawberry and raspberry," she says, pointing to the fat glass jars of jam. "Homemade. And butter, not margarine." She puts out her cigarette, blowing the last bit of smoke to the ceiling. "I never use margarine," she says and then shrugs, "It's my token attempt at self-destruction."

Elizabeth and Tupper laugh, reaching for the muffins. The three talk for a while about the city and the fall tourist trade and the problems of running a guest house in a town with only one season ("One season that anyone *knows* about," Hedda says. "As if we all disappear when it's over, like in *Brigadoon.* "), and Elizabeth decides that she likes Hedda. There is, she thinks, something strong and clean and wholesome about the woman. Despite the cigarettes, something terribly healthy, terribly attractive. The muffins are warm and the jam is rich and sweet and she can easily imagine that Hedda made both herself, that she mixed the batter with her hands and licked her long fingers as she stirred the jam.

She tells them that she lives here alone, has lived here alone for nearly six years now, since she divorced her "last husband," and gave up her job as an illustrator in New Haven. Although, she confesses, lowering her foggy voice so that the words seem to break on the air or slip, unheard, back into her throat, sometimes, when she has a boarder who seems a little "shady," she pretends there's a man living here. Sometimes she leaves out a pipe or a pair of men's shoes, and once she even closed the kitchen door and had a long conversation with him, talking first in her normal voice and then, "In a deep, mumbly voice like this."

"Sounds like it would be easier for you to just get married again," Tupper says, smiling. He has loosened in her presence, appears even to be enjoying himself.

Hedda shakes her head, looks at him sternly, but fondly, as if he were a favorite son or lover who has spoken out of turn. "No, dear," she says. "Never again. It's been my experience that it's woman's happiest state, not marriage, the single life." She leans closer to him. "It's men who thrive in marriage." She makes *thrive* sound like some kinky coital position and Tupper smiles stupidly, as if he is about to agree to try it.

"What brought you out here?" Elizabeth asks before he does.

Hedda lights another cigarette. "I was on vacation, right after my divorce, at a friend's house in Sag Harbor. I told him I wanted my own place and he took me to a real estate agent who showed me this."

Elizabeth imagines that the friend had something to do with the divorce. Hedda, she thinks, is not the type of woman who is left.

"Do you like it?" Hedda asks.

"Oh, yes," they both say.

She gets up quickly, goes to the stove for more coffee. "I think it's a great house," she says as she pours. "It really should be haunted." She brings the pot back to the stove and sits down again, blowing smoke. "But with my luck, the ghost would be some sea captain like in—what's the movie, *The Ghost and Mrs. Muir*—and after three bad marriages, I'd be stuck with a man in my house again."

They laugh. She is, Elizabeth feels sure, one of those women who must flick men from her, whose life is a series of lush dinners and European vacations and summer houses in Sag Harbor. A series of gifts from men. A never-ending series of various and limitless possibilities, for in every ordinary male she meets she discovers, like a jewel in a box of Cracker Jacks, the offer of love.

One of those women who will claim, of course, that looking back, she would have preferred one normal husband and a quiet life.

"Do you know anyone around here named Nelson?" Tupper asks suddenly. "Or Neilson, Nevelson, something like that?"

She takes a long drag from her cigarette, lets the smoke out through her nose. Slowly, she shakes her head. "I can't think of any. Are they friends of yours?"

Tupper smiles. "No. Elizabeth had an uncle who used to live here, and her father grew up here. We were just curious about where his house might have been."

Hedda turns to Elizabeth, sympathetically, she thinks. "Is your uncle dead?"

She nods, she's never thought of him as *her* uncle. "A long time ago."

"Check the library," Hedda says. "Or the newspaper office. One of them has all the town's obituaries on file. You might get an address from that."

"Great idea!" Tupper says, and, to Elizabeth, "Want to try it?"

She smiles, finishing her coffee. "If you like." Although she'd prefer to stay here, get the details of Hedda's three marriages, her single life, her discovery that only men thrive.

Tupper gets up, thanks Hedda, offers to pull the car around front so Elizabeth won't get too wet. When he's gone, Hedda turns to her and smiles, but with a funny, rounded, almost frightened shape about her mouth.

"You're not looking for your father, are you?" she asks.

Elizabeth's own mouth seems to fill with salt water. "Pardon?" she says, politely. The politeness taking over like a cartoon ghost rising up from the prone, unconscious body.

Hedda puts her elbow into her hand, holds the cigarette near her ear. Shakes her head to dismiss the question. "My daughter," she explains, "she's about your age, went on a kick last year about finding her father. My first husband. We were divorced when she was two and he took off for God knows where and never bothered to see her again. It never seemed to matter to her when she was growing up—my second husband adopted her and the third couldn't do enough for her—but all of a sudden, she wanted to see him. I don't know if it was the whole Alex Haley bit, or because someone on one of the soaps, *Days of Our Lives* I think it was, was doing the same thing, or maybe because she started thinking about having children of her own. But, whatever it was she started calling up relatives and visiting strange towns, libraries and newspaper offices, checking obits, because I told her that as far as I knew he could be dead." She stamps out her cigarette. Elizabeth hears the car pulling around the drive.

"Did she find him?" she asks.

Hedda throws her head back over her shoulder, as if to indicate that he's in the living room. "Oh yes. Right here on Long Island. Well, actually in Bayside. They had lunch together and she met his family, but all she told me about it was that he had an awful Queens accent and a son with the thickest neck she'd ever seen. She said she was sorry she wasted so much time. They had nothing to say to each other." She looks at her nails. "Of course, part of it might have been my fault," she adds. "I probably made him sound a lot better than he was, over the years." She smiles, to herself. "How do you tell someone about some poor man you once loved desperately without lying about him a little?" She laughs. "At least in *Days of Our Lives* the girl discovered that her father was in prison on a murder charge. Katie was a little disappointed in comparison."

She looks at Elizabeth, smiling. Her eyes are dark brown and terribly bright; sharp, as if a thousand fascinating memories and thoughts milled around behind them, catching light like cymbals and sequins and small bits of glass. "That's why I asked," she says. "When your friend mentioned your uncle." She sighs, an apology. "It does seem to be the latest fad."

A man at the newspaper office sends them to the library, and the librarian sits them before a TV screen with a dozen reels of microfilm. Both seem slightly amused by their requests, as if Hedda's daughter, or someone like her, had been in with the same questions just a day or two before—as if they'd been having a run on obituaries—and their amusement, as well as their serious willingness to help, only increases her sense of bulky foolishness. Surely she is too big to be playing Nancy Drew to Tupper Daniels' Hardy Boy.

They find a Nelson who died in childbirth and a Neilson who drowned in 1935, at age 27, and a Nicholson survived by twelve children, and read fifty other stories of the dead before she sits up, shaking herself as if from some absorbing bad habit and declares that she has had enough.

"This strikes me," she tells him, whispering, slipping into her jacket as he sits blinking at her, the greenish light from the screen still on his face, "as a particularly morbid way of spending a weekend."

He laughs, and, returning the reels to the librarian, follows her out into the rain.

They have lunch at a small bar with hanging plants and Tiffany lampshades—a reproduction of every bar on the Upper East Side—and then he drives her slowly through town, up and down past the huge summer homes of the wealthy and the small, inhabited homes of the year-round people, suggesting that she might, just might, see something she had forgotten or been unaware she ever knew, that would identify the house where her father lived.

She looks carefully, but sees nothing: her inheritance.

Later, they park at the ocean, where the rain and fog obscure the sea and most of the sand, and Tupper Daniels talks about immortality, one hand on the wheel, the other on the seat beside him.

He says it is all wrapped up in his writing, it is why he writes and what he writes about. It is, he says, the only thing that anyone ever really strives for and as far as he is concerned, the only thing worth achieving: The certain knowledge that when I die, all does not die with me.

She watches him while he speaks. Watches the dunes that line the beach behind him, and which are only slightly more substantial than the fog. At first she wonders what he's talking about. Hadn't he, after all, sat beside her as one page after the other of names of the dead was pulled up before them? Hadn't he heard the monotonous hum of the screen that lit, one after the other, that monotonous list of ordinary deaths, as if it were some final rolling of the credits for some long-forgotten variety show? How then could he talk about immortality?

But slowly she realizes he's referring to his book—or maybe all books, she can't tell—and the realization comes to her sadly; fills her not with a profound, but a helpless, loving kind of pity, as if he were a child insisting that a pet, long dead, had only run away, would be back any morning barking and wagging his tail.

He says: "To me art, especially literature, alone is immortal. Nothing else lasts. Even science can become outdated and obsolete; even political and social achievements. Even love. To me," he says, "to stop writing would not only be to admit defeat, it would be to admit death. To say there is no hope for immortality."

He looks at her. The fog seems to press at the windows, even the sand has given way beneath it.

"That's why I'd hoped," he says, "that out here you'd see something, or, I don't know, regain something of your father. Something that I could put in my book. I'd hoped, for you, to give him some of that immortality." He leans closer to her. "It's really the only gift I have to give someone I love." His pale face moves closer; with his hand on her neck, he presses her toward him. "I love you, Elizabeth," he says.

And she answers, mouth to mouth, both to keep him from kissing her and to send the moment from sentiment or farce into reality, to turn off the fog machines, to clear the air so that the words might have a chance at true meaning, a chance to change everything. "You realize Vista is a vanity press."

"Yes," he says, smiling just a little and then kissing her

anyway, deeply. Crushing the stick shift between them. His hand very lightly brushes her breast, and then he pulls away, still smiling.

"Vista is a vanity press," he says. Slowly, he begins to unbutton her jacket. "And vanity presses—of which Vista is only one —are not taken seriously by the rest of the publishing world, right?" He looks up at her, raising his eyebrows. She feels ill.

"Except for 1976," he goes on, "when the president of a very large, very American organization published a bicentennial book with Vista and made it required reading for his many members, employees and associates, Vista has never had a best seller, right? In fact, Vista books don't even get reviewed. Right?"

He pushes her jacket aside, begins working on the buttons of her blouse, slowly. "Yes," she says. With the fog and the sand, the car's white interior and his sweater, his hair and face, the blue eyes seem to be the only spot of color in the universe. And they are on her.

He stops, sits up. Her blouse is opened to just above her breasts. "You must know I looked into all this—long before I came to New York."

"Well," she says, coolly, "I'd presumed . . ." But she can muster no authority, or indifference.

He shakes his head, the smile getting slightly angry, battling with insult. "I do know what I'm doing by publishing with Vista," he says. His fingers return to her blouse. He suddenly reminds her of a gynecologist, making conversation as he works.

"To write a good novel is one thing," he explains. "You get a few nice reviews, your books hang out on the racks for a while, and that's that." He pulls her shirt up out of her jeans, unbuttons the last two buttons. "But to change the course of one certain publisher. To be the first best seller of a house that's known as a joke, to make publishing history, *that's* news. That's lasting notoriety."

He parts her shirt as if it were a delicate curtain, and, sighing a little, moves his fingers over her chest.

"Vista doesn't sell any books because it doesn't advertise or distribute, not enough anyway. My father has controlling interest in a very large ad firm that will handle my account once the book is published and he's willing to put his own money into it. We're going to hit TV mostly, and the women's magazines."

He leans forward, pulling her close, and slowly runs his tongue between her breasts. "I'm going to do my own distributing, too," he says into her throat. "Make sure the book is available everywhere." He kisses her chin and then pushes her shirt and jacket from both her shoulders. Kisses them. "After that," he says to her collarbone, "it will start selling itself." He places his open mouth over her left nipple, breathes softly through his nose. Reflexively, she puts her hand to his hair. She remembers seeing an article somewhere about a man who printed his own book, loaded his car with thousands of copies and drove cross-country, promoting it. After three or four trips, the book became a best seller. Was it possible?

She is about to ask when he suddenly pulls away from her, quickly opens his door, gets out, slams it behind him. She watches him walk around the car. Her blouse is still open, her breast still wet from his mouth, and she believes for a moment that he is leaving her for good. But then she sees the trunk open and sees him standing behind it, a green blanket in his hand, when it slams closed. He opens her door and, taking her wrist, pulls her out. With one hand, she holds her blouse and jacket around her, off her shoulders like a stole.

"But it's raining," she says, not sure it is rain or just a mist from the sea, or the fog. He takes her down the beach, up into some small dunes. Lays the blanket down between them. Grinning, he unbuckles his belt, slips off his shoes, then his pants. His penis springs out with a quick rigidity that lacks only a *boing*.

She begins to laugh. Sitting on the damp blanket, she laughs quietly, her shirt and jacket still wrapped loosely around her, dipping down her back, gathered at her elbows, like a blanket worn by the survivor of a shipwreck. She laughs, shivering a little as the rain hits her skin. He sits beside her, sweater and socks still on, smiling at her over his raised knees.

"What's so funny?" he asks, taking her shoulder, pulling her back. "Hmmm? What's so funny?" She lies back on the blanket, he leans over her. "What's so funny?" She knows he doesn't ask the question to be answered, but only to make some noise at her, the way one might speak full sentences to a newborn and so she says nothing, merely puts her hands to her sides, letting her jacket and shirt once again fall away. He puts his mouth to her breast as if to pick up where he left off. She puts her hand to his hair.

Above them, the sky is low, gray, limitless. It doesn't relent at some horizon or bank of clouds, but instead moves down around them, becomes what's before and behind them, becomes the ground where they lie. Even Tupper's head on her breast is vague, the breast itself the color of sky.

She would be a fool, she decides, to look for a dead father in this fog, when a lover, his heart beating against hers, so easily floats away. She would be a fool to think, pressed under such a sky, of future or past or a present that endures.

And yet, when he moves up over her, his hair already caked with salt, brushing her lips, she whispers, "I love you too," closing her eyes slowly, as in a fadeout. She imagines a young boy, dancing on some invisible dune above them, claiming it goes on and on and on.

"You, I hadn't counted on," he tells her over dinner. "The book is for women and I wanted a woman editor—that's why I came to Vista, not the other vanities, since all their editors are men, but I never thought you'd be *you!* I knew I needed a woman's sense of how it should end, but God, when you mentioned your father, it seemed too good to be true. I sensed you were skeptical, but I was positive, even though you weren't, that you had my ending somewhere within you."

She smiles. "Kind of like a diaphragm."

He smiles too, cracking open a lobster claw. "I like to think of it as a fetus," he says. "And I planted the seed."

She grimaces, gripping her stomach, and then pours him more wine. "But you still haven't got it," she says. "How can you pull off this great miracle of publishing with a book that has no ending?"

"It'll have one," he says. "And I just know we'll find it here. This weekend."

"We've only got tomorrow."

"And tonight."

She concedes, as if it were simply a matter of time.

The restaurant, a small, many-windowed place full of candle-light, is nearly empty, but the few patrons are elegant and handsome. She notices one couple in particular, a broad, high-colored man with an ascot and pure white hair brushed back and worn long, and a thin, dark woman dressed in black and silver. The waiters move silently, in and out, and the talk is low, only a murmur, but full of importance.

Tupper is wearing his blue blazer, a white shirt and khaki pants, and what looks like an old school tie. His hair is neatly combed. Anyone could mistake him for an ivy league author. A young man with talent and bright prospects.

And she, in her simple wool dress, navy trimmed with gray, four tasteful buttons at the yoke, she (if only she wore glasses) could be his young editor. Or wife. A literary pair; after all, the Hamptons are famous for them.

(As she was dressing this evening, Tupper was in the kitchen talking to Hedda. She heard him tell her that he was an author

and Elizabeth his editor. That they were actually here to research, not her uncle, but his book. When she came into the
kitchen, Hedda looked at her with what seemed to be new
respect.)

"You said this afternoon that the book would sell itself."

He nods.

"I'm not sure I know what you mean."

"Word of mouth," he says, through food. He bows his head
to swallow. "No, that's not it, really. It's the whole bigamist
thing. And women."

"I still don't see."

He drinks his wine, then presses his lips together, thinking.
"Well, you're the perfect example," he says. "You read the
book and thought of your father. And most women, I think,
will react in the same way. Every woman, or almost everyone,
has a bigamist figure in her life. Usually, it's a lover, but father,
friends, even uncles will do too. For most women, it's the man
who got away, the one they couldn't quite put a finger on.
Maybe their first love at camp, or a teacher in college, or the
boy who lived next door who never noticed them. Every
woman I've ever met seems to have some man who touched
her emotionally and then went away. My book is about that
man."

"But how does it sell itself?"

He leans forward. There's a confidence in his manner and
his speech that she's never seen before: he has it all worked out.
"What the book will provide, for all those women, is an excuse;
a reason, an imagined reason, but a reason still, why that man
disappeared. It will absolve them, show them that their love for
him was noble and his leaving nothing personal. He leaves
everyone sooner or later. And, at the same time, it will offer
them a hope of his return. A hope, I think, that every woman
harbors for some man."

She thinks of Bill and suddenly he holds up his hand. "I

know what you're going to ask, 'Don't some men harbor the same sort of hope for some women?' "

"Yes," she says, as if he had indeed read her mind.

He sighs. "I suppose they do, but for men it's just not that important. If a man fails to connect with a certain woman, he just goes on to someone else. But women—and I'm not condoning this, I'm just talking about the way things are—women derive so much more of themselves, their identity, their self-confidence from men. They just can't forget a man who left them because they always take it to heart. They take it personally. But my book will help them place those men in the proper perspective. Help them to retain their dignity. And the dignity of their emotions."

The heavyset man with the long white hair is having trouble with his bill. He shows some item to the waiter, raising his voice, and the waiter, shaking his head, snaps the check from the man's fingers. His companion covers her eyes with her hand, apparently unconvinced of the dignity of her emotions.

"And besides," Tupper is saying, "you've got to appeal to women these days. They buy more books, they're more imaginative. They need more reassurance."

"So women will buy it like one of those self-help books?"

He laughs, softly. "I guess I am making it all sound too clinical. The truth is I believe in this book. It's a good book and it's about a man all women—for whatever reason—will be intrigued by." He smiles slyly. "You were intrigued, weren't you?"

She lowers her head, wishes she had read it all. For it could be true, it could be a good book. There was that article about a man who printed his own book, made it a best-seller. It's possible. "Yes," she says. "I guess I was."

He reaches across the table and takes her hand. "And as soon as we discover my ending and get the book out, you'll see you were right. You'll become the editor who turned vanity publishing on its ear."

The woman in black and silver sweeps past them, sparkling, sprinkling her perfume over their table like fairy dust.

"I hadn't thought of that," she says, smiling. Lying.

He winks at her, Tracy to Hepburn. "Think of it," he says.

XVIII

A DULL LAMP GLOWS IN HEDDA'S living room and a tiny nightlight illuminates the narrow floor of the hallway upstairs. There is a bottle of brandy, its seal unbroken, and two large snifters on the dresser in their room. A note in flat, long, somewhat Oriental print that says: Help yourself to a nightcap and a fire. See you in the morning—H.C.

Elizabeth and Tupper smile at each other silently, knowing there's no need to say how perfect it all is. When she comes back from the bathroom in her long flannel robe, he has lit the fire and placed the two glasses on the floor beside him. They sparkle in the firelight. The rest of the room is as dark as a cave.

She sits beside him and immediately, a little awkwardly, they lean together, as if someone were about to take their picture. As if, after today, they feel it is important to keep in touch. Then Tupper stretches out his legs and leans down on his elbow. She draws her knees close to her, feeling the fire on her hands.

"Talk to me," he whispers.

"About my father?"

He shrugs. "About all the men in your life. Everyone before me."

She puts her chin on her knees. The fire is just beginning to catch. Thin flames reach up and around the logs, tremble and retreat. Flare up again. There is, she knows, a book in the making here. Anything she says may be used, may be made immortal. He will know her worth by the ending he finds within her.

She begins with the Beatles.

But he turns his head to look up at her as she speaks and before she's even gotten to "A Hard Day's Night," he begins to laugh.

"Be serious," he says.

"I am being serious," she tells him, although her voice is coy and her lips form a make-believe pout. "It was important. It was training."

He shakes his head. "It was adolescence. It doesn't mean a thing." He puts his hand on her leg. "Please," he says. "I asked you seriously. Be serious."

She smiles at him. It occurs to her that although women are held responsible for what they have done to males through infancy and childhood, men will take no blame for anything they've made women feel before twenty-five. They will claim women's silliness is inherent, not learned.

But that's not what he wants to hear; certainly not what she'd planned to say.

She tells him she met her first lover at a peace rally.

Again he turns to look at her. "Were you active?" This like an embarrassed intern checking on last night's bowel movement.

When she says, "Not really," he seems relieved. "Neither was I," he says. "We did take over the cafeteria at Andover once, but I was a bit too young for most of it."

"Wasn't everyone?"

He shakes his head, staring beyond her. "Christ, it was a *vital* time. There's been nothing like it since."

She smiles at him, feeling thwarted.

"It was really a Renaissance of sorts."

She nods.

"I often wish I'd been old enough to participate, either in the protests or the war itself." He sips his brandy. "Nearly every great writer has had some war experience to draw upon." He sounds wistful. She feels forsaken. "I've even thought of basing my next novel on my father's experience in World War II. He was in Navy Intelligence. He's got great stories. But I'm afraid that research will never replace actual experience. Not when you're dealing with war."

She nods again, sipping her brandy which burns her tongue and nose and settles like hot iron on her stomach. A nightcap before a blazing fire had sounded so appropriate she'd forgotten that she usually avoids brandy.

Tupper lowers his voice. "But you were saying?"

She looks at him, a little startled. She suddenly wonders if her own stories can compete with the shot and shell and bombs bursting in air of his next novel. "I was saying." She pauses, mysteriously, she hopes, and looks down at the shadow of flame on the floor between them. Already she has made two false starts; what she tells him now must hold him, must have meaning and significance and whatever it takes to compete with Navy Intelligence. Must make her, indisputably, part of it, the bright young editor. He will know her worth by the ending he finds within her.

"I was saying that maybe my father wasn't the only bigamist figure in my life." Her voice is a whisper and she pauses again to discover just what she'll say next. She looks into the fire, feels it on her face. "I suppose my first real lover, the man I lived with for a while, could be called a bigamist figure too."

She feels him watching her but he says nothing and she continues to watch the flames. "He was tall," she whispers, trying to begin. "And good-looking, extremely good-looking. The kind of good-looking that makes other men shy . . ." She feels herself approaching the subject as if it were a long-imagined reality finally seen. The way a soldier in a movie, returning home, might approach his own front door. Walking slowly at first, breaking into a run. "He was arrogant too. And charming."

He charmed her, she tells him, the first night she saw him, in a bar outside Rochester, her senior year at college. He was with another woman, a beautiful woman, and even in the dark, they seemed to glisten—both of them—as if they'd just stepped out of a sauna or had spent the afternoon rubbing each other with baby oil.

She had long, strawberry-blond hair and very fair skin. He was darker, with thick hair and light eyes. They were both very tall. She always carried a red rose, twirled it between her fingers, dipped it into her beer, brushed it against her lips, his lips. They always stood in the same place, leaning against a wooden post between two booths, whispering to each other in a way that made her feel that whatever they had to say was inconsequential, only an excuse to put an open mouth to the other's skin.

"They were there every Friday night for nearly two months, and every Friday night I was there too—watching them."

The first time she saw them part, she says, it almost surprised her. They seemed so joined, she almost expected even their physical separation to be somehow incomplete, like a photograph that can't be split fully in two because the man's hand will appear bodiless on the woman's shoulder or her arm will remain wrapped in his, and the first night they failed to return she felt a sad, hopeless kind of disappointment, as on a clear night with no moon. She broke up with Jeff, the boy she'd been dating, and slept with no one else all that year. With them in mind, she tells him, she began to see something pathetic, even unworthy, in all other pairings.

"Strange," he whispers, but she shakes her head.

He had charmed her. Charmed her so that all other men

were diminished in her eyes, so that she moved through those months she didn't see him as if in an aura of light, unable to see anyone clearly, but vaguely aware of a certain, peripheral beauty, the certain knowledge that soon she would see him again.

"I'd never felt anything like it before or since," she says, and, effectively, her voice drops, almost with fear. She feels that slow, lovely, even sexual stirring of final revelation, unveiling. "After I graduated, my mother moved to Maine and I moved to the apartment in Flushing. I found a job with a paper company on Park Avenue. My official title was Gal Friday, but I comforted myself with the fact that paper was the staple of publishing which, along with social work, advertising and professional fund-raising, was something I'd said, in college, that I'd like to get into. I'd been there about a month when I saw him again."

He was sitting on a short, concrete wall outside an office building on Madison Avenue. He was leaning back, his elbows propped on the concrete planter behind him, and he was watching the people walking by so intently, she felt sure he was waiting for his girlfriend. Although she'd already had her lunch, she went into a coffee shop across the street and took a seat at the counter, where she could watch him through the window and the traffic. He was wearing a beige suit, his tie was pulled down, his collar opened. Because of his thick mustache, he seemed to be frowning, and she imagined how his face would change, light up, when he spotted the girl, her yellow/red hair shining in the sun.

But a few minutes later, he simply stood up, stretched, and then, straightening his tie, walked into the office building behind him.

She drank none of the coffee she'd ordered, but when she raised the glass of water to her lips, she saw her hand was trembling.

She began to take her lunch hour at the same time every day, and, as long as the weather held, he was there. He would arrive at about a quarter to two, smoke one cigarette, watch the people walking by, and then, at two o'clock, get up and go into his building.

Once she saw him return from lunch with two other men, and, after chatting with them for a while and then shaking their hands, he turned and sat down on his wall, smoked a cigarette, watched. He was twenty minutes late returning to work, she was fifteen.

"A man of routine," Tupper says.

She nods.

"And then?"

She pauses, runs her fingers over her lips.

It had been a long, boring morning. It seemed years between nine and ten and another six months between ten and eleven. She was filing, trying to play games with herself that would make the time go faster. She slowly counted out what she thought was five minutes and then glanced at the clock and found only two and a half had passed. She tried to remember, scene by scene, line by line, last night's episode of *Barney Miller*, but got to the end of the show in a mere six minutes. She imagined Bill (although she didn't know his name) in his office three blocks down, smoking a cigarette, giving dictation, stroking his thick mustache.

When lunchtime finally came, it seemed nearly anticlimactic, as if being assured that all mornings do eventually end was somehow disappointing.

Outside, it was a bright day, terribly hot; the sun glaring off the buildings and the sidewalk made her dull headache suddenly sharp, painful—the way a bright light turned on in the middle of the night is painful. Instead of going into the coffee shop, she bought a can of soda from a street vendor and sat on the stone wall, just where he usually sat. She closed her eyes for a minute, trying to relax her face. She didn't want to be squinting when he saw her.

He arrived with his coat off, his shirt sleeves rolled up, but the sun allowed her only a brief glimpse of him, in the moment before he was absorbed by the bright electric blues and yellows and greens. He sat on the wall, further down, on the other side of the planter, and lit a cigarette, bending into his cupped hands. He flicked the match out into the street. She heard him sigh, saw him lean back, and she stopped thinking about herself.

"Excuse me?" Her voice was small. She changed it. "Excuse me?"

He peeked around the planter. His face was serious, but pleasant.

"You'll probably think I'm crazy, but were you ever in the Golden Door, in Rochester?"

He smiled a little and his eyes went from her knees to her face. "Yes," he said. "Plenty of times. Do I know you?"

She shook her head. "No," she said. "I don't think so." She shaded her eyes with her hand in order to see him better. "You just look somewhat familiar."

His eyes combed her again, head to knee this time, and then he put his cigarette in his mouth, biting it, and moved down the wall, close enough for his shadow to fall over her face. His eyes were terribly bright. "How familiar?" he said, smiling. And when he leaned closer to hear her reply, she felt as if he'd pressed his palm into her stomach, low, and that all her pulses had gathered under it.

They began to meet like that every day: fifteen minutes on the concrete wall in front of his building while he smoked a cigarette and she drank a soda.

The strawberry blonde, she learned, was Sarah, the woman he'd "been with" for the past two years. She was a nurse, just graduated from the University of Rochester, and the two were now living together in Forest Hills. He'd gotten his master's in engineering from RIT two years ago and had spent every weekend last year upstate with Sarah.

He spoke her name as, she has since discovered, so many men speak of their wives: without drama or emotion, as if he were simply naming the floor he worked on or the subway he rode home. Much later, when she tested him about what he remembered of their early days on the wall, he told her that he alternately felt she was either infatuated with him or totally bored. She had told him in one of their first lunchtime meetings, lying to offset what might seem to him the imbalance of Sarah, that she was seeing someone regularly (she used Jeff's name and description for the lie) and Bill said later that knowing she had a boyfriend confused him when it came to figuring out just what she wanted from him. It didn't occur to him that Sarah could have been equally confusing to her.

At the end of August, they finally agreed to meet one evening after work for a happy hour and hors d'oeuvre supper at a small bar on Fifty-first Street. He seemed to know everyone there. Men and women came to him from across the dining room, along the packed bar. He laughed easily with them, getting serious only when he introduced her, as if she were some puzzling coin he had just found in the street. She ate nothing, drank heavily. She supposed that being with him in a dark bar, with his arm around the back of her chair, his eyes going to hers while someone else spoke, their thighs always touching, she should have felt like Sarah, slim and beautiful; should have felt she had somehow usurped her, won out.

But instead she felt, once again, that she was watching him: that he was far away, in another corner, across the street, for his nearness—the faint laugh lines around his eyes, the large, round nose, the slight, bluish shade of a beard that brushed his white collar—seemed somehow unreal, unearned, as if she was merely watching him through field glasses or on a videotape.

As if touching him was still an impossibility.

She got very drunk. Leaving the bar, she stumbled and nearly fell, and he took her arm, laughing, and insisted he take her home.

On the way to the subway, just around the corner from their concrete wall, he turned her around and kissed her, putting his right leg between both of hers so that she stumbled again. He bit into her lip, pressed her into his thigh. With anyone else she might have called such a kiss awkward, pawing, but with him she called it passionate.

She thought of lovely Sarah with the single red rose.

They took the train to Sixty-third Drive where his car was parked, and then he drove her to Flushing. She didn't turn on the lights when they came in, but there was enough pink light from the window for them to see their way to the bed and for her to watch him as he undressed.

She told him she loved him. Not because she was drunk enough to be excused for it in the morning but because he was rough and his beard was harsh and he bit into her in a way that made her feel her flesh would snap. Because the pain somehow jarred the phrase from her.

She woke when he leaned over to kiss her good-by. He was fully dressed, with his shirt unbuttoned and his unknotted tie draped around his neck like a priest's scapular. Her room was just getting light and she was somewhat disappointed, even offended, that he was dressed and ready to leave; as if she'd thought that once she brought him home, he'd stay forever, like a stray cat.

"Sarah," he whispered, "gets home at seven."

He kissed her again. His face was drawn, tired, darkened by his beard. "I'll see you at lunch."

So she'd gotten what she'd wanted, what she'd dreamed of. After he left, she lay in bed, repeating the phrase to herself. She had wanted something and she'd gotten it. There. Finished. But even as she thought this, she imagined him driving down the road, onto the Parkway. The sun would just be rising. There would be little traffic. When he got home he would let himself into their apartment, shower, get into their bed, rubbing his arms and legs against the sheets to quickly make them warm. An hour later he would raise his head from his pillow, wearing a smile she had not yet seen, and welcome beautiful Sarah back to their home. All of her time with him shaken off like a dream. Not finished. Not ever really begun.

She slept no more that morning but took a shower and dressed carefully. She rode the subway to work with more pleasure, expectancy, than she'd ever known and as she climbed the steps to the street, she felt an ache, a tightness in her groin and her thighs and low in her back, as if, she thought, she already had some part of him held inside her; bound by muscles and tendons, by her own tissue; as if there was something her body was learning to accommodate, straining to hold.

"You truly loved him?" Tupper whispers, his voice almost reverent.

She nods. "Yes. I loved him very much." She could be Ingrid Bergman.

They are silent for a while, their heads bowed. Her tale has done this to them.

"Do you know the story from mythology?" he asks. "About how man and woman were created as one being, joined, androgynous, but that Zeus, seeing that they were arrogant, split them in two. And ever since the two halves have searched to find each other, to be joined again?"

She watches the fire. "I've never heard it."

"It almost seems that's how it was, with you two."

She nods. Between the logs, the embers are red hot, glowing. She thinks of all the stories that have been told around fires: stories of hunts and battles and ancient ancestors, stories of undying love. She thinks of all the facts that have burned while the stories were getting told. "Yes," she says again. "It was almost like that."

"And when did you go to Buffalo together?"

She licks her lips and tastes the residue of brandy. "That winter. He was transferred and asked me to come along. He'd left Sarah by then."

"And you lived together?"

"Nearly two years."

"It was unhappy?"

She looks at him. Even in the light of the flames, he looks pale. Or maybe just pale in comparison. "We were very happy," she says, as if he has missed some essential point. "I loved him."

He leans closer to her, looking both curious and sly, like a detective, not quite sure, but, yes, perhaps, coming across some clue. A critic slowly recognizing some false turn in the plot. "Then what happened?" he asks.

She looks at her glass. "It didn't work out."

"Why not?" He moves closer to her, hot on the trail. "It all sounds so perfect. And you say you loved him. You lived together, so I presume he loved you. What went wrong?"

She raises her glass again, feels the warm path the brandy makes through her. The flaw would be to say she left him. Despite his beauty, despite her love, despite the fact that he alone was her mythical other half, she left him. It is a contradiction that the story cannot bear.

"It was just one of those things," she says, knowing he'll want her to do better.

"Another woman?" he whispers. "Did he meet someone else?"

She looks at the fire, hears the wood snap and hiss. To say that she left him denies all the rest; but to say that he left her, he was wonderful and he left her, implies no contradiction.

"Was it Sarah?" Tupper whispers. "Did Sarah come back?"

She raises her head and nods once: Anne Boleyn signaling to the executioner, crying "God Save the King!" "Yes," she whispers. "Sarah."

He touches her arm. "I'm sorry," he says and his voice is filled with pity and love and, although she suspects not for her, a certain respect. "He was no bigamist then," he says, leaning back. He seems relieved. "He was too loyal. A bigamist would have known how to keep you both. He would have made both of you his wife and kept you both." He smiles and leans to kiss her thigh. "His loss."

She looks down at him and then suddenly lies back, the room tangibly cool behind her, the rag hearth rug beneath her somewhat damp. Her story will not do. It is, for him, without significance, without nobility. Tupper stretches out at her side. She closes her eyes. Listens for some other sound, something from the house, the barn, the road outside, even the ocean. But there is only the sound of the fire, like a slow, faraway wind. The sound of his breath. For the past hour their two small voices had been all there was to hear, and now, she thinks, it's as if they'd never spoken. Now there's nothing. Now she could tell the story again, tell it differently, change the names and the places and the outcome (What happened? We married and he thrived. What happened? I grew tired of hard winters. What happened? He died in Wisconsin.) and there would be nothing left in the air to contradict her. Nothing of the first story that could bend or shape the second or the third. Only he could point out that certain details had been changed. And it would be his word against hers. The air could not testify, and no evidence could be found. They are, after all, two strangers, in a stranger's home, in a town where no one knows them.

She could tell him, for instance, that there was no loss involved. She had made *herself* his wife. It was a private ceremony, she could say, attended only by the bride. She had bought the ring in a Buffalo jewelry store and outside in the parking lot, alone in the car, she had taken off her glove and slipped it on. She closed her eyes and spoke words to herself about loving him for the rest of her life. Everything will change but this, in me. Although the steering wheel was cold, she left the hand bare. She watched it moving to the window or the horn, saw it choose boxes and bags from the supermarket shelves, open her purse, accept change. She noticed it each time it flashed like a beacon through the cold dull fog of housekeeping and job-hunting and all the hours she waited for him to come home.

She could say she had made herself his wife and so she became not the precarious live-in, second choice, but the eternal, duty-bound mate. Became not one of those timid lovers who sleeps with a packed bag at her side, one shod foot on the floor, or one of those cautious, passionless women who refuses to say forever (as if her life will never end, never consist of more than those tiny stepping-stones of the present), but one who has claimed, for the rest of my life, all but this, but me.

She made herself his wife and so could smile at the innocent indifference of busy husbands, smile when she found herself, like a wife, feeling neglected. And at night, while they sat together watching television or while he slept heavily beside her, she could finger the ring and feel like a woman with a double life, or a spy from another planet: If only you knew what this ring means, where it has come from. Like an assassin gone underground: If only you knew what I am capable of.

She could say she had made herself his wife, forever, and so there was no loss involved.

Or, she could tell him: Sarah was always there; he was, indeed, loyal. She could tell him of a rainy afternoon in summer when she was looking through his bookcase (she would say for something to read) and among the hardcover textbooks from his business courses and a few paperback thrillers, she had found a slightly oversized book that he had slipped sideways into the back of the shelves. A photography book called *Nurses*, that showed nurses at various times, in various places: caring for men during World War II, walking together through a slum at the turn of the century, graduating, picketing, laughing together over a patient's birthday cake, embracing each other, assisting at operations, crying. Nurses who were nuns and nurses who were men; nurses who looked like grandmothers or sex symbols or harbingers of death.

In the front of the book there was written, in black ink, in a long, graceful hand, "Gaze at this and think of me. I love you, Sarah." It was dated three years before.

She could tell him how she had sat and looked at the book for a long time. Of course, it was not the first trace of Sarah she had seen. When they moved in, Bill had not hesitated to point out what pots and pans and coffee mugs and bath towels he had taken from Sarah. And he proudly showed her a pen she had once given him and a small sculpture they had bought together and he had "gotten away from her" when he left. But the book, she'd say, somehow touched her. Made her breath come short. Maybe it was the "I love you," so simple and assured. The date, three years ago, before she had ever seen either of them. Or maybe it was the nurses themselves. Since Christmas, Elizabeth had been working in a large department store, in an alcove called "Enchanted Evenings," where she sold bright gowns to what seemed to her like the same four Polish women about to take a cruise to Bermuda, and with the summer she had gone from full-time to part-time because, as she'd told Bill, she needed to think about what she wanted to do with her life, although all she'd really done was think about him. But here before her were all those photos of all those women with a profession, a most important profession. Here was Sarah (and—she'd never thought of it before—how lovely she must look in her white dress and white stockings and soft white shoes, her hair braided and twirled into a thick gold bun!)

showing him the range of her expertise, her emotions, her long history. Showing him that she was a professional woman who necessarily must have more on her mind than love but who would manage to love him still.

She sat on the couch, the day low and heavy against the sliding glass doors behind her and thought how dull her own love, which was all her life, had made her.

She could tell him: She had asked Bill once if he ever thought of Sarah and he was silent for a moment and then said, "No, I don't think I ever do." It was the hesitation, of course, that convinced her and she brought her ring to her mouth.

She asked him once, after an elaborate lead-in: What was Sarah's birth sign? and he pretended not to remember the month or day she was born.

He answered once that he thought she was Swedish. Or Scots.

He said he vaguely remembered bringing her a rose when he came to visit, but he was sure he didn't bring one every time.

She was afraid of deep water, he said. Or is that you?

Thinking of Sarah one night as they held each other, she began to cry. He was startled; he may have been asleep. When he asked what was wrong she said, "You'll never love me enough." Stroking her, laughing a little, he said, "No, I probably never will."

She could tell him that gradually she came to think of them both as victims of the same disaster. The unwilling survivors of a tragedy that had deprived them both of all but their lives. He longed for Sarah, she for him. She came to think that if he was not her lover he was, at least in love, her brother.

She could say that she began to measure their love-making, which, from the very beginning, had veered and swayed unpredictably, according to what she imagined were his thoughts of Sarah. When he was rough and passionate and impulsive, he was trying to forget her. When he was gentle, inquiring, loving, he had decided he never could. When he pulled away and laughed at her enthusiasm, he was feeling both guilty and ashamed and, perhaps, a little repulsed by her dark hair, her hips which were growing a little too fleshy, her legs that were not quite long enough, not Sarah's.

She could tell him of their last evening together when he had come home from work, his tie off, his shirt sleeves rolled up, his brief case under his arm and his jacket over his shoulder and she'd said, as he came into the kitchen to kiss her, "Sarah called."

How he'd grimaced and said, "She probably thinks I owe her money for something," and, in the same breath, "Are you making potato salad?"

How he had refused to call her back, claimed he no longer remembered her number. How she had started out being understanding, "Call her, I don't mind. It doesn't bother me." (Planning to say, when he called and found Sarah had never called him, "Well, it sounded like Sarah.") How she had grown sarcastic, "Why are you so afraid to talk to her? Can she still affect you so much?" and had finally cried, "I won't live with her ghost any longer!"

How he had watched her, first startled by her outburst, then amused, and finally, when she threatened to leave him, angry.

How he had leaned across the table, one fist clenched, saying, "Look, I love you. I once loved Sarah, I won't deny it, but I don't anymore. I love you now, okay? All right? I love you. I don't know how many ways to say it. You want me to marry you? Christ, I'll marry you, if that will make you believe me. Anything so you'll believe me and we can drop the subject and get on with our lives."

She could tell him that at that moment she believed it. He loved her, not Sarah. He had loved Sarah once but now he loved her. At that moment, she believed it. And she also understood that to say she believed it would mean the subject could be dropped, ended; and the subject, she understood at that moment, was all her life.

How she began packing at midnight. Bill lying in bed, his voice low. "I'm not entering into your little drama, Elizabeth. I know what you're doing and I won't play along. You've got no reason to leave and you've got no place to go. You're acting. I've got meetings tomorrow. I can't spend the night battling your made-up problems. This is not *The Late Show,* for God's sake." And later, "I love you. I love our life together. What more do you *want* from me?"

How she was crying when she walked out the door.

She could tell him that she left because she was willing to admit that Sarah was the love of his life, but not that there was no love of his life at all.

She could say that she left because he believed that his love, which was smooth and featureless and solid as a wall (a blank wall where she was pinned, where he stopped at the end of a day), which had been worn so smooth by others whom he once had loved but now loved no more, was enough to sustain her.

Or she could tell him again (for where is the evidence to contradict her?) that it was Sarah who parted them. For he had loved her first and he was a romantic. Tall and handsome and too loyal.

Instead, she tells him, lying in this strange room, the arc of firelight making the ceiling seem high and touched with gold, "Even now, I'm not always sure I'm over him."

She tells him, and there is nothing in the air, in her memory or his, to contradict her, that there was no loss involved, she had made herself his wife. She recalls that even on the train as she was leaving him, even now in this dim room, her love could bring tears to the eyes of strangers.

XIX

S HE WAKES WITH SOME DREAM of Bill, Bill talking to her, talking endlessly. Tupper Daniels sleeps beside her with his mouth closed and his hand over his heart. If the revelations of the night are still with him, they don't disturb his sleep. His face is serene, neither his mouth nor his eyelids twitch or tremble. All she has told him is safe, well below the surface.

And she'd said he was her mythical other half. Said: Even now, it isn't over.

The light behind the heavy curtains falls softly, weakly, into the room, dulls the edges of the dresser and the tops of the bedposts, fills the room with odd shapes. Staring hard, she can see the shadow of a fish, what seems to be a distant line of mountains at the foot of the bed, a dark madonna in a corner, a long shadow boat, perhaps a battleship, on the ceiling. She closes her eyes for a moment and when she opens them again, the images have disappeared.

She would like to wake him, to ask, What next? What should I tell you next and when will you find your ending? And what after that? When does it all take shape, the ads, the distribution, the bright young editor who turned vanity publishing on its ear?—but she has never been good at waking her lovers. She has always wanted either to shake them or to kick them, or, as with Bill, never to wake them at all, and so she merely lies beside him, thinking how she might some day describe this moment to her children, to the press, to some future biographer who asks about the weekend in which she discovered the first best seller of a house that until then had been known as a joke.

She imagines Bill reading it, wondering why he isn't mentioned, and then smiles at her own dreams. She smiles at Tupper in his dreamless sleep.

Later, she gets up quietly and slips into her robe, walks down the silent hallway. In the bathroom mirror, she looks different to herself. Somehow sharper and more clear. It may only be the strange surroundings, the wide bevel on the mirror, the blue-tiled wall behind her (although, she realizes, she doesn't feel strange, feels quite at home among all the small surprises of a place she's never seen before). She brushes her hair, holds it for a minute in a ponytail at the back of her head and lets it fall to her shoulders. It may just be that she always looks better on a morning when she hasn't slept well.

As she opens the door, she sees Hedda in a loose black robe with long, winglike sleeves, going silently down the stairs. There is something gracefully feline about her movements; as Elizabeth steps from the bathroom, she stops, and, like a cat, slowly turns her head.

"You're up," she whispers hoarsely.

"Yes," Elizabeth says.

"Good. Come have coffee with me." Without waiting for a reply, she turns again and moves slowly down the stairs. Elizabeth glances down the hall to their room. Last night he had asked her, If you're still in love with him, where does that leave me? You also said you loved me. She hadn't answered, but perhaps, she thinks now, waking alone he'll begin to understand: She is no ordinary lover. Her love for Bill hasn't ended; her claim to love Tupper ends nothing. She follows Hedda to the kitchen.

They take their coffee into Hedda's library, a small room

lined with books on brick and plywood shelves and centered around a large stereo/television console. The rain has stopped and bits of sun, full of shadows from the trees, stream through the mesh curtains. Hedda sits on the plaid couch, putting her feet up on the seat and pulling her black robe over them. Elizabeth sits on a brown leather recliner beside her.

"Your friend tells me you didn't quite find what you were looking for yesterday."

Elizabeth smiles. "No, not quite. Although we did take your advice and check with the library."

Hedda nods. "So he said." She lights a cigarette, blows the smoke to the ceiling. Her neck is long and freckled and taut. The wide yoke of her robe shows the deep, tanned hollows around her collarbone, and Elizabeth feels certain that she is naked under the robe. She imagines that Hedda spends a great deal of time naked, wearing her freckles like a fur.

"I think your job is fascinating," Hedda says.

Elizabeth laughs, modestly.

Hedda puts her fingers to her breasts. "Well, to me it's fascinating." Moves the same fingers to her mouth, touching them to her tongue. "The book's about bigamy, then?" she asks slowly.

Elizabeth sips her coffee. "Yes."

Hedda laughs or says *Hmph* and shakes her head. "About a man who commits bigamy?" She leans forward, hands on her knees. "Is that correct, you *commit* bigamy?"

"Yes," Elizabeth says. The editor. "I believe so."

"But you don't commit monogamy." She pulls her lips together, makes her eyes wide. "Do you? Or marriage. You don't *commit* marriage."

Elizabeth laughs, "No, that's true," and Hedda looks at her for a moment, frowning, as if she has just corrected her in some obvious error. "The language is biased," she murmurs, putting an elbow to her raised knee and resting her head upon her hand, a pinkie to her forehead, the cigarette dangerously close to her dry red hair. "His wives must be very patient," she says, eyebrows raised.

Elizabeth nods over her cup, smiling wisely. "Like Penelope," she says.

"Who?" Smoke curls from her cigarette.

"Penelope. Ulysses' wife. From mythology."

Hedda brushes some smoke from the air. "Oh, yes." She takes a final drag of her cigarette and leans to stamp it out. "I suppose she was patient"—smoke pouring from her mouth and nose—"if you call filling your house with boyfriends while your husband is away patient." She lifts the cup, blows. "I call it a romp."

Elizabeth is uncertain that she follows and Hedda, looking up at her, throws her head back and barks a deep, dry laugh. "Well, anyway, I'm all for it," she says. "Bigamy. I think it would make me feel positively ambidextrous."

Elizabeth tries to remember the story, Ulysses, Penelope. She recalls that he killed off all her suitors as soon as he got home, but she is uncertain of Penelope's reaction. *Did* she consider them boyfriends? She hears the toilet flush upstairs.

"And it makes so much more sense," Hedda says, standing. "Simultaneous husbands." Her eyes go to the ceiling. "There he is, I'd better tell him we're here. What's his name?"

"Tupper," Elizabeth says. She feels she is handing him over to her.

"Right." Hedda leaves the room and Elizabeth hears her call from the stairs, "Tupper, darling, you haven't been deserted. We're down here in the library. Can I get you some coffee?"

Elizabeth can't hear his reply, but she hears Hedda in the kitchen and then hears the phone ring and Hedda's bright, "Why it's *you!*"

She thinks it a wonderful thing to be able to call someone darling, so naturally, without even making it a joke.

She reaches for one of Hedda's cigarettes, lights it, and then leans back in the chair, putting her feet up and her robe over them. She tries to imagine what it would be like to live here, alone, lovely, smoking cigarettes, reading books. She sips her coffee and stares at the books along the wall. There's Hemingway and Mailer and Ian Fleming. And Solzhenitsyn. Other books whose authors she doesn't recognize, but whose names imply cowboys *(Catch the Wild Appaloosa)* or soldiers *(The Bloody Stand)* or spies *(To Save the Munich Papers)*. There is also a number of history books and movie-star biographies (Gable, Bogart, Montgomery Clift, Gary Cooper), but nothing she would call a woman's book. Perhaps, she thinks, because Hedda doesn't need that kind of reassurance.

Or perhaps this is her own way of filling her house with boyfriends.

She hears Tupper come down the stairs and Hedda call to him. A minute later, he enters the library, a steaming cup of coffee in his hand. "She's on the phone," he says. "She'll be off in a minute." He kisses her head and sits on the couch where Hedda had sat. He is wearing blue jeans and a pinstriped shirt. His feet, like hers, are bare. They have both made themselves at home.

"You didn't wake me," he says, surprising her with his smile. After last night, her story about Bill, her refusal to make love, she'd expected him to be cool, even distant.

"You looked so peaceful, I didn't want to disturb you," she says.

He winks. "There are nondisturbing ways to wake someone."

She shrugs. "I don't know any."

"Remind me to teach you some."

She wonders if this friendly intimacy isn't their own kind of distance.

Hedda walks quickly into the room. "Sorry," she says. "That

was an old beau of mine out to ruin my peaceful Sunday." She looks at them both meaningfully. "He's coming over at noon."

"We've got to get going anyway," Tupper says.

Hedda stands before him with her hands on her hips, her shoulders slouched, her pelvis thrown forward. The shadows of the sunlight and leaves fall over the hem of her robe and her just-visible white feet. "Yes," she sighs, almost regretfully. She looks at Elizabeth over her long black arm. "They're so adorable," she says, as if Tupper were a piece in a museum. "But so impossible to live with. It's a shame we can't bottle them or do without them completely—or maybe keep them in the attic and just take them down when we need them."

Tupper blushes and Elizabeth laughs. She likes Hedda's *we*. "Like *The Ghost and Mrs. Muir*," she says.

Hedda throws her head back. "Yes," she says. "A ghost might be the answer after all!" Her eyes flashing: "*Two* of them!"

Tupper says later, as they change in their room, that for a woman who claims she'll never marry again, she sure was excited about getting laid.

And later still, as they pull away from the house, Hedda in her "riding clothes," a man's long sweater and blue jeans, waving from the drive, "Something tells me we just spent the night in a one-woman whorehouse."

"Let's try to follow it through," Tupper is saying. The day has grown bright and she digs in her pocketbook for sunglasses. "We need to give Beale a past, a logical past, so let's try to follow it through. We've got a man like your father, right? A man who begins traveling when he's fifteen, gets his wealth from a man like your uncle, conceives this sense of wanderlust, continues to travel . . ."

Falls off the edge of the earth, she thinks, steps through the looking glass. Who cares? She has put Bill between them, claimed she still loves him so that, last night, she brought tears to his eyes, and today he hasn't said a word to protest it. He hasn't said a word, not when they dressed in their room, not through brunch, not during their short walk through town, about loving her. Who can look for a father when a lover so easily disappears. Becomes all business.

Let's talk about us, she wants to say. That's enough about him, what about us?

She wonders if she should bring up Bill again, tell the story a little differently this time. Retell it. Say, perhaps I only think I love him. I'm not sure. Help me forget him.

But, as she finds her sunglasses and puts them on, and turns to watch him driving beside her, she feels again what she felt so surely last night, feels it again like the pain from a muscle tested after a night's rest and found still sprained. She loves him, always will, and even to admit the possibility of change, of being talked out of it, seems a grave betrayal.

Tupper Daniels is too pale; or he pales in comparison.

"Here it is," he says and pulls the car onto a grassy shoulder. Across the street there is a high knoll and just behind it, the first few rows of stones.

"And you take me to too many cemeteries," she says out loud, getting out of the car.

He says, "What?"

The sunglasses make her feel like a framed camera shot, hand held, walking toward some terrible fate. She blinks to become less aware of how she is seeing. "Nothing," she says. "Nothing at all."

The cemetery is busy with visitors this Sunday afternoon. A tow-headed family stands around a bright stone, heads hung a little, faces dumb, like passers-by stopped outside a TV store, watching the movements of a colorful, silent screen. A middle-aged woman on her hands and knees crawls around a tomb-stone, clipping grass. An old woman in a purple velvet hat sits on one of the stone benches that line the path and reads a thick paperback.

Around the cemetery are the fading trees and another field waiting to be filled. This, Elizabeth thinks, is what they should be like, spacious, out of the way. As serene as a golf course. Her glasses suddenly seem appropriate.

They walk toward what seems to be the older part of the cemetery, Tupper checking the dates on each stone as they pass, murmuring, "Nelson, Neilson, Nicholson, Nevelson," as if he were looking through a phone book. Her boot heels sink into the mud and the wet grass as if the earth just below it were hollow. They walk slowly through one row and then turn and go back down another. The styrofoam forms of old wreaths are at some of the graves. Green pots of withered chrysanthemums are at others. One has a plastic lily covered with a dirty glass jar, another a feeble American flag. She watches a squirrel, its movements so slow and graceful they almost seem stylized, mechanical, hop down the grass before them. They turn again, pace another aisle, reviewing the troops. She begins to wonder why she is here.

"Neilson!" Tupper cries. "Here's a Bridget Ross Neilson, died 1947." He holds out his arm, like a surgeon demanding a scalpel. "What was his wife's name, the uncle? What was your father's aunt's name?"

Elizabeth frowns. "Betty."

"Was her maiden name Ross?"

She shrugs. "I don't know. Is that an Irish name?"

Tupper shrugs too. "I don't know. But then I'd say Neilson was English, like Admiral Nelson, not Dutch."

Elizabeth looks at the stone. It is pale brown, with a small cross and "J.M.J." chiseled at the top—what the nuns used to tell them to put on all their test papers, for good luck. Not much of an epitaph.

"Well, Bridget is an Irish name." She looks at Tupper, not

sure that she wants this to be her aunt, but sure, somehow, that she wants him to believe it is. If only to get this over with.

"But Betty usually comes from Elizabeth," Tupper says. "Doesn't it?"

She adjusts her glasses. "My father's mother's name was Elizabeth. This aunt," she nods toward the stone, as if it were indeed hers, "lived with them in England before she came to New York. They were sisters. They couldn't both be named Elizabeth."

"Maybe your father was saying his Aunt Biddy."

She nods. "Could be. But you'd think I'd remember a funny name like that."

"You'd think," Tupper says. His enthusiasm seems to falter. "What else do you know about her?"

She looks at him. She is bored, sick of this. "Nothing," she says.

He slaps his thigh, "Great," and walks a few feet down the path to a small stone bench. "You're proving to be a great help, Elizabeth," he says, sitting, clearly annoyed. "You're really trying to help me." He hunches over his lap like *The Thinker*.

She looks at the wet grass, the crushed, somewhat silverish imprint of Tupper's shoes. She wants to say, All right, then, let's forget about it. Let's talk about us instead. Let's go home. But she also wants, still, and even more, to be part of it. The bright young editor.

She walks slowly to the bench and sits down beside him. The stone is cold and the cold seems to soak through her jeans.

"My father once told me," she says, in a tone she might use for an apology, an offering, "that his mother, in London, was always trying to pass herself off as English."

He turns to watch her. "So?"

"So maybe the aunt did the same thing over here. Maybe she wanted people to think she was English so she said her name was Betty, not Bridget."

Tupper sits up a little, hands on his knees. "Why would she want people to think she was English?"

She touches her glasses. "Well," she says, improvising. "She was a maid for a while, when she first came over. Maybe English maids were more in demand—you know how you WASPs are about the English." He is about to speak and she puts her hand on his sleeve. "Or maybe it was because of the uncle," she says. "He wasn't Catholic and he didn't like Catholics, my father told me that. Maybe she told the uncle she was English and Protestant and that her name was Betty just to get him to marry her."

He frowns. "Sounds like an awful lot of trouble to go to just to marry someone."

She nods. "It does, but maybe she loved him." Maybe crowds parted, their eyes met, he fell on his knees.

Tupper puts his hands under his thighs, raising his shoulders, and looks out across the stones. "It hardly seems likely," he says, dryly. And she had to agree. The uncle, she knows, would be a ridiculous figure in such a romance. Old, stern, bigoted. Puzzled to find himself, so late in his life, no longer a bachelor, no longer childless. Struck dumb by the miracle of her father riding beside him.

She crosses her legs, folds her arms over them. Her story, or, this time, her mother's story, of their first sweet meeting, will not do. She looks across the cemetery, feels the weak sun on her hair, although through her glasses the place seems sunless. She watches an older couple pass by, pausing here and there, bending, as if in a garden. She glances at Tupper beside her and wonders again why they are here. It was, after all, her father they were supposed to have been looking for. Her father's story that was to have been told, blessed with immortality.

She looks again at the pale stone, the sharp, bevel-cut of the words. Bridget Ross Neilson. J.M.J.: Jesus, Mary, Joseph.

Joseph: A man puzzled to find himself, so late in his life, no longer a bachelor, no longer childless.

"All right," she says slowly, smiling a little. "It wasn't because she loved him," she says. "Maybe she lied to him about herself simply to get him to marry her. So he could help her out."

He turns to her again, smiling kindly, as if he appreciates, but has little hope for, her efforts. "Help her out doing what?"

"Sending for my father."

He presses his lips together, swings them to one side, considering. "She cared that much about seeing your father?"

She nods. "He'd been her favorite, back in England. Before she moved to New York. My father told me that. Maybe she'd planned to send for him from the very beginning, as soon as she got married and had her own home."

Tupper laughs. "Very Jane Austen."

She smiles, coyly. She could be offering him peeled grapes. "You said you wanted to appeal to women."

He laughs again, folds his arms before him. "So you're saying that the aunt here married old Neilson just so she could send for her nephew, your father?"

"Right."

"The son she never had."

"Yes." Although she doesn't like the phrase. It reminds her of silent-movie captions and Catholic euphemisms for aborted babies. Melodrama. And yet, she is sure, it was the phrase her father had used, telling her the story. And she had thought it a lovely story.

"Or did have," she whispers.

Tupper pulls his head back, "What?" and a laugh, unbidden, rises to her throat. Feels more like a blow. Why not melodrama?

"Yes," she says. "Why not? Remember I told you that his parents gave him up easily? Well, maybe it was because he wasn't theirs, he was hers!"

"Her son?"

"Yes," she goes on. "And remember," having fun now, surprised herself at how she can make it fit, "my father said that the uncle was a little in awe of him when he first arrived, he didn't know quite what to make of him when they rode out to the Island together?"

Tupper nods, but uncertainly. And yet curious, she is sure. "Yes," he says slowly. "So?"

"Well, maybe it was because he knew." Like Joseph, awed by the miracle of his wife and this child, of where the child had come from, of the way his wife must have loved. "He knew my father was his wife's child by someone else."

Tupper is squinting at her. "By *whom?*"

She hesitates. "God" would be the consistent answer. "Someone in England, I suppose." Someone who had appeared before her once and had fallen on his knees. Someone who had done great things to her. "Someone she'd had an affair with. Someone who'd gotten her pregnant."

"Someone she never got over?" he asks, that facetiousness again in his eyes—gray eyes through her glasses.

She nods. The miracle of his wife and the way she must have loved. "All right."

"Someone she continued to love even after she met and married the uncle."

"Maybe," she says.

"Which would make him *her* bigamist figure, right?"

She studies her hands. She should say, Yes, that's right, let's go. One bigamist bagged, let's go. "Or else it would make her the bigamist," she says.

She looks up at him, the small eyes, the pale lashes. He is biting one side of his lip. "No," he says finally. He straightens up, shaking his head. "No, that's no good. A man like the uncle wouldn't put up with that, a wife with a lover and an illegitimate child. A bigamist wife."

Her story will not do. "Why not?"

"It's just no good." He raises his collar against the growing wind and looks at her over the felt undersides of his lapels. "What would be the appeal of a woman like that? Especially to a man like the uncle. Why would he marry someone who says she's still in love with someone else?"

She presses her hands between her knees, shivering a little, studying the dew that has beaded across her boot. "It might have been reassuring to him," she says, slowly. "To know that she was capable of loving in a certain way."

"Yeah," Tupper says. "But with someone else."

She looks up again. He is smirking at the stones. "You never know," she insists. "The uncle had been a bachelor all his life, he'd lived alone, maybe someone like the aunt would have appealed to him precisely because she did have a lover and a child. Because she told him that her life had been tragic and romantic, and maybe that would have appealed to him, filled him with awe."

One corner of his lip remains twisted, as if he were smiling at something at the edge of his vision. "The same way your father, her son, filled him with awe that first day?"

She nods. "Yes. Could be."

"Which," he adds, "might be why the uncle left your father all his land. Almost as a tribute to what your father represented, his wife's great love for someone else."

"Yes," she says again.

"Because, you're saying, what really appealed to the uncle, what he really worshiped in the aunt, was the way she had once loved someone else. And still loved someone else."

She watches a line of clouds moving swiftly over the trees. A voice from another part of the cemetery is suddenly caught and snapped by the wind.

"Could be," she whispers. "Could be that's what appealed to him."

For what magic had touched her, through all her dull life,

except that she had met him and he had fallen on his knees?

Tupper suddenly smiles his square smile, slips his hands into his pockets. "Could be," he says. "But only if the uncle was willing to believe her, and all the stories she told him about how she was still in love."

What magic except in the stories she told? "Sometimes," Elizabeth says, slowly, feeling a slow pulse rising, beating softly in her ears, "people are willing to believe anything about someone else if it makes their own lives more interesting."

Willing to believe in the stories she told, recited like prayers. Stories, like prayers, that recounted for him the way she had loved; and redeemed the way she had suffered. Stories whose meanings, if they had meanings, he alone knew because she had confided in him.

"You don't think the uncle might have seen through her?" Tupper asks.

She shakes her head. For what else could her mother have told him to make herself seem, to him, such an extraordinary woman, starting her life over. Why else would she have left Long Island where she had spent her life, left the prosaic death, the bishop-blessed funeral at St. Elizabeth's where still she would have been called "good Mrs. Connelly," the widowed virgin, the saint, if not to start her life over again with a man who would worship her for what she said she had been, how she told him she had loved? A man who would hear her call, after everything, her lover's name.

Tupper slides close to her, puts his hand on her thigh. "You don't think," he says, leaning so close that she can smell the sharp odor of his breath, "that the uncle, at some point, might have asked her, 'Well, if it was such a great love, where is he? Why didn't he marry you? Why'd he get you pregnant and leave you?' "

He presses his lips together, but, it seems, with a great effort, as if he can barely fit them over his small teeth, barely contain his grin. "Don't you think he would have asked what happened, why'd he leave you?"

She shrugs again, elaborately, shaking him off. "I don't know," she says. And when he doesn't move away from her, she stands. The breeze lifts her hair and she steps back, as if to catch it. She looks down at him, through her dark glasses, and suddenly longs to be alone, to return to her own thoughts as if to a sleep.

But Tupper persists. "You don't think he would have seen through her stories a little? And maybe asked why he left her?"

She looks down at him. "We don't know who left whom, do we?"

"All right then." His square chin raised toward her, his smile saying he's got her. "Even stranger, don't you think the uncle might have wondered why, if she had this great love, and still loved him, she would have left him? Don't you think he would have asked why *she* left *him?*"

She digs her hands into her pockets and feels a slight, sickening chill tremble down her spine. Asked why, if she loved him, she had left him, loving him still. Or why, loving him, she had let him leave her. Time and time again had let him leave her. Until the last time, which she also allowed, accepted without tears. Asked why, if she'd had this great love, the pictures and the bedspread and the sweet stories of their beginning only reappeared after she'd moved to Maine, after she'd found Ward.

Why she'd left Bill, come to New York alone.

"Yes," she says, fingering sand. "All right. He might have asked her that."

"And what do you think the aunt would have said?"

She walks past him, to the grave, and stands before it where, perhaps, her father once stood, his footprints pressed silver into the grass. She reads again the slight epitaph—Jesus, Mary, Joseph—and recalls that the sponsor of it all, the one who had filled her womb, filled poor Joseph with awe for his son and his wife and the way she had loved, is not mentioned, not present. The silent Partner. The quintessential Lover. The absent and so irrefutable Husband.

"She would have said that her love went beyond that," she says, turning to Tupper.

"Beyond what?" he asks from the bench.

"Him." She thinks of Bill, Bill himself, Bill telling her that she shouldn't let loving him become her whole life. That she should get a job, a hobby, a dog. Bill himself reminding her that he was just an ordinary man, no prince, no god, no one capable of utterly changing her life by falling on his knees.

Reminding her that the ring she wore had meaning only in her wild imagination.

The ring that, when she left him, could bring tears to the eyes of strangers.

"She had to leave him," she says, "because her love had gone beyond him. It had surpassed him. She had to leave him to be free to keep loving him the way she wanted to. So she could continue to believe in him."

Tupper laughs a little, stands, squeezes his fingertips into the front pockets of his jeans. He walks toward her. "You mean so she'd be free to tell all her stories about him, to make him into some kind of myth."

She nods. Joanne had said: It has nothing to do with Tommy, meaning the disappointment, the discovery that he could not, after all, utterly change her life. But maybe the hope, the desire, the expectation itself had nothing to do with him either. Maybe it had only to do with all the stories she'd been told, the myth: Love will come to you, love beyond everything. It will change your life forever.

The myth he alone can refute; that his absence alone can make irrefutable. The myth in which he is best left in shadow, best left imagined, or remembered, or told.

Told in the darkened bedroom, told to the warm, the homely, the necessary husband: the myth of another—Husband, Father, Prince.

"Yes," she says, thinking not my father then, but my mother. My mother who needed the myth of Husband, eternal Husband, and the other, ordinary husband who was willing to believe in it. My mother who could start her life over again simply by retelling it, by waking in another man's bed and telling him: I love a man, a charming man, a man with a thousand different lives. And everything will change, but this, in me.

Her mother, who could be reconciled to her life, to his life, to all that through him she had lost, by the lovely story it made.

"Because some love," she whispers, feeling him beside her, "goes beyond even the lover himself. Some love can surpass even him, the real lover, until his real presence is no longer required for the love to last. Love that's like a spiritual life, like pure faith." She hesitates, but his head is bent as if he were a priest in a confessional, or a pilgrim at a shrine. "It's love that can't be ended," she goes on. "Or replaced. It's the way my mother loved, the way she, the aunt"—and yes, why not, she wants him to believe it—"my grandmother loved. The way I've loved."

The wind stirs and a red plastic flower, perhaps a carnation, rolls along the grass. Tupper raises his head, slowly, not smiling, not quite serious. His eyes pale and round. "Whose novel are you writing now?" he asks, a small twitch at his mouth. "Not mine."

She nods, the pulse at her throat and her ears, her spine straightening. "Mine then." She puts her hands to the front of her jacket and feels her own soft breasts. He will know her worth, the way she is capable of loving. She and all the women before her. He will know what magic has touched her by the story she tells. "Because that's the way I love Bill, the way I'll always love him. It's the way I love him and it will never change. No matter what. Because it's in me. It's mine."

"Your fiction," Tupper adds, leaning close to her.

"Yes." Hesitating, his square smile suddenly making her fear the word. "Mine." The foolish, passionate word of all her silly authors.

His dry lips are to her cheek. "But not," he says, his breath warm, sharp, "a particularly good one."

He steps in front of her, laughing softly, and puts his arms around her shoulders, forcing her hands to her sides, knocking her glasses with his cheek. "Oh, Elizabeth," he whispers into her ear, fondly. "You are so transparent sometimes." He steps away, still holding her shoulders, shaking his head. "Don't you see what you're doing? You love me and it scares you. All right," he shrugs. "It's okay to be scared. I'm a little scared too." Kindly, "But don't try to handle it by running away. By claiming you still love someone else—someone you'd barely mentioned until you'd admitted you were in love with me. Don't try to put me off with some eternal-love fiction." Chuckling, shaking his head. "I know you too well for that. I see through it. I see through *you.*"

He embraces her again, and her story, all she wanted to believe, is suddenly reduced to something simple and pathetic: an excuse, a contrivance, a pitiful cry for sense. *Now I know why it happened to me.*

Her single laugh is like a stab. He loves her, he sees through her. He sees through all the stories she has told. "Yes," she says, holding him tightly to keep her fingers from his small pale eyes. "Yes, you probably do."

She watches suburbia creep back into the landscape, irregular fields and trees giving way for homes and hamburgers and piles of crushed auto bodies that flash their former bright colors between scabs of orange rust. He has found his ending, he said.

The bigamist is her father, he said, and for his ending he will use her father's past. He will show, in the last chapter, how Beale came from England and was raised by a man like the uncle. The aunt will be mentioned, but she will be dead already. ("This is a book for women, but not necessarily about them.") There will just be the two men in the house. Then the scene will change to England, where a man, leaving one wife, walks across London to the home of another. ("I may fly over just to check on street names and details.") On the way, he wonders about a woman he'd once married and given a son. He thinks he heard she moved to America. The man will be described in the exact same words as Beale, her father, so that it is clear that the bigamist in the book is a bigamist's son.

"You'll see his past," he said proudly, "and you'll understand his whole life."

She said, "It's silly."

He said, "It's exactly what you were talking about, with your aunt and uncle, how the past explains everything, how there are bigamists everywhere and women just have to learn to make the best of them. I've changed the details but the theme is the same. It's exactly what you were talking about."

Now, riding in silence, watching the sky grow dark and the small blue lights come on in every home, watching the stars, also blue, but weak competition, appear slowly above them, it occurs to her that every great realization given up, spoken, placed in another's clumsy hands is, at heart, silly; every message from the grave a stale sermon or a slick song; every fiction, with all its attempts at sense and order, climax and resolution, words that mean something and change everything, laughable. Terribly laughable. Merely an excuse for fear, for laziness, for bad luck.

It occurs to her, returning to the frightened orange lights of the city, the air made dull by far too many lives, that Vista is, after all, the sanest, clearest place to be. *Her* side of Vista, where they take it for granted that whatever is shared is marred. Where they understand the tyranny of what lovers do to each other.

"Will you call me tomorrow?" he asks at her door, and she nods, smiling. She knows he would interpret the truth as a mere challenge, another transparent ploy. She has confided in him; he will now want the heart of everything she says.

"Sure," she tells him. "I'll call you."

XX

WE SAT ON HER PORCH, MY MOTHER and I, in the green wicker chairs where Ward and I had sat waiting for her just the night before. Where I had listened to him talk about my father—his long absences, his constant distractions, the life he had lived without us.

It was early morning, and the chairs were still damp from last night's rain. The sun that cut through the leaves had turned the shadows around us a deep, mossy shade of green but had failed to warm the wet odor of the woods.

We sat in silence, drinking coffee and looking out at the trees. I found I was playing an old, familiar game.

When my father was alive, I would sometimes increase the pain or the pleasure of waiting for him by trying to capture, exactly, the one moment before the moment he arrived. I would close my eyes and say now, *now.* Now it is quiet and everything is the same, but in the next moment—or this one, or this one—a door will swing open, a car will pull into the drive, a word will be spoken and everything will change.

I would try to transform each moment as it passed, make each a threshold, bless each with the significance of all it had not yet become.

I found I was doing that now, sitting with her in silence, where I had sat just last evening and listened to Ward. Listened to him talk about my father and my mother and the stories she had told, as if I had thought that between us some word could be formed, in the air or on our lips, that would define forever the life they had lived.

As if, like a child, I had thought I would be appeased by her stories only when I'd learned what parts of them were true.

I found I was thinking: Now she is silent and everything I know is memory or story or hope, but in this next moment, this one, this one, there will be the sound of her voice. It will be softer and slower than even Ward's had been. It will find, as Ward's could not, the one word that will define him.

I waited. There was the sound of the woods: birdsong, a slight stirring of the leaves.

In this next moment, I thought, there will be the thrill of his definite presence, of her single, definite word. In this next moment, she will begin to speak and whatever word she choses will cut through all her stories, all my memories, all interpretations and speculations and hopes. It will be final, whatever she says in this next moment. It will be true.

I looked at her as she watched the trees. I saw her head tremble, a slight, involuntary nod: now, *now.*

But each moment passed. We sat in silence. A silence marked only by the form and the timbre of all it would not and yet might, still, at any moment become.

XXI

———— ·•· ————

*E*VERY CONTRACT SIGNED BY A
Vista author contains a paragraph that is known around the
office as "the cancellation clause." It states that the Publisher
shall not have the right to terminate the agreement until two
full years after the date of publication. "At any time thereafter,
however, should the Publisher determine that the demand for
said Work be insufficient for the Publisher to continue to
handle same profitably, the Publisher may then terminate this
agreement and return to the Author all rights granted here-
under by giving the Author notice thereof by first-class mail."

As Mr. Owens first explained it to her, the need for this
clause is both clear and logical. As soon as Elizabeth signs an
author and receives payment, Vista's profit has been made.
After that, every penny that is put into production, or advertising, indeed, every book that's sold (for if they sell out the first
small binding, they must dig into their pockets to pay for the
second) chips away at that profit. But as soon as a contract is
canceled and all rights are returned to the author, Vista's profit
is frozen, the author with all his troublesome questions about
sales is disposed of, and the stockroom can be cleared of yet
another stack of books.

It is merely a matter of course, then, Mr. Owens had told
her, that each Vista author, two years after a contract is

signed, receives notice thereof by first-class mail.

At the time, she had thought two years a terribly long way away.

"You said you believed in it," the woman on the phone wails. "Don't you remember? Those were your exact words. I even saved your letter."

"I remember," Elizabeth says, sincerely. Ann is still in the file room, looking for the woman's data. Elizabeth can remember nothing about her.

"When the letter came this morning," the woman goes on, her voice twirling down into a tight, desperate sound, "I was so excited. I had to sign for it, and my hand trembled. I saw it was from Mr. Owens. I thought it was good news. I thought you were going to make it into a movie or something."

Ann rushes in with the pale folder. Elizabeth grabs it from her, making it clear she is annoyed. Ann should have screened the call, kept the woman on hold until Elizabeth had figured out who she was and what she might want. What she could say in reply.

The woman begins to read from Mr. Owens' letter. " 'I am sorry to note that your book has not been selling well. While no one can predict such an unhappy circumstance . . .' "

Elizabeth opens the folder. There are copies of all her letters, dated two years ago, praising *All's Fair in Love* and welcoming Mrs. Lorraine Webb to Vista. Letters from Mrs. Webb—yellow, slightly scented stationary with scalloped edges and small white doves in each corner—thanking Elizabeth for her "kind kudos," asking, if she's ever in State College, Pa., to come and spend an evening with them. "P.S. Enclosed is my check."

" 'It seems best at this time,' " the woman continues to read, " 'that we cancel our agreement and, if you wish, send you the remaining bound copies of your book for your own personal use.' "

There are other happy letters to Production—thanking Ned's predecessor for sending her the galley proofs, for making the few changes. An ecstatic letter praising the lovely book-jacket design they so kindly showed her. A polite, inquiring letter about how much longer it will take for the book to be printed and bound. ("It has been three months since I last heard from you and I'm beginning to think it may have all been a dream.") A slightly less-patient letter written a month later. ("I fear I'll meet with some accident and never see my book . . . ") And then, "Just got my first copy of *All's Fair in Love* and my feet still haven't touched the ground!!!"

"You said you believed in it," the woman cries again. "You said it was good. You said it would sell!"

Elizabeth knows the woman is lying. One of Mr. Owens' cardinal rules: When they talk sales, just smile. Promise nothing.

"I don't understand why you want to cancel my contract!"

She sighs; What to say? "It's not my decision, Mrs. Webb," she begins. "I did think it was a good book. It is a good book." She quickly skims the woman's summary. "Even now I remember that powerful scene on the mountain when Agatha thought her husband was trying to murder her." She is reading from her own letter. "It was chilling, beautifully rendered."

"It was true," the woman interjects. "It's a true story."

"Yes," Elizabeth says, going through the letters once again. "It was chilling, brilliant I thought." At the back of the folder is the original copy of the woman's dust-jacket photo. It shows a blond, fortyish, carefully made-up woman leaning over her typewriter, looking serious, books piled all around her. There is a pencil stuck over her ear. "A rare piece of real literature, I thought."

"Then why are they canceling my contract?" Her voice has softened, sounds more defeated than outraged. And, Elizabeth notices, the *you* has gone to *they*. "Why didn't it sell?"

Elizabeth sighs deeply, as if she too were about to cry. She notices that the photo seems to have been taken in a small room, full of books. A room, no doubt, the woman has set aside for herself, for her work, her career. She says in her questionnaire that she has taken many writing courses. "Oh, Lorraine," Elizabeth says, "Who buys books anymore? Who, in this television society, is even interested in literature?"

"But no one even hearheard of my book."

"People heard," Elizabeth says wisely. "You're not aware of it, but people in New York, in publishing, heard. And for a new writer, that's sometimes more important than sales, notoriety, lasting notoriety."

"But I didn't even make my money back," the woman goes on. "You promised me I'd make my money back."

Another lie: Even the Vista brochure says, in very large print, We cannot guarantee a return on your investment. But then, given a chance, they'll always choose the lie. It is, after all, what she and Mr. Owens depend on. "Look, Lorraine," she whispers, as if she is suddenly making some confession. I'm an editor. Not an accountant. When I read a wonderful book like yours, a real contribution to women's literature, I can't worry about how much money it will make. I just have to get it into print, for posterity, if you will." She waits. Mrs. Webb is silent. "And do you know, Lorraine, to tell you the absolute truth, although I'm sorry you're so upset, I don't really care that your book didn't sell. In fact, it only confirms for me that it is not an ordinary book, that it is too deep, too good for the general public." She is still silent. "And *I* have no regrets about publishing your wonderful story. Do you?"

The woman hesitates. Elizabeth smiles at her office. "Well, no," she says. "It's just that . . ."

"Personally, I think it's a travesty that accountants, those soulless, emotionless dolts, are the ones who finally judge a book's worth. As if monetary profit is all a piece of literature is created for. If I had my way, accountants wouldn't be allowed even to speak to artists like yourself."

Mrs. Webb chuckles a little. "Well, I suppose publishing is a business, too."

"Please!" Elizabeth cries. "Don't remind me. But I'm not a businesswoman, Lorraine. I'm an editor, and it breaks my heart to think that a fine writer like you can be so discouraged by the decree of the accountants."

"Oh," she says, bucking up. "I'm not discouraged. I did read somewhere that even Jacqueline Susann's first novel didn't do that well. Not as well as the others."

"That's true," Elizabeth says.

"It wasn't until her second book that she really started to be popular."

"Yes."

"They said some authors just take a while to get a following. They said some need to develop a momentum."

"Yes." There is, she knows, no telling the limits, or limitlessness of their hopes, what they will chose to believe. "Lorraine," she whispers, gambling, but somehow perfectly assured. "You wouldn't happen to have another book, would you?"

There's a pause. "Yes," she whispers. "I do."

She wonders why she doesn't feel like laughing. "Do you think, do you think I might see it?"

"Well, I don't know. It's a sequel. *All's Fair in War.* I must admit it's much better than the first—that one may have been too short."

"Would you like to send it to me? Would you like to try again?"

More silence. Elizabeth can almost hear her making the leap, reweaving the dream: If not this time, next time. If not this one, then another. She can almost hear in the woman's shallow breath, the tight, restless sound of hope. Hope springing, like a Jack-in-the-box.

"All right," the woman says. "Yes. I'll send it to you. I'll send it to you tomorrow morning."

"Wonderful," Elizabeth says. "I'll look forward to it."

"Yes," says Mrs. Webb. "Thank you. Thank you very much, Elizabeth."

Elizabeth bows her head. "You're very welcome, Lorraine."

As she hangs up the phone, she glances at her calendar. Mrs. Webb is only the first of her authors to be canceled. In the next two years, every author she's ever signed will receive Mr. Owens' letter. And by the time she's heard from them all, Mrs. Webb will be calling again, asking why her second book has been canceled.

She makes a note to herself to find out what famous authors had unsuccessful first *and* second books. What famous authors died penniless and unknown and yet never, never gave up hope.

She throws Mrs. Webb's folder into her OUT box, stands, straightens her desk. It occurs to her that she is becoming a real master of literary name-dropping. A real master at her trade.

Mistress, she corrects herself. Mistress of hopeless cases, of eternal optimists. Mourning and weeping in their valley of tears. She picks up a stack of manuscripts and walks into the hallway. Someday they'll erect a shrine.

Ann is just coming to see her. "Sorry about that call," she says. "But it wasn't my fault. The woman asked for Owens first. He took it and then told me to pass it on to you, without even talking to her. I thought it was something you already knew about."

Elizabeth smiles. "That's all right."

"Is she going to sue?"

"Sue?"

"Yeah, she told me she was going to sue us."

Elizabeth turns up the corner of her mouth. "She's sending me her new novel," she says. "She'll probably sign again."

Ann frowns. Then laughs a little. "Slee-zee," she says, rolling her eyes. "How the hell did you accomplish that?"

Elizabeth shrugs, passing her by. "It's an art," she says.

Ellis is on the floor of his office, on all fours, tucking a small yellow wire under his rug, perspiring. His tie hangs before him like a broken leash. "For my speakers," he says to her, over his shoulder and his plaid rump. He raises a paw to the windowsill where there are two small stereo speakers. "Thought I'd get some music in here," he says, standing, his face flushed, "now that I'll be here more." His face, like his body from the waist down, is large and round, fleshy, his graying hair almost unnaturally bouffant, and although Marv has told her that he is the scion of a wealthy Midwestern family who, until he became editor-in-chief at Vista, had considered him their golf bum, their failure, she can only think of him as one in a long line of Fuller Brush men. Perhaps it is his plaid suits, or his ready smile.

He turns the smile on her now, brushing his hands together. "Those for me?"

She puts the pile of manuscripts on his desk. "Yes." She has a sudden vision of breaking down the wall between their offices, throwing Ellis out, taking over the larger space. She could, she knows. She's better at this than he is. Better than Owens himself. Her own, unique talent. "I'm giving you each of their manuscripts," she says, "their questionnaires and the correspondence thus far. They should all sign within the next two weeks."

He nods, lifts the manuscripts one by one. Tupper Daniels' is in the middle. He picks it up and puts it down as if it were exactly like all the rest.

"This all you've got?" he asks.

"All I've got pending."

He nods, grunts a little, and then smiles at her with all his teeth. "Hey," he takes her hand. "Have a good trip and if you've got any questions, you know where to find me."

"Thanks," she says. "I'm sure I'll be fine."

Back in her office, she combs her hair, puts on her coat. She checks her desk again and then, lifting her manuscript bag—a black, square case that makes her feel like a musician—turns off the light.

Owens calls to her from his office.

"What time's your train?" he asks, reading a letter.

"Five," she says.

"You sure you wouldn't rather drive?"

"No."

He looks up at her. "Where's your suitcase?"

"I checked it at the station. This morning."

He throws the letter onto his desk. Leans back, putting his hands behind his head. He stays that way for a few moments, staring into space. She watches him.

Finally, he looks down at her, says *huh* as if he's surprised she's still there. "And sweetheart," he says, "when you're on the road, remember the accountants, emotionless dolts that they are, who'll be looking over your expense account when you get back."

He winks and she feels herself blush, feels some strange intimacy between them.

He closes his eyes slowly, slowly opens them again. He smiles at her, points a thick finger in her direction. "You see," he says. "I'm keeping track of you."

"Good," she says, smiling too.

As she walks through the office, Ann is on the phone, already saying, "Ms. Connelly is out of town. May I take a message?" She mouths something as Elizabeth walks by—maybe "Tupperware," maybe "toodle-ooo"—rolls her eyes and waves. Elizabeth waves back.

The ladies in the file room are holding up small mirrors, putting lipstick on at their desks.

Bonnie is at the board, paging through a copy of *Vogue*,

waiting for five o'clock. She says, "Have fun," as Elizabeth goes out the door.

She takes the elevator down alone and walks to Penn Station. By the time she gets there, she remembers that she'll need gloves and that she forgot to bring them. She decides, as she boards the train, that she'll buy a pair in Hartford, and then realizes that from now on, many of the things she owns, small pieces of clothing, cosmetics, jewelry, will be inadvertent souvenirs, picked up here and there across the country.

She imagines herself, like some tattooed sailor, meeting strangers and showing them how these shoes are from Philadelphia, these gloves from Hartford. These panty hose I got in Albuquerque—oh, what a night that was—and this ring, well, it's from Milwaukee. Milwaukee, Wisconsin, a town of some significance to me . . .

The train starts with a jolt, as if it had broken off something, and then moves slowly through the tunnel, out past the dark train yard, the black outline of the city. The businessmen in her car reach up to turn on the soft reading lights above them, clear their throats, rustle their newspapers. Somewhere behind her, two of them laugh, one talking through the laughter, all his words ending with *eeesh*. When they are silent, the train is silent.

And her father was a businessman who traveled. Left again and again. Carried his history with him like a tattooed sailor. Left nothing of himself behind. When she asked him what he did on those long trips away, he said he was a gigolo and she had to imagine even the meaning of the word. She chose to believe it was something unique and wonderful. She chose the lie.

As, no doubt, he knew she would.

She sinks down into her seat. Below her is a yard full of Greyhound buses, their backs humped, their windows only reflecting light. Beside it, a field of mail trucks. Then what seems to be a power plant. They pass a highway crowded with cars, white lights on one side, red on the other. Men coming home for the evening, only to leave again in the morning. To return, to leave. And all the wives waiting in their kitchens, listening to traffic reports, fearing the worst until he comes through the door. All the wives creating those small domestic dramas that can transform their day, shine through its dullness like fools' gold.

She looks around the car. In a little while, she'll get up to get a small bottle of wine. Maybe even meet someone on the way, invite him back to her seat. He'll see her manuscript bag and ask, What are you, a musician? A doctor? A traveling saleswoman?

If she likes him, she'll say she is an artist, a mistress of her art. A hall of mirrors and secrets. A mystery.

If she likes him, she knows she'll lie.